Richard John Knight has lived on three continents and his education includes the Duke of York's Royal Military School in Dover Kent, Royal Military College Duntroon Australia, and the Chartered Institute of Loss Adjusters UK. Richard spent nearly 50 years of his life investigating, handling, and settling major insurance disaster claims and writing reports often for legal processes. It was therefore an ambition to write an exciting work of fiction covering the areas that he knew and countries he had researched.

To my wife, Christine, for putting up with the hours I have spent locked away with the computer, researching, drafting, and redrafting this novel.

Richard John Knight

FAR BEYOND DUTY

A Story of Titus Lovell

AUSTIN MACAULEY PUBLISHERS™
LONDON * CAMBRIDGE * NEW YORK * SHARJAH

Copyright © Richard John Knight 2024

The right of Richard John Knight to be identified as author of this work has been asserted by the author in accordance with sections 77 and 78 of the Copyright, Designs and Patents Act 1988.

All rights reserved. No part of this publication may be reproduced, stored in a retrieval system, or transmitted in any form or by any means, electronic, mechanical, photocopying, recording, or otherwise, without the prior permission of the publishers.

Any person who commits any unauthorised act in relation to this publication may be liable to criminal prosecution and civil claims for damages.

This is a work of fiction. Names, characters, businesses, places, events, locales, and incidents are either the products of the author's imagination or used in a fictitious manner. Any resemblance to actual persons, living or dead, or actual events is purely coincidental.

A CIP catalogue record for this title is available from the British Library.

ISBN 9781035869060 (Paperback)
ISBN 9781035869077 (ePub e-book)

www.austinmacauley.com

First Published 2024
Austin Macauley Publishers Ltd®
1 Canada Square
Canary Wharf
London
E14 5AA

To the unnamed editor at Writers SA who challenged me to lose 90 pages, tighten the story, lose some unnecessary characters and add more dialogue. The final novel therefore bears little resemblance to the original draft, except the storyline.

Prologue

Titus was very uneasy.

He had never been so anxious about anything in his life but of course, it was 1980 and he was now a civilian, after years of military service, and so options previously available to him were physically and legally out of reach.

A month ago, his life was orderly, sane and safe, but all that changed very rapidly.

He'd been attacked and had had to fight off a knife-wielding Yemeni assassin.

On top of all that, the managing director of the company he had been tasked to investigate had been brutally murdered, on the very day he was instructed to act in the matter. By the same man, he wondered?

British Intelligence was heavily involved but as expected remained in the background.

He would end up in turbulent times in the Middle East, in yet more danger.

All a little too dramatic for his taste!

But there was now a girl in his life, and he was desperate to keep her safe from all this.

Chapter 1

The grisly murder of a well-dressed, middle-aged man initially went unnoticed in the wet and dark railway yards, behind Richmond Railway Station, in London's west.

The victim had been savagely and repeatedly hacked across his body, and then almost beheaded by violent slashes across his throat.

Robbery didn't appear to be a motive, as the victim's watch and wallet were intact.

The next day, at the Richmond office of New Giffin-Sen PLC, a quickly convened, but extremely devious meeting was taking place. It involved their UK manager, Efraim Khoury, and a senior staff member from Ecothan plc, who had come in through Khoury's private entrance, by-passing the front office. The two were well known to each other but there was no sense of closeness between them, rather a tolerance born by a deceitful necessity; or perhaps just greed.

New Giffin-Sen PLC was a mid-sized mining contractor, based in Jordan and involved in mining phosphorite ($Ca_5(PO_4CO_3)_3(F, OH, Cl)$.), commonly referred to as phosphate rock, near the small settlement of Wadi al-Abyad, set in the eastern desert.

The business was primarily involved in mining the fertiliser and then shipping on to customers in India and Japan, making the shipping aspect secondary but still quite lucrative as there were many 'back-handers' to be extorted along the way; and Khoury knew how to extract more than his share!

Khoury was not a miner or a banker but appeared to be somewhere between a salesman, a conman and a thug. His slicked-down greasy hair, his goatee beard and the £1,500 Italian suit he was wearing did nothing to make him any more appealing to the visitor.

The pudding of a man was splayed out, slouched, in a wide leather chair, in a most undignified position and a very un-business-like manner. He didn't bother to get up, or even sit up properly as his guest came in, displaying great disrespect, probably deliberately.

He rudely gestured to an upright chair on the opposite side of the small table, almost as a command to sit there.

There was a huge knife on the coffee table between them, which the Arab pointedly glared at several times, menacingly.

The visitor felt like an intruder, most unwelcome and nervous. He was telling Khoury of recent happenings. "An insurance investigator has just commenced sniffing around my office and we should now be especially careful. He seems quite persistent and it worries me."

The fat man sagely pointed out, "There is too much money involved to back out at this stage. We should continue our scheme until he steps too close and then maybe shut it down and disappear. I think that we should continue to discreetly keep in touch but never be seen together in public anymore, or be directly connected in any way."

Khoury's observation was rather chilling when he hissed, "Through my associates in Yemen, we could easily arrange to dispose of any threat to our clandestine operation."

After a moment's silence, the visitor enquired what he meant by 'dispose', despite having more than a sneaking suspicion of what he meant, nevertheless was shocked by Khoury's action of a finger slashing across his throat.

He felt sick.

Surely this wasn't what happened to his boss, James Kingwell. Surely not!

"Life is cheap, my friend!"

"It is not easy to make nearly £3 million, per year, each; for as long as we can keep it off the records."

"Do you think that we can keep this going now that your own company's head office has issued a writ against mine and is suspicious? We do not know what they may have discovered," said the visitor.

"The fact that you and I are still employed seems to suggest that they have no real idea of what's going on. We should ensure that we keep it that way," snapped Khoury, but the implications made the other nervous, although there was no walking away from this enormous flow of money now.

Even just one more payment would turn all his aspirations into reality.

He was too committed and he knew it!

Hell, he'd already made purchases and advance commitments; so the next instalment, hopefully soon, was essential for him to complete his escape. His wife did not have the slightest clue about his nefarious dealings. She didn't care about him and this was the reason he was planning his getaway from her, to the sun. Neither did this repulsive creature in front of him have any idea how far advanced were his plans, nor of the illegal passport he intended to use to cover his escape.

"Let us not concern ourselves at this stage my friend, we will have tea!" and with that, he clapped his hands which caused a swarthy, heavy-set woman to immediately appear in the doorway. She looked directly at the visitor and then dropped her eyes, as she knew that he had come in through the private entrance so it was not her business. Nevertheless, she drank in his details, as it may be useful to her for later, perhaps. Yes, she was certainly a cunning one.

She took Khoury's order for a pot of coffee and slid away silently, returning shortly with a tray but this time avoiding eye contact.

He knew that under Arabian hospitality conventions, he would cause great offence by refusing and as he was now in a very delicate relationship with Khoury, he gave all the signs of graciously accepting.

No more was said and after the ritual of drinking several smallish cups of the sugary, thick, mud-like coffee, he was pleased to shake hands, rather than the traditional kiss on both cheeks, and leave Khoury's office via the same inconspicuous way he'd entered.

It was just after 5 pm so there was no point in going back to his South London office, which would involve a torturously slow drive at this time of the day, from these rather plush offices at Richmond-upon-Thames. He decided that before he set off for home he'd call in at the nearby Olde Shippe to steady himself with a stiff double malt whiskey, or two!

Watching from his second-floor office window was Khoury, taking note of the departing dark green Morris Mini Cooper sedan and its identification plates.

"This might be useful later," he mused aloud to himself, feeling that the visitor, who had been pivotal to this exercise, was becoming unstable and may also have to be dealt with in some form or another.

There was too much at stake he thought to let this venture slip away from him now and besides, Khoury didn't like this man or his weakness.

"Christian infidels are weak and are of no consequence," he sneered out aloud, as he stared down at the departing vehicle.

The Ecothan employee drove away, oblivious to the piercing black eyes watching and the potential danger hanging over him and possibly his family.

This criminal operation was heading nowhere good for some people!

At The Olde Shippe, the double malt whiskey gave him some relief and courage, however temporary, as he sat alone and alarmed by recent developments.

A swarthy individual entered the bar, stopped, and after eyeing him, sat down staring his way. Oh, god, is this it? He didn't dare move.

He grabbed a second drink, swallowing it in one gulp and shivered. Time passed slowly but eventually, he felt a wave of relief when a woman entered and sat next to the Arab, who seemed to lose interest in him.

He made the decision to escape straight way and walked out of the bar.

There was nothing here for him except danger.

He would disappear forever, within a few days.

He climbed into his car, feeling much better after pulling the door closed and locking it.

Looking over his shoulder he was relieved to see nothing! No one followed him into the car park.

He thought that he'd have to abandon the car, which he really loved, as it made him feel young, but it had to go.

He'd leave it in one of those giant 24-hour shopping centre-free car parks, and hopefully, no one would notice it for weeks. Or maybe someone would notice and steal it; all the better. It was under a hefty financial lease but he would walk out on that too—abandon the bloody lot!

Someone had once told to him, "It is no good being half bad; you may as well go all the way, otherwise you'll end up paying for it." Now it finally made sense to him.

Then in a special news flash on his car radio, the police announced that they had now identified the recent murder victim. Named as James Kingwell.

The murder occurred only a mile from Khoury's office.

Filled with dread, he opened the car door and vomited.

Chapter 2

Titus Lovell was well respected as a successful specialist Chartered Loss Adjuster usually working around London, after a stellar career in the military. He was well qualified and highly sought after, working all over the UK and a fair proportion of Europe on instructions from London underwriters. His firm had even sent him out on exchange to their Australian division twice, to extend his experience and for some cross-pollination of techniques.

Most of his work involved the investigation of large insurance claims,

He was personally briefed by the senior partner of Brown, Collins & Knox lawyers, Mr Deacon Collins, who explained, "The claim involves a client with the business name Ecothan," which he spelt out aloud.

Titus was given a copy of rather scant documentation which consisted of a writ and an accompanying letter, with an indication that the matter was not due in court for about six months.

He returned to his office on foot after the conference and then studied the file in detail, making only a few notes because the documentation was not particularly illuminating or useful. The allegations related to the past two years, 1978 to 1980 and they were currently in September 1980.

He made a phone call to the Ecothan's offices and an appointment was fixed for the following afternoon.

It wasn't much good having a car in London for work and the rail network, together with the traditional London black cabs gave him all the transport he needed for a city job, or even away to other cities.

At 1 pm the following day, he walked the short distance to Tower Hill tube underground, which after a quick change underground brought him to Southwark station, the closest to his appointment. He knew the area reasonably well and that Emerson Street was tucked behind the old Bankside Power Station.

He found Ecothan's offices in an oldish, yet stylish stone building occupying a prominent position on an upper floor.

"Good morning, my name is Titus Lovell and I have an appointment to see Mr Kingwell," he said, introducing himself to the receptionist and passing her his business card.

The receptionist asked him to take a seat for a moment and Miss Lang would come out and speak to him.

He had hardly done so when he heard the clicking of high heels on the pinkish Italian marble floor, coming towards him, off to his right. An immaculately dressed, absolutely stunning young woman approached, with her hand proffered for a handshake and introduced herself as Rhoda Lang.

Titus quickly rose to his feet to greet her. From her voice, his quick assessment suggested to him that she was originally from Australia or had at least lived there for some considerable time but she had acquired a 'business' type of British accent.

Her mannerisms seemed very defensive when she enquired, "May I ask the nature of your call, as there seems to be no record of any appointment?"

She appeared to accept the fact that he was genuine and ushered him through a pair of large mahogany doors into what was obviously the boardroom.

She asked, "Again could you please explain the nature of any business with Mr Kingwell and with whom you say that you made the appointment?"

"It relates to a very large insurance claim reported by Ecothan plc to their insurance underwriters whom I represent."

On flipping open his thin file, he was able to tell her, "Yesterday I spoke to a young lady named Kim who set an appointment for 1:30 pm to see Mr Kingwell. Kim said she would block off one and a half hours in his diary, as I requested."

"Is there a problem, Miss Lang?" This seemed to fracture her facade altogether and her eyes reddened as she turned away from him to dab her eyes and regain control. When she turned back to him, she asked that they both sit down, whereupon he filled a glass from the water jug on the boardroom table and passed it to her.

It took a few more minutes before she told him three staggering facts.

"Firstly, we do not have any record of an appointment having been made for anyone to see Mr Kingwell in the diary, which I personally keep for him."

"Secondly and very tragically, Mr Kingwell was brutally murdered last night and the matter is being handled by the London Metropolitan Police Murder Squad."

"Thirdly, as PA to Mr Kingwell and keeper of all his files, I am unaware of any writ or pending insurance claim and certainly not a very large claim as you have suggested."

Although this seemed simply a puzzle then, it was to become the beginning of a nightmare, which would soon lead him and others halfway around the world into dangerous situations.

Chapter 3

Sitting in the boardroom feeling sorry for Miss Lang but still trying to elicit some useful information from her, he was surprised when the double doors were thrown open and a bull of a man stormed into the room and headed straight for them.

He seemed to have taken offence at Miss Lang dealing direct, in perhaps his area of control. He bellowed at her, "**Get out, now girlie!**" and she fled.

Titus introduced himself saying, "It seems there's been some misunderstanding. I'm Titus Lovell, Chartered Loss Adjuster. I'm investigating a large insurance claim that Ecothan reported to their underwriters last week after a writ was issued. I had an appointment with Mr Kingwell, but have just learnt that he's died."

The bull started to raise his voice again and stepped closer to Titus in an effort to intimidate him but Titus simply raised his hand, palm forward in the traditional stop sign. The face became even redder but at least the mouth closed!

It seemed that calling the man's bluff had cooled him down a little and when he replied his voice was about 50 decibels lower in volume, *thank god*, thought Titus.

"My name is Pieter Coetzee and I am Head of Security for Ecothan plc. Our managing director has not just died, but has been bloody well murdered! The police have been here all morning and I find you unauthorised in my boardroom speaking to a mere secretary, so what am I supposed to think?"

Holy shit! thought Titus what an unbelievable arse of a man and this is the contact that I may have to deal with. *How am I going to get this back on track,* he thought and perhaps get at least a half-decent individual to speak to.

"Now what the hell is this about an insurance claim of millions of pounds and what has it got to do with you?"

How did he know it was millions of pounds if he knew nothing about it?

Time for some home truths and take control of the situation if it was possible.

"If you are the appropriate person, I should be dealing with, perhaps you could retrieve your company file and we could discuss it to see how I should commence my investigation and who I should see. If not, perhaps the deputy managing director or chief financial officer or similar may be in a position to discuss this with me."

"The deputy MD is on assignment in a secure African facility for the next week, and I'm not sure why you suggest the CFO who is nothing but a bloody accountant. If anyone does investigations for Ecothan it will be me!" he spat out.

Charming, thought Titus, *it is going from bad to worse.*

"Mr Coetzee, believe it or not, but I am here to help. If you do not have access to the file would you, please find me the CFO? I can then commence to at least consider the financial dimensions of this investigation?"

"I'll get the damn CFO who will be of no use and don't think you've heard the last from me, man!" he shouted over a shoulder as he exited the boardroom, slamming the door loudly.

After a couple of minutes, the double boardroom doors were pushed open gently and a tall lean man in a grey pinstripe suit eased himself in, closing the door carefully behind him. He walked almost silently up to Titus and introduced himself in a quiet professional voice as Peter Moles. He had a firm handshake and furnished him a black-and-white embossed business card which identified him as the chief financial officer. However, he was carrying no file of papers with him and had a perplexed look on his face.

Moles explained that he could not trace any papers in the office that could be related to anything Titus had raised or that Coetzee had just told him about.

With that, he opened his file and took out the three pages of the writ issued out of the High Court, Westminster, confirming this matter must be of some considerable size and intricacy.

The writ itself really only contained the basics of who and when and in generalities the amount involved. It named Ecothan plc as the defendant whilst the plaintiffs were jointly listed as:

Plaintiff one-New Giffin-Sen PLC.
Plaintiff two-Abdal-monem Twal.

Moles looked at the names on the writ and threw up his hands in exasperation responding, "We have no business that I know of with the first plaintiff and the second name likewise means nothing at all to me."

"Where to next?" Moles enquired obviously becoming intrigued and clearly doing his best to assist.

"Well, let's look at other details on the writ," suggested Titus looking for a location or date of an occurrence but there was more frustration when it referred to various dates over a two-year period starting in 1978 and occurring in Jordan, but in particular Wadi al-Abyad.

"I guess the reference to Jordan might explain the second plaintiff because it sounds like an Arabic name," suggested Moles.

"The writ's allegation refers to various losses both individual and cumulative, amounting to no less than £3 million but up to £10 million over a two-year period, plus legal costs and ongoing losses," explained Titus.

None of this really explained the what, where or when and didn't actually suggest an 'accident' as such, but what did it suggest?

Moles looked genuinely bewildered. "As CFO, I should be made aware of any financial liabilities and their implications on our publicly listed company but am one hundred per cent sure nothing has come across my desk."

Chapter 4

At 17 years of age, Titus had been restless, having completed his schooling to a very respectable educational level, and shortly after, he had enlisted in the Royal Engineers (REs) as a Sapper (Private), holding a hope of training to become an army combat engineer. The first seven months of service had involved him in recruit training, basic training, and then Corps training which was spread between depots throughout the UK, including Malvern and later at Cove, at 6 Training Regiment. He was kept far too busy to be either restless or bored or to get into any trouble.

Soon he was pleased and relieved to receive his first overseas posting in 1959 to 36 Corps Engineering Regiment stationed at Osnabruck Garrison, BAOR (British army on the Rhine) as part of the occupation forces, some dozen years after the end of World War Two.

Here, he learnt the more practical use of explosives, fuses, detonator cords and all manner of detonators and trained on a myriad of heavy equipment, including bulldozers.

His personal skills were expanding rapidly and he was becoming well respected and was promoted to the rank of corporal.

His next posting was to Gibraltar for nine months, which by comparison was almost a sunny holiday camp, having an altogether lighter atmosphere. Not being in an occupier's role and being totally welcomed by the population was an appreciated change to his off-duty hours.

However, dealing with WW2 unexploded floating sea mines was quite a different challenge. It became an all too regular and pretty hair-raising, sobering exercise, especially since the steelwork was so corroded that the mines could be unpredictable, difficult to work with and just plain dangerous. There were accidents resulting in several deaths plus some very nasty and permanent injuries in his and other RE squads.

Titus survived unscathed and another skill was added to his increasing repertoire.

Then he was posted again, across the Mediterranean to the island of Cyprus, quite briefly, fortunately, because these were very difficult times in 1963. This was followed by a posting to a nicely peaceful and welcoming Island of Malta for nearly two and a half years where he worked mainly around the large military/naval hospital at Mtarfa, supporting the 1st King's Own Malta Regiment.

Life was rewarding at work, and he was promoted to sergeant.

Then, there was the posting to India!

Chapter 5

Despite his misgivings, Titus asked Moles to invite Coetzee back to the boardroom and to put the names of the two plaintiffs to him to see if he showed any recognition.

He wasn't sure he could read Coetzee's facial expression but the answer surprised him greatly. "No, I know nothing and as you have chosen to deal with Moles, rather than me, and as this is clearly a security matter, then I'll do it my way! Therefore, I have nothing to say on the subject, at least for the moment!" He abruptly turned away and exited the room.

No need to comment further on this, thought Titus but he was struggling with where to go next.

Moles explained, "We are an international company and although I'm not aware of all individual contracts, we could well have dealings underway but not formalised in Jordan. However, I doubt whether they would be a multi-million-pound contract without me knowing, for you see, we are what I would describe as a 'facilitating' company. That is to say, we assist others to achieve their goal. An upmarket middleman, similar to a specialist merchant bank."

"Do you have any literature on the town of Wadi al-Abyad, just to see just where it is and what its claim to fame may be, if any, please?"

Moles called in their records clerk/librarian who very efficiently delivered an impressive atlas and they found Wadi al-Abyad to be situated 84 miles south of Amman, the capital of Jordan.

It was listed as being rich in potash and phosphates deposits, currently in big demand worldwide for agriculture and industry. Again searches failed to reveal anything on the country, the town or the individual's name referred to in the writ.

Unspoken, but hanging over the two men was Kingwell's murder.

Eventually, Moles offered, "I hate to voice this, but could Jimmy's death somehow be involved in what we are looking at here?"

It was a question Titus couldn't answer, but it did concern him.

In his past, he had seen plenty of danger, destruction and death, and really didn't want to go back there.

Chapter 6

Titus' thoughts drifted back to 1965, in North-Western India, on the Pakistani border and the prelude to a horrific tank battle.

The unit he was with was an Indian Army Special Forces infantry unit, heavily armed, obviously expecting similar opposition from the Pakistanis.

However, what ensued in the next 24 hours was to become part of military history and the biggest tank battle since World War II in North Africa.

The area just inside the Indian border was an agricultural area with much of the ground used for growing sugarcane, with a village close by.

Situated near the Beas River, which was subject to annual flooding, meant that proper reconnaissance by the Pakistanis would have shown that certain sections of it were basically unsuited for tanks, as the ground was either boggy, flooded, or simply too soft to carry their weight at speed.

Their unit was to be positioned near one of the two bridges over the Beas River, not much more than a mile from the village and that was just inside the Indo-Pakistani border, but at the beginning stage, they were to be held back in reserve, several miles east.

They were aware that the First Armoured Division of the Pakistani Army was close to the Indo-Pakistani border, but its strength was unknown to the troops on the ground at that stage and they had no idea a major battle was about to unfold. In general terms, it was known the Pakistani Army was equipped with modern American tanks including the Patton M-47 and M-48s, plus older M4 Sherman heavy tanks which had been up-gunned with the most modern French high-velocity CN75-50 guns, making them very formidable. They also had lighter Chaffee tanks, for quicker deployment.

On the other hand, India's First Armoured Division was regarded as the pride of the Indian army, having a mixture of Sherman tanks plus a large number of British-made Centurion mark 7 tanks, which had also been 'up-gunned', but with the latest 105 mm Royal Ordnance L-7, and backed up with a number of M3 Stuart light tanks.

The Pakistani Armour had exploded onto the scene at dawn, in a blitzkrieg-type action, taking the town, but slowing to consolidate their position before the next stage of advancing over the Beas River.

Titus' unit was immediately brought forward towards the bridge but the shells from the tank battle were flying indiscriminately and at that point, the Indian Armour seemed to be coming off second best. Their job was to hold the bridge if necessary, for sufficient time to allow the withdrawal of the Indian Armour, and then to prevent Pakistani Armour from crossing the bridge by disabling it, as best as possible.

It seemed clear that the Pakistanis were well aware of what his unit was there for, and the gunners from the tanks were focusing their range on his side of the river.

The Indians had done their homework by blowing a number of irrigation canals, thereby flooding certain areas of the plains between the town and the river. The advance by the Pakistani Armour forced them to simply cut through the fields of very high sugarcane and sweet corn crops, without realising the ground had in fact been deliberately flooded. The result was that the Pakistani Armour was slowed to such an extent that they were distracted. When they eventually moved forward it was into a horseshoe formed by four squadrons of Centurion and two Sherman tanks, in their concealed 'hulled-down' position within the high sugarcane.

Lying in wait for the Pakistanis were not only tanks but also infantry anti-tank units who together successfully ambushed the Pakistani Armour but both sides suffered a massive loss of life and equipment.

Despite this, Titus's group at the bridge suddenly found themselves under new fire from the north-east, across the river, where five squadrons of fast-moving Pakistani M24 Chaffee light tanks approached through the smoke of battle, obviously with the intent of capturing the bridge and isolating the Indian tanks from their rear, from the far side of the river.

As the Chaffee tanks approached, reaching within 900 hundred yards, they too were slowed by the boggy conditions but their firepower was laid devastatingly accurately across the river on their position, causing many Indian casualties.

Dangerous heavy machine gun fire was being sent their way.

It was getting very hairy!

It was at this moment it became obvious that the bridge should be blown thereby isolating the Chaffee tanks in their boggy and treacherous position, which would allow the Centurion tanks of the Indian army to turn on them and with any luck wipe them out; and at the same time save his men.

Every effort to approach the bridge more closely was thwarted by the machine gun fire on their commando unit, as the Pakistani tanks crawled slowly through the boggy conditions towards them, maintaining their intense fire.

The Pakistanis, with their range finders and their long-distance lenses, were most likely able to see them quite clearly at 900 yards and predict their next movement, making their approach to the bridge unachievable.

It was at this stage that Titus suggested to Subedar Major Gill that if the main body of their two platoons were to withdraw to the east, it may distract the Pakistani tank commanders, sufficiently for one man to slip away towards the bridge. He volunteered to do this, as the acknowledged demolition expert and so, after quickly conferring with the captain commanding their unit, it was agreed.

With much noise and movement of abandoning their position, they hoped that it would have been clear to the Chaffee tank commanders that they were all forsaking their defence position at the bridge because of the heavy gunfire raining down on them.

Titus went to the ground, laying very still for a couple of minutes, until the platoons were well away from him. He then raised his head slightly but it brought a hail of bullets in his direction and so he was forced to commence to zigzag his way, in a leopard crawl. He was in the slightest of depression, with heavy gunfire just over the top of him.

He had to drag his explosives with him, towards the south-west side of the bridge. Shells and machine gun fire continued to strafe his side of the river bank almost indiscriminately and his progress was slow, causing him no shortage of concern.

He knew that he not only had to reach the bridge with the explosives intact but had to detonate his charges before the tanks crossed it and time was becoming precious.

Then the rather sobering thought passed through his mind, "You wanted to be a combat engineer! Well, here you are, armed with a Webley Mk IV .38 service revolver, during a tank battle—bloody brilliant!"

His progress towards the bridge was painfully slow on the rocky ground, added to which the weight of the box of explosives was almost becoming too much to drag. His elbows and knees were raw and felt like they were on fire but he had no option but to keep crawling.

He could hear live rounds passing very close to him but fortunately, the shells were not so close, as they were now redirected mainly towards the platoons acting as decoys, moving to the north-east.

He eventually reached the edge of the river bank, with his face and hands stinging from the sand kicked up by the rounds zinging all around him. He again peered over the lip of the shallow ditch which had offered him scant cover during a slight lapse of gunfire but knew that he must now leave his barely covered position.

This was not going to be fun!

He rolled over the lip of the depression, dragging the box and trying to keep as low as he possibly could, sliding down the bank. Eventually, he reached a point where he was obscured from view by the bridge's southern pylon, enabling him to slide further down the embankment to a position behind a large concrete buttress.

Now, completely hidden from view, he peered around the massive buttress, and finally scrambled up, alongside the steelwork. Still out of sight of the approaching tank crews, who by now were about 800 yards away and advancing slowly; and struggling in the flooded terrain, but not slowly enough for his liking!

He had earlier observed the bridge from afar, through the smoke and had already formulated his plan regarding which part of the structure he could blow for immediate effect.

He quickly flipped the catches to open his steel box of goodies, viewing the range of explosives, detonating cord, fuse cord and detonators, all neatly laid out. Working quickly but carefully, he selected the appropriate charges, which he attached to the centre two legs of the bridge's southern pylon about four feet up. Checking charge sizes and shaping carefully, time seemed to be passing all too quickly for him.

Once satisfied with their placement, he attached the detonators ultra-carefully, followed by a good length of det-cord and next he joined that to the fuse cord. He then trailed the fuse cord behind him as he crawled up the river bank, keeping as low as he possibly could, because the general incoming fire across the bank was becoming more intense than ever. However, the worst was to come when he had to leave the cover of the concrete buttress.

As he emerged over the lip of the embankment, the dirt kicked up all too close to him and he had five metres of unprotected ground to scurry across before slipping into the shallow ditch which he'd used for protection on his way to the bridge. The gunfire was merciless, with one round striking his right boot, feeling like a sledgehammer, but fortunately, it only ripped off the rubber heel and part of the sole, of his newly issued desert boots.

At this point, he thought that at any moment a shell or round would collect him as the noise was hell!

About 40 yards from the bridge, the ditch opened up into a deeper hole created by a recent shell exploding and this offered slightly more safety. He knew that he was lucky to be alive as he rolled into it. He needed the space so that he could assemble the firing mechanism, needing a bit of headroom to do so.

He sneaked a look over the edge of the ditch and could see that the tanks were now within about 100 yards, and realised that he had better get a spurt on, but there was never any room for error with explosives and he did not want to go up with the bridge!

Titus hoped that he was now far enough away from the bridge because there was simply no time to set a delayed timing device to enable him to shift further away. He hoped that if kept his head down he would be able to detonate the charges from where he lay, without too much direct impact on him.

His brain was starting to go numb with the noise and tension.

His fingers were turning to rubber.

Drawing on all his training, he worked steadily, hearing the closeness of the tanks' turbocharged diesel engines screaming as they slugged their way through the boggy flooded territory. The engine noise level then changed as the tanks suddenly gained harder ground, and so he knew they were now moving much more quickly, on the hard roadway approach to the bridge.

A quick glimpse over the edge of the ditch brought fire directly on his position and so it was clear that his location was known to at least one of the tank commanders. What he did establish was that one Chaffee was already on the bridge and three more were close on its heels.

He threw himself flat, wishing the hole was twice as deep and he flicked the detonator switch. He immediately placed both hands over his ears, waiting for the inevitable explosion and trusting he had in fact made all his connections properly.

The sound of the ensuing explosion dwarfed the entire battle for that moment as he lay there getting sprayed with the smaller debris and sand from the bridge and the embankment.

He was thankful that he was wearing a steel helmet as all sorts of debris landed on and around him with quite some force. Once the dust had settled, he struggled up from under the rubble, which had half buried him and dared to peek over the edge of the ditch. A plume of dust and black smoke was rising quickly, hundreds of feet into the air, but more importantly the closest span of the bridge was missing.

The Centurion tank commanders, alerted by the noise, were already swinging their gun turrets around 180°. They were able to re-set their gun-sights; and what followed was them setting about wiping out the entire five squadrons of light tanks, which stood exposed on the riverbank and at the bridge entry, within 300 yards of their formidable guns.

Titus crawled carefully towards the riverbank and could see that three of the light tanks must have been on the bridge at the time of the explosion because two were now down, on end, in the swift-flowing river and the third was trapped on the partially demolished bridge. Its crew was standing on the road surface beside their undamaged tank, with their hands high in the air, hoping to stay alive and to be taken prisoner.

The sounds of the now one-sided battle, from the Centurion tanks' 105mm guns became even more deafening. It was followed by the ear-splitting sounds of the Chaffee tanks exploding, from the ignition of their internal stocks of ammunition and diesel fuel, as they were impacted by the 105 HE shells.

Titus again threw himself flat on the ground in another deep crater, in an attempt to avoid sound waves, heat waves and debris flying in all directions.

Intense red and orange balls of fire erupted from each tank as they exploded one by one and these were followed by intense black plumes of smoke from each, rising high into the air, in mushroom formations.

The noises, brilliant colours and smells were beyond description, and the general devastation was horrific: something never to be forgotten.

Above all that, he could smell burning flesh.

Sickening!

Including several separate battles, some 92 Pakistani tanks were destroyed in total that day and although it was difficult to tell, because of their concealed position in the sugarcane crops, it appeared to Titus that the Indian army had probably lost up to 10 tanks.

This was later declared by the Indian Armoured Corps as 32 tanks either damaged or destroyed over the next few days, here and elsewhere.

Whilst the Centurion tanks and infantry anti-tank guns were completing their task, the Special Forces platoons made their way back quickly to the bridge, by which time tank shelling and machine gun-fire had ceased, leaving the perfect calm after the storm.

After securing the area and posting guards, the troops swarmed towards Titus patting him on the back, shaking his hand and chairing him on their shoulders whilst shouting 'TeeGee' in their sing-song English. It was pretty embarrassing for Titus, and he had no idea what it meant. Fortunately, Gill intervened with a sharp command and they snapped back into their duties, for the day was far from over.

Gill shook his hand solidly, looking him in the eye and saying, "A credit to Britain and the Royal Engineers. Thank you."

As Titus had deliberately blown only one section of the bridge to disable it, he was able to quickly and effectively plan a temporary repair procedure.

An engineering unit from the Pioneer Force of army engineers from Jhansi Army Camp was already in transit and arrived on site within an hour. Under Titus' direction, they made the bridge negotiable within 24 hours, initially for only light traffic, nevertheless adding further to his kudos.

The Centurion tanks would have to remain there for the moment or travel some 20 miles to the next bridge to cross the river.

In fact, they stayed there for several weeks to guard the village and the nearby border area.

Further plans to strengthen the structure were discussed so the Centurions could cross the river at some later time but at least it was repairable.

His remaining time in the border regions of India, after that episode, was only a little less dramatic, being involved in a number of very dangerous skirmishes over the next eight months. One in particular involved two Pakistani Sikorsky H-19 helicopters fitted with three separate 20mm canons and a 12.7mm machine gun.

Helicopters could still give him nightmares, from time to time.

Chapter 7

Needing to clear his head after seeing Moles, Titus decided to walk the few yards to the Thames, which as a Londoner he always found soothing. He sat on a bench outside the land on which an American millionaire director, Sam Wanamaker was proposing to build a replica of the original 1599 Shakespeare's Globe Theatre, possibly in the next 10 years.

He elected to take the tube back to Tower Hill Station. This would give him almost equal opportunity to stop by the office or just walk past the Tower of London taking him to his apartment just off St Katharine's Way in the Docks.

He was a calm man by nature but he felt the frustration rising in him, as his very nature demanded that problems put before him be solved, especially when he was engaged to do so.

The thought struck him that if Kingwell's murder had anything to do with the writ, then he'd better watch his step too.

He loved his apartment which he'd managed to buy after his last trip working in Australia. He had saved heavily, both in the army and in civilian life, leaving him currently in an enviable position of having only a nominal mortgage.

Titus was not much of a drinker, having seen far too much excess drinking during his service, so made himself a pot of tea, to sit and contemplate. He was listening to 'Wings', the Regimental March of the Royal Engineers, on his small cassette player. This made him swell with pride, but friends would look at him quizzically, even pitifully, at what they considered his old fashion and staid music tastes.

The current popular music of the day included songs by Queen, ABBA, Kenny Rogers, Blondie and The Police, amongst others.

He smiled to himself enjoying the RE's band's strident marching music, when his new, very expensive Nokia portable phone burst into life with its shrill new ringing tone. It gave him a start because it was newly on issue to him, as the latest technology and he was far from accustomed to the demanding ring.

It was cumbersome, almost the size of a house brick, but it could be taken to most places around the City of London. He really wondered if it would lead anywhere or perhaps it was just another 'fad' from the IT people at work, who seemed to need to justify their very existence by changing everything, where no one else thought it necessary.

A young female voice spoken very softly pleaded with him, "Mr Lovell, its Rhoda Lang here, can I meet with you after I have finished work because there is something going on at Ecothan that I don't understand and I think it might be pertinent to your enquiry?"

He assumed that she was probably still at work and whispering so that nobody could overhear. He readily agreed, asking, "Where would suit you and what time would be best?" Titus asked her, "Which bus or train do you take home?" and on hearing her reply, he asked, "Could you get off the tube at Covent Garden station perhaps and meet me at Cardone's Restaurant almost alongside the station? Then we can have a drink whilst discussing what is worrying you."

She hesitated for only a moment saying that she did not expect a drink but it would be fine to meet there at about 6:30 this evening.

Why the secrecy? He wondered.

He exited from his third-floor apartment at 6 o'clock with the intention of catching the tube to Covent Garden but at that very moment a black cab was dropping off a fare and so on a whim he decided to travel by taxi, which he didn't need to do very often. As he would have expected the Cockney cabbie knew the address for Cardone's Restaurant without being told, but suggested, "I can take you somewhere better, with good English grub, not that Eye-Tie spaghetti muck!" He smiled to himself but so as not to offend, he indicated that someone else had picked the location and he was stuck with it, so with a shrug, the driver set off for Covent Garden.

These drivers were extraordinary, being right up-to-date on any road works or road closures and able to pick their way through smaller streets and lanes to avoid heavy traffic at this time of the evening. His driver was as good as any and he arrived in record time, being able to stop within about three car lengths of the restaurant. He paid the cabbie, with the usual 'keep the change, mate' as he exited.

He had eaten here once before, with a client, and knew it was pleasant, and somewhere neutral, with a safe feeling for Miss Lang.

He quickly ducked inside to book a table for two, well away from the front windows and then stepped outside again to look for her. She arrived a few minutes later hurrying towards him, already apologising, looking flustered and glancing over her shoulder. She seemed very concerned, *but god, she was gorgeous*, thought Titus.

He guided her to the table, which she seemed to approve of, because of its privacy and was now looking a little less anxious. She declined the waiter's offer to take her coat but soon removed it herself and hung it carefully over the back of her chair.

The fact that they were quite early meant that there were very few people in the restaurant and little chance of being overheard, accidentally or otherwise he thought and it made them both feel more comfortable. The waiter was still hovering so Titus requested a jug of water and two glasses, plus the menu so that they could consider their options.

She suddenly seemed embarrassed but Titus gave her a sympathetic look asking if she would like a nice glass of Australian 'red'. Her face brightened up immediately and so he ordered a bottle of a two-year-old 1978 Cabernet Sauvignon from South Australia's Coonawarra area, famous for its red soils. He knew 'Rouge Homme' as a superb, soft but full-bodied dry red wine made by the Redman family, hence the name.

"Let's take our time and have a drink," Titus said as there was no need to hurry through any of this as he certainly didn't have plans for the evening.

The waiter reappeared with the wine and two glasses and set about removing the foil cap followed by the cork and then offering Titus a sample of the wine. After his approval, the waiter began pouring out two glasses of the rich, deep plum-red wine. It was smooth and soft with a beautiful bouquet and was altogether a delightful drop of wine.

He lived alone, with his work currently being his life, which didn't trouble him because it was so interesting and took him all over the world but he had to admit that sitting in this restaurant with a lovely girl, maybe 10 years younger than him, gave him at a buzz. *Let's not get carried away here*, he thought, *this is business, as delightful as it is.*

He decided that because of her nervousness, he would slow the proceedings down and not talk business for the moment but enjoy the wine and order a couple of serves of bruschetta to soak up the wine. She initially suggested that she wasn't really interested in eating but once she started nibbling on the bruschetta it was clear that she was hungry and so when he suggested that he order a large pizza to share she readily agreed.

He asked her whether she had any favourites and enquired politely, "Perhaps vegetarian?" but this brought out a stunning smile and a comment, "Really! You must be kidding! I was brought up on a farm, so the more meat, the better."

Just what he had wanted to hear! They jointly selected an extra-large pepperoni and ground beef pizza, with a thicker crust; he called the waiter to place the order.

I'm really starting to like this girl, thought Titus, comparing her to some of the girls at his office who ate two dry biscuits and drank a glass of water for lunch, whilst talking incessantly about being 'fat', when they actually looked like pencils!

It wasn't until they were well into the pizza that he felt that she was at the point where she would open up and voice her suspicions. He had been watching her visibly relax for over an hour or so, as he chatted to her about Australia as they had this in common. She told him that she had come from a small country town named Laura in the mid-north of South Australia where she was brought up on a farm with three older brothers, before setting off to the capital city, Adelaide, to train as a nurse. The two older boys worked on the cereal crop and sheep farm with their parents but the youngest was a self-taught mechanic, maintaining the machinery and vehicles at the local ice-cream factory which was famous throughout the state.

"I love their honey-flavoured ice-cream!" she said with delight.

On arrival in Adelaide and prior to taking up the nursing opportunity, a businessman, originally from her hometown, saw her and offered her a job as a receptionist in his agricultural machine manufacturing business, at a very acceptable salary. She took evening classes in legal studies and office management, excelling at all and soon became the personal assistant to her mentor, who acted like a second father to her.

She initially lived in a rented one-bedroom flat, organised through a friend of her father but it was tiny and in a suburb which made her feel isolated, especially at night.

Later, she shared a three-bedroom house, with another country girl at Glenelg.

"I just loved living near the beach at Glenelg, as I got to watch the sunsets from the shore most nights. I'm really an outdoor girl!"

She said that she was well paid but her boss said that she was worth it and she found the work stimulating and rewarding.

After nearly three years, all this came to a painful ending, when her mentor died suddenly, leaving her personally distraught. This was compounded when his avaricious family summarily sold the business to a multinational company based in Sydney. Her boss had rebuffed the takeover bid twice, but they accepted simply to get their hands on the cash, without the need to work for it themselves!

It did not take long to decide that it was time to move on and it was at that stage she elected as her rite of passage that she should travel to London and see if her skills could be useful there.

Rhoda said that she was only 20 years old when she left Adelaide and had loved her for almost 10 years in London since then. "After a series of short-term appointments, I was eventually offered a full-time position as PA to the managing director of Ecothan plc, James Kingwell, whom I found to be very much like my previous mentor in many ways."

"I settled into this senior position well and found myself privy to all of the company's files, no matter how sensitive. With my previous experience, I had no trouble in maintaining confidentiality on all that I dealt with."

Her life became an open book to Titus when she said that she had a couple of short-term boyfriends, who she described as 'lightweight' and so, similar to Adelaide, she tended to socialise in groups, if at all.

He had been watching her chat, now in a more animated fashion and was fascinated with everything he saw and heard. She was beautiful in every sense of a word. She had dark mid-length hair which glowed in the restaurant lights and her lightly made-up face was entrancing: But it was the eyes that floored him, completely!

He was trying not to stare at her but she was talking directly at him, looking him in the eye, apparently quite unaware, he thought, of the effect she was having on him.

By this time, she invited Titus to drop the formality of 'Miss Lang' saying, "Please call me Rhoda," which was an affectation by my mother, who thought it sounded much grander than simply 'Rose', which is really what it means!

"Would I be too cheeky calling you, Rose?" to which she smiled, saying, "Only my three brothers have ever called me that, just to wind-up Mum! It would be lovely to be called Rose again after so long," and so it was decided but only if she agreed to use his Christian name too.

After that was settled, she thought that perhaps she was ready to tell what she knew, or rather about her suspicions.

Chapter 8

It was by now nearly 9:30 pm at Cardone's Restaurant and it was buzzing with movement, laughter and loud voices all seemingly in good cheer.

Rose was more relaxed and confessed to him that nerves had got to her at the office when Coetzee appeared shouting, but was now wondering whether she was being a little paranoid when she phoned Titus. She said that Mr Coetzee had totally rattled her and that it was not until later that day she collected her thoughts, to review the happenings of the last week or two.

She was genuinely grief-stricken and still red-eyed about the manner of death of Mr Kingwell, which had been told to her by Coetzee, in detail, somewhat unnecessarily. She had now suffered the loss of two very close and decent bosses and she felt very alone.

"I checked carefully through his desk and his files, feeling like a thief in the night," she said, "but there was nothing that could be linked to the issue of the writ, or the country of Jordan."

She next decided to look at his diary and on the day that the writ was served, there was a single jotting on his diary at 10:15 am, in his usual tiny neat print saying, "Writ."

A couple of days later, there was an entry reading, 'See PC and RN', which Rose said she knew nothing about nor did she understand what it meant or whether it was connected to the previous entry.

The initials 'PC' could be a match for any number of people including Pieter Coetzee and also the in-house counsel, Pat Curtis, both of whom would have had regular contact with him, as they reported to him weekly.

At this stage, she said, "My nerves were electric, my eyes were flitting everywhere and I just couldn't stand it any longer and so I left and locked up."

Coetzee's dealings with Mr Kingwell had always seemed to be satisfactory and she had no reason to think that he was anything but good at his job. "You can't like everyone," but showing her personal distaste for the man, she concluded with a small shrug of her shoulders.

Yes, she had a beautiful figure too, thought Titus, more than a little distracted by the gentle bouncing of her breasts as she shrugged.

The other item she found was a blank manila folder containing a dozen or so hand written sheets of paper and several photocopied pages dealing with various subjects including phosphorites.

"I have not had time to read anything properly but simply took them to the main office photocopier to make copies. I was so nervous whilst making the copies I actually spilt half a dozen sheets onto the floor and was near panic at being seen. Right at that moment Mr Coetzee came storming by, pausing momentarily and towering over her. 'Be careful girl' and continued on."

"As calmly as I could, I picked up the papers, completed the copying, walked back to my boss's office and buried the folder back where I found it."

Rose had taken the quarto-sized pages, rolled them up and placed them in a narrow cardboard cylinder which fitted neatly into her handbag. After having a quick nervous look around the restaurant she took it out, on her lap, and passed the cylinder to Titus under the table, looking relieved that she had got rid of this hot potato! Titus in turn was able to palm the cylinder and slip it subtly into the inside pocket of his jacket, without any fuss at all.

They spoke in general for another half hour or so about the office and its characters but nothing of interest to Titus' investigation arose, although all in all, it had been an interesting evening and he was desperate to read the papers in his pocket.

Titus couldn't keep his eyes off her and hoped it wasn't too obvious.

By now, the time was a little after 10 pm and he was concerned about her welfare in getting home safely but he was unaware where she actually lived. She said that she was accustomed to travelling home late from work on public transport but currently, she did feel a little nervous but felt silly about that.

Titus told her she had already been a great help and that she should be careful and not put herself or her employment in jeopardy by playing the amateur detective in the office. Nevertheless, if she could discreetly find out more from Kim, who'd made the original appointment, it may be a help. She too was puzzled regarding Kim and would quietly review staff records, as there were temporary staff changes happening quite regularly.

He invited her to keep in contact with him should anything come up, or for that matter worry her. She suggested, "If you need to speak to me directly, I'd suggest that you do not use the switchboard but call me on my direct outside line installed so that Mr Kingwell could bypass reception at any time to speak to me discreetly."

She handed him a black-and-white business card, but before doing so, she deleted the office number and neatly wrote in her dedicated office number, which she asked him not to disclose.

She indicated that she was now quite relaxed about taking the train home to Holland Park, as she always felt safe on the tube. Similarly, the short walk from the station to her flat was well-lit and did not cause her any concern, as she felt quite unperturbed.

He offered to hail and pay for a cab but she insisted that all was well and she was happy to travel by herself.

Titus paid the account and then walked with her to Covent Garden station where they would head in opposite directions shortly. As is often the case, at the moment of parting, the 'goodbyes' were awkward and so Titus' proffered a hand, to shake hands with her. There was an uncomfortable moment, which was resolved by Rose stepping closer and giving him a quick peck on the cheek before she darted off to her platform and he turned the other way.

What a great girl, was all that he could think as he waited the four minutes for his train. He did not have her home telephone number but resolved to call her in the morning, at work, to ensure that she was okay, or was there another reason?

Sitting on the train he reviewed the highs and lows of the day and rather wished that he was maybe six or eight years younger when he thought of Rose, but realised the truth of life and pushed the thought from his mind.

Chapter 9

Sitting on the train, the cylinder of papers in his pocket seemed to be burning a hole in it but he resisted the urge to remove it and take a peak.

He was acutely aware of the other passengers around him but saw nothing sinister in their movements.

On arrival at St Katharine Docks, he decided that he needed a clear head to review the papers and he would start on them fresh in the morning.

This was typical of his self-control, that he could push it from his mind and simply go to sleep.

Waking at 6:30 am, without an alarm, he followed his trusted routine of exercise, ablutions and breakfast, ready to start the day properly.

Sensing that this was going to continue to be a difficult case, he decided to maintain complete control of all information and rather than going into the office, he would spend the morning looking at the papers at home.

He popped the red plastic end cap out of the cardboard tube and found about two dozen sheets of quarto paper, some hand written, some copies and some that appeared to be originals, so Rose must have mixed them up after dropping them. After a short time, he had sorted them out into a number of basic subjects.

Phosphorites
A list of overseas phone calls from the office.
A list of overseas travel and associated expenses.
Some general information on Jordan.
A Company's Office search on New Giffin-Sen PLC.
A list of out-of-hours alarm codings for entry/exit from the building.
A list of all existing clients/contracts.
A list of any known or proposed new clients or contracts.
A small hand written note reading 'query PC & RN'.

He then started reading the information in detail and making mental notes only at first, as was his habit.

He turned his mind back to the papers, in particular, the handwritten note referring to the initials PC. He resolved that he would have to return to the Ecothan's office in the next day or so to see Pieter Coetzee and Pat Curtis, both of whom could have been taken into Kingwell's confidence.

Suddenly his Nokia phone rang, startling him with its shrill demanding tones. It was Rose, sounding quite bright and confident. "Titus, I had a fabulous night last night with you, and it left me feeling on top of the world, compared to my despair when I arrived. Thank you."

He added that he was pleased she had a nice evening with such 'an old bloke', at which she laughed, reassuring him that he wasn't old.

Was he fishing for a compliment? He wondered.

Then she became serious and told him that there was in fact no one named Kim on their permanent staff, but there was a girl from an agency who'd been around for a couple of weeks, called Kimberley Philpot.

"To my surprise, I found Kim was still somewhere in the office and so I decided to dig a little further and try to casually speak to her, ostensibly about how she is getting on."

Titus enquired about Nicholson (RN?) and was told that he was involved in sales and overseas matters, although she admitted that she didn't know quite what that meant.

She said, "I don't really know him and without being rude, he seems rather dull and boring to me. He doesn't dress very smartly and he looks sort of drab and out of place too, but I guess his work must be okay."

Strangely he thought that Rachel Noll also had the initials RN and wondered whether that was significant or not. This lady was involved in organising overseas travel for the executives so she may well have some ideas about Jordan.

Rose then stammered and asked Titus whether he had read today's tabloids, which had a fairly sensational story about an as yet unnamed middle-aged man, found dead in the railway yards at Richmond, with his throat cut. Obviously, Mr Kingwell, but not yet been named publicly.

He asked whether this area was close to Kingwell's home but Rose said, "No. He lived in Tonbridge Wells, in Kent, about 40 miles away and he used to take the express train home every night, from London Bridge Station."

So what was he doing there? Was he pursuing his own investigation? Or more to the point was this of any relevance, thought Titus!

This seemed to be drawing him into something that may or may not be pertinent and so he had better tread carefully.

She confirmed that the only two people with the initials PC were indeed Pieter Coetzee and their in-house counsel Pat Curtis, whilst the initials RN revealed Ron Nancarrow in the accounts department, Rachel Noll in the travel department and Ralph Nicholson in overseas sales/promotion.

He thanked her for all this fresh information and again cautioned her that she should not stick her neck out for fear of endangering herself, or her position in the company, especially since her boss was now gone.

She said, "I have a couple of other areas I could check out, without calling attention to myself and will ring you in a day or two, if that is okay with you, Titus?"

Chapter 10

For the moment, Titus passed over the pages dealing with phosphorites and the general information on the country of Jordan.

He picked up the three sheets stapled together, being a Company's House search on New Giffin-Sen PLC and read it thoroughly, without a pen in his hand, to ensure he was not distracted.

He concluded that it was a mining company, with its head office in Amman, Jordan but had a representative office in the UK, at Richmond-upon-Thames, to the near the west of London. The company president and main shareholder with 95% holding was listed as Abdal-monem Twal at an address in Amman. The minority shareholder with only 5% was listed as Ephraim Khoury whose home was listed at Queens Drive, Thames Ditton, in Surrey.

Next, he selected the list of after-hours alarm operations, which seemed to show the comings and goings of staff after about 6 pm. It appeared that Kingwell had jotted initials beside each code.

There didn't seem to be any particular patterns of note either.

What next? He thought, putting his hand on the nine-month period of overseas phone call listings. Kingwell had already worked on this list because a number of phone calls, with Middle East area codes, were highlighted. The majority of them were to one particular number, alongside which he noted Amman and one to Sana'a.

Amman he understood perfectly, but what was Sana'a about?

He knew where to find out!

He called his last OC, who now worked in a hush-hush quasi-government security business, based somewhere in London, as a Middle Eastern expert, having served in the area many times.

Bob Truscott-Browne had been a Lt Colonel and Titus, after his stellar eight months' Indian service, had just been promoted to Warrant Officer Class One (WO1). He'd come home with medals and a hero's welcome.

As a team, they worked together closely, planning advanced high-profile military joint exercises all over the world, for almost two years and despite the discrepancy in ranks, they became close friends.

"Sana'a," he was told, "is the oldest continuously inhabited city in North Yemen and also the capital."

The countries of North and South Yemen had been known previously as the British Protectorate of Aden, situated south of Saudi Arabia, and bordered by Oman to the east and the Gulf of Aden/Arabian Sea to its south. He described Sana'a in even more uncomplimentary terms than the southern capital of Aden in South Yemen, which Titus knew from other servicemen was the arsehole of the earth.

"Sana'a is an elevated city, sitting at 7,500 feet above sea level, but well inland and well away from the coastline. It has no rail connection and incredibly poor roads so the 520km drive from Aden city could take between seven and ten hours by car, depending on a million frailties. The road journey was considered a 'No-go' zone for foreigners or anyone with a brain!"

Titus thanked Bob and promised to tell him more later.

So what did North Yemen have to do with Jordan, with the latter regarded as a pleasant, safe and trouble-free country?

The obvious follow-on to that list was the overseas travel and associated expenses for the past 12 months. This list was quite extensive and again Kingwell had isolated a number of items, although Titus thought he had to be careful not to dismiss the others.

Coetzee 'starred' in many of the trips visiting Germany, Bulgaria, Algeria, several African countries and one trip to Singapore but none to any Middle Eastern country.

There were five trips by Nicholson to Lebanon, which was only separated from Jordan by the Golan Heights.

Was this the key? He would scrutinise all expenses carefully to see where and when Nicholson actually journeyed.

Rose had seemed vague about just what Nicholson's position and duties were in overseas matters because she was not really involved in his activities at all. His reaction was that he would keep this information from Rose.

He was quite impressed just how far Kingwell had progressed and Titus was now starting to wonder whether his death may well have been associated with his enquiry, where there were many millions of pounds involved. People had been killed for much less.

The dots were starting to connect, but slowly.

Titus went back to the travel expenses papers and after about half an hour felt that he had found a deficiency which he believed was putting him on the correct road. Each of Nicholson's trips to Lebanon was for four days but only one night's accommodation and meals expenses had been claimed, but in Haifa, whereas Nicholson flew into Beirut.

Why?

This was indeed intriguing because he could have flown directly into Haifa so where did he go from there, as he claimed no hotel bookings, or expenses for meals, taxis and other sundry travelling expenses on any of these three or four-day excursions.

Again he was back on the phone to Bob, who readily agreed to assist. He explained, "The obvious flight would have been into Haifa because the road journey from Beirut to Haifa, although only 120 km would take about three hours to drive, providing you did not get caught up in sectarian violence. The old peaceful holiday and business haven of years ago have long since gone and Lebanon is semi-permanently involved in a long ongoing civil war."

Having 100% confidence in Bob, Titus then gave him an outline of the matter he was investigating, outlining the details and names on the writ.

Bob told him, "The distance from Haifa in Lebanon, to Amman in Jordan, is about 150 km by road, via Syria and would take only about three and a half hours, providing you had not visited Israel, in which case, you would probably be held at the border and eventually turned back!"

He said that he would make some discreet enquiries and let Titus know if he uncovered anything useful.

So, thought Titus, *Nicholson could have been going into Jordan covertly, after booking trips to Lebanon, when it would have been much more convenient to fly straight into Amman on BA, Royal Jordanian Airlines or even Turkish Airlines via Istanbul, all of which flew out of London daily. This was certainly something to consider especially with the connection of RN noted in Kingwell's diary.*

Where did Coetzee feature, if at all?

Suddenly he heard noise outside his apartment door. Then it went silent.

Just a neighbour passing?

Still, he was now on full alert.

Again!

A scraping or scratching sound? Definitely at his door.

He listened more intently. Yes, someone or something was there.

Was it sinister?

Suddenly the door flew open and a knife-wielding man rushed in.

Fortunately, Titus had moved to one side, and a Middle-Eastern-looking man ran straight in and passed him, waving the curved knife, like a sword. He was looking left and right but Titus was behind him. Once he would've had weapons, but not now as a civilian.

Titus grabbed a coffee table and rushed the intruder, pinning him hard against the wall, keeping well away from the knife. They were eye to eye with each other and pure hatred emanated in his direction. At a stalemate now, Titus kicked him in the knee, causing him to scream in pain and drop the knife, but also dropped down under the table which had been securing him to the wall. He was scrabbling on the floor, trying to regain a grip on the knife, so Titus strove to smash the coffee table downwards onto his back.

At the last moment, the assailant twisted out of the way and only took a glancing blow on his side, enabling him to move out of Titus's reach.

Titus pivoted around to catch him again, but he was out of reach.

He held the coffee table in front of him but the assailant was still out of reach. The slippery individual scampered towards the door, picking up and hurling a large vase, striking Titus in the leg. Fortunately, he was on the run and didn't see Titus drop to his knees, otherwise he may have continued the attack.

As Titus regained his feet, he was aware that the knifeman had run to the stairs and disappeared.

He made a 999 emergency call to alert police, who attended very quickly but found no one in the area.

Titus informed the detective inspector of his own investigation and suggested the knife and assailant may be linked to Kingwell's very recent murder in Richmond.

They identified the curved knife as a traditional Janbiya, from the Middle Eastern countries, and took it for forensic examination, noting the possible connections.

He also informed Bob of the attack, who said he'd organise better security for him.

It took less than an hour for two brilliant technicians to arrive, to repair and reinforce his door.

They also fitted a second lock, where the tumbler arrangement was so sophisticated that it added another key, to his ever-expanding key ring.

Whilst this was happening, the second man checked the entire apartment for any concealed sound recording devices, quickly giving the all-clear to Titus.

Why all this special attention? He wondered.

By the time the two technicians left, he was feeling considerably more comfortable in his home environment. A few deep breaths later, he was back to the documents, now concerned where the case was leading.

He hoped Rose wouldn't be drawn into any danger.

Chapter 11

He made a call to Moles indicating that he would like to see him straight after lunch, say 1:00 pm, asking him to keep the visit confidential for the moment. Requesting him to make appointments to bring Rachel Noll to his office at 1:30 pm, Ralph Nicholson at say 2:15 pm, and Pat Curtis at say 3:15 pm, without alerting them to his presence.

On arrival, Moles shook his hand and said that he was pleased to see him again. He expressed concern that the matter in hand and the death of Jimmy Kingwell may well be linked.

The police had told him their enquiries seemed to be leading to a swarthy man, of Middle Eastern appearance, seen in the area at the time.

Titus told him of the attempt on his life, by a similar character.

He was visibly shocked.

Moles indicated that it looked as though it was going to be a complex and perhaps a long-winded investigation and wondered whether they would be better off on first-name terms, rather than 'Mister' all the time.

Titus asked if he could be given an office for a couple of hours, without interruptions, to which Peter replied he could have his office, so he set himself up.

Soon there was a knock on the door, heralding the arrival of his first witness, Rachel Noll.

He asked, "Did you facilitate any business trips to anywhere in the Middle East or other Arabian countries?"

Without delay, she indicated, "Ralph Nicholson travelled regularly to Lebanon in the last year or two, with perhaps four or five visits recently."

Jotting down notes as he went, Titus showed no particular interest, other than to ask what business interests they had in Lebanon.

Mrs Noll smiled and replied, "Strangely, I have no idea what any of our people actually do when they travel overseas but I've often wondered! It always sounds so exotic to me to be a jet setter!"

She then said, "It was only a couple of weeks ago that I prepared a list for the late Mr Kingwell. He was such a lovely man and I was so very sorry to hear about his horrific death, but if you wait a brief moment, I can recover that list from my office, if it will help."

He was pleased with the offer, which would put the list in his hand as being legally properly discovered, again removing any attachment to Rose. As a bonus she asked him, "Would you be interested in the other list Mr Kingwell asked me to prepare, being a listing of all overseas phone calls for the past two years?"

He thanked her when accepting the papers, and requested that she keep this conversation to herself, saying, "Chit chat amongst younger inexperienced staff often leads to difficulties later."

Promptly at 2:15 pm, there was a timid knock at the door and he invited entry, for his first meeting with Nicholson.

Average was the word that struck Titus.

A very average man in every way he concluded.

Medium height, medium weight, slight pot belly, light brown, thinning mousey hair, sallow complexion. He was wearing a very plain off-the-rack brown woollen suit, with a well-worn white shirt and an unremarkable beige tie. He was surprised to see Titus in this office, obviously expecting to see Moles and abruptly stood quite rigid, half way between the door and the desk.

Titus walked around the desk to meet him offering his hand and introducing himself by name and occupation. He found Nicholson's hand was clammy and weak, not something he would expect to see in a sales manager or whatever he was supposed to be. He invited him to sit at the desk and returned to his position behind it, to explain about the writ and how he had been tasked to solve the riddle, ready for a massive court case in a few months' time.

He opened by asking Nicolson, "Do you know either of the two names listed in the legal proceedings; they being New Giffin-Sen PLC and Abdal-monem Twal?"

Nicholson replied, "Su...su...sorry neither name rings a bell with me," stuttering out his unconvincing answer.

He watched as Titus jotted something down and then paused as though fumbling for the next question. Out of the corner of his eye, he could see

Nicholson relaxing a little so he told him, "I'm really struggling with this matter altogether, so perhaps to give me a better idea of what this company does, could you explain your position here and exactly what your duties are please?"

Titus knew the best way to relax someone was to ask them harmless questions where they knew the answers and felt comfortable talking and this was one of the best.

As Nicholson started to talk, he relaxed quite visibly, telling Titus, "I've been with the company for 15 years and in the last three years have operated as a sort of an unattached sales/procurement manager, seeking out new overseas opportunities and contracts; as a liaison to facilitate them moving forward."

Time to drop a bombshell, asking Nicholson, "Please explain the contract you have been working on in Lebanon for the past eighteen months or so."

The change in appearance was dramatic as Nicholson turned white and immediately was bathed in sweat, with large unpleasant wet patches now appearing on his shirt underarm areas. He seemed dumbstruck because he had been lulled into a state where he had felt comfortable and now he simply stuttered, without making any sense.

He then repeated the question suggesting that he would like to see any preliminary work, legal opinions or even contracts to see whether there could be any connection to the Jordanian matter that he was investigating.

When pressed again, he mumbled, "It, umm, involves working between several countries, but is highly confidential, with huge monies involved. Off the top of my head, I couldn't possibly put my finger on any names."

Pressing again Titus asked, "Is it possible that New Giffin-Sen PLC or a Mr Twal are involved?"

Whereas Nicholson's whole demeanour screamed yes, the shaking of his head said no!

Titus said, "I have another interview in just a moment, so I must insist on at least the name on the contract now."

However, Nicholson stalled and stammered without any sensible reply. In the absence of any useful information from Nicholson, Titus said that he should return to his office, collect the appropriate files and return at 4 pm with those files and they would continue the interview.

With that, Nicholson literally fled out of the door leaving Titus about five minutes to complete his notes, think about what he'd just heard and be ready for Pat Curtis.

Chapter 12

With precision, at 3:15 pm, there was a stout knock at the door, which was immediately opened and in walked Pat Curtis, without waiting for an invitation. She was of an indeterminate age which Titus thought could have been anywhere from the early 30s to early 40s. She was a professional woman and dressed as such, giving an air of complete confidence in herself, which he considered impressive.

She articulated, "Mr Kingwell briefly mentioned to me that a writ had been served on Ecothan. He said that as soon as he had referred it to our liability insurance underwriters and when he had made his own basic enquiries, he would need to involve my expertise. He didn't sound overly concerned about it, saying that none of the names were at all familiar and so it may not actually involve Ecothan."

"In the meantime, I should explain that I have been on three weeks leave, travelling in the United States and have only just returned to work this week to hear of the tragedy of Mr Kingwell's savage death."

She stated that she had never even seen the writ and so Titus placed his copy on the desk for her to scrutinise. She ran a practised eye over it, looking at the important areas rather than all the padding and legal mumbo jumbo, thought for a moment and declared, "Nothing in it rings any bells with me about any contract that I have ever examined, and they all come my way numerous times before being signed off. None of the names are familiar nor are there any contracts in the country of Jordan to my knowledge, because I would have had to research local laws before sanctioning Ecothan's involvement. These types of contracts are very complex and require months of negotiation and refining to be brought to a proper conclusion."

Titus said, "Jordan is very close to Lebanon and I understood that Ecothan is currently working on at least one new contract there."

She replied, "It has been a long time since we have been involved in war-torn Lebanon and certainly nothing for that country has come before me in the last two years. Furthermore, the civil war situation would put any potential contracts there well outside Ecothan's company risk management profile."

He referred to Ralph Nicholson as travelling there a number of times recently and she replied it was news to her. "I have not worked on any contracts at all for Nicholson for at least 18 months, which makes me wonder what he actually does, because he certainly wasn't bringing in any new business."

She seemed very precise and factual, with no wasted words. He then refocussed sideways and asked about Coetzee's role referring directly to the difficult time of their first meeting.

"I do not particularly warm to him but think that apart from his arrogance, he seems to carry out his duties for the company quite efficiently and honestly; just not very pleasantly!"

Titus confided in her, "Both Peter Moles and I are suspicious of the connection between the murder of Mr Kingwell and this investigation, so you should be vigilant and particularly discreet, in case there is any staff involvement or leaks of information."

Titus then took the unusual step of warning her not to involve Nicholson, reminding her that of course his request was strictly in confidence.

Pat Curtis was a no-nonsense straightforward young woman, obviously competent and had left the office saying that she would confide in only him and Peter Moles.

By now, it was 4 pm and he was expecting Nicholson any moment. He was carefully concluding his notes of the Curtis interview, ready to turn a fresh page and continue with Nicholson. The next time he looked at his watch, it was 4:11 pm, causing him to wonder where Nicholson had got to.

As he was unfamiliar with the telephone's internal intercom system, he could not buzz a reminder to his office. So after waiting a few more minutes, he walked next door to Kingwell's old office, knocked and entered to speak to Peter Moles. He gave him a brief summary of the interviews but said he had been waiting about 20 minutes for Nicholson to produce the Lebanon proposed contract and documentation and he didn't know how to buzz him, nor the location of his office.

Moles picked up his telephone handset, dialled a two-digit extension code and waited. He then flipped open a small in-house directory, rechecked the number and dialled again but still without an answer. Looking puzzled he said, "I'll call reception and I am sure that they will know Nicholson's whereabouts within the office."

"Nicholson left the office in a hurry at just after 3 pm telling reception that he was unwell and would not be back today! He must have walked straight out of the interview with you and left the building immediately! I do not like the potential of that," said Moles, addressing Titus.

Titus also expressed some concern saying, "He appears to be the only staff member who visited the Middle East and he may be the key to this whole issue. This all ought to be kept particularly confidential between the two of us and we should not alert Nicholson about our suspicions, agreed?"

Titus asked that he be informed in the morning, as soon as Nicholson arrived and he could be at Ecothan's office within 20 to 25 minutes, to continue this enquiry and examine any potential contracts in Lebanon.

Titus indicated, "I think that I am just about finished for today, Peter, but wonder if it would be prudent for me to see Miss Lang, to see whether she has any inkling about this matter?"

Peter said, "I'll buzz her, requesting that she come to my old office, so perhaps you can wander down there now and meet her."

Titus waited only a few moments in Moles' office for Rose's arrival.

She was surprised and pleased to see him, indicating that she did not know he was in the building but was expecting to see Mr Moles.

"I'm trying to minimise your personal involvement and so I made my appointment directly with Peter Moles. How are you coping, Rose? Is anything in particular concerning you, apart from the obvious loss of your boss."

She replied, "Yet another news report on this morning's radio upset me again when it confirmed Mr Kingwell's murder and highlighted its gruesome nature. The police have spoken to me briefly again today by phone, but since I had left the office before Mr Kingwell on the fateful day, I could not even tell them what time he set off for his home."

She continued, "I can offer no explanation as to why he was in that area because he always took the express train each evening."

Suddenly she remembered and was bubbling over to tell him that she had made a point of bumping into Kim. She is an average receptionist, photocopier and filing clerk but not a very good typist, she herself declared.

As she seemed quite genuine, Rose asked whether she had ever made appointments for staff members and the girl suddenly flushed, saying she had once made an appointment for Mr Kingwell but rather casually said, "Oh yes. I forgot to write it down, but it doesn't matter now because he is dead!"

Rose looked even lovelier today than she had last evening and suddenly he found himself blurting exactly that sentiment to her but then feeling embarrassed. She was very sweet about it and thanked him for the compliment, repeating that she had no social life to speak of and couldn't remember the last honest flattering remark that had come her way.

Smiling, she recalled, "I have three big brothers at home, who always teased me about my tomboy looks as I was growing up; but I once heard them talking together saying, she is the best looking bird in the Laura area, so we'd better keep the boys away for a while."

She fondly remembered this as the best compliment she had ever received and coming from her own quite shy, rough and-tumble farm boy bachelor brothers it was extra special, and they were always very protective too!

She stood up to return to work with Titus standing beside her, simply enjoying the innocent closeness to her. He smiled, saying that they would speak again and for the second time she reached up and gave him a quick kiss on the cheek, saying it would be nice for them to get together again, before blushing slightly, spinning on her heel and disappearing through the door rather quickly.

He didn't tell her of the attack at his home.

And he didn't know that Nicholson and just driven straight to New Giffin-Sen's office in Richmond-On-Thames.

Chapter 13

After his posting to India, he returned to the UK, a minor celebrity in the army generally and especially in his Corps, The Royal Engineers. Initially, he was made a recruiting 'pin-up' boy, which role he did not identify with at all.

It was not his style of soldiering at all.

After the fuss died down and the army had used up his two minutes of fame, he was posted to Lt. Colonel Robert Algernon (Bob) Truscott-Browne's special development unit at the Aldershot army barracks as a WO1.

This posting was rather benign but allowed him to gather his thoughts and consolidate what he may do in perhaps a future civilian life. The 'think tank' he was in was strictly an office hour type job, and even then he had considerable 'spare' time.

A chance meeting with someone he had not seen since schooldays led him to consider a career as an Insurance Loss Adjuster/Investigator, which he understood had a good mix of the outdoors, meeting people, plus time in the office. He was told of the pre-requisites for the job and so immediately enrolled in the Chartered Insurance Institute's Associate course. With all his spare time, he was able to complete the course in record time, giving him a deep understanding of most facets of general insurance.

He had just over a year to complete his service and so decided to make an appointment to see the chairman of the largest Chartered Loss Adjusting company in London for some advice. He took along his CV and his recent insurance qualifications and was very pleased to find the chairman had been a major in The Royal Fusiliers, City of London Regiment, during World War II, and as they say, 'once a soldier always a soldier', so they got on like a house on fire.

Cyril Blake said that if he was really keen, he would personally seek a special dispensation from the Institute of Chartered Loss Adjusters for Titus to commence their studies and examinations, which were only open to individuals already working for a member company, under proper supervision. If Titus was prepared to commence such studies and showed some aptitude, Blake, was prepared to offer him support initially and then employment upon his discharge from the army.

By the end of 12 months, he had completed five subjects of the eight, with distinctions and knew so many people in the office that he felt quite at home there.

He had a real feel for the job even before he started.

His discharge from the army, after years of service, came with little fanfare, as was the norm, with him checking in all his gear, undergoing medicals and other formalities, followed by a few handshakes and then marching out of the gates for the last time. He was of course placed on the Army's Ready Reserve for a period of six years and therefore compulsorily available for re-activation in the case of conflict, or if otherwise deemed essential by HM's Government.

It was a strange feeling leaving this all behind but he believed that his future in civilian life was assured and he had no regrets.

The new chapter started as promised, with Blake signing him on as a trainee loss adjuster, initially assisting others with assessing property loss issues.

His ability to quickly and efficiently determine facts and resolve complex issues led him to investigate major liability matters.

After five years, Blake approached him saying that they could all benefit greatly from him undertaking a 12-month exchange with their Melbourne, Australia office. As a single man who had travelled a great deal in the army, this came as a welcome distraction and he readily agreed.

He accepted this as simply another 'posting', true to his army training; telling Blake that once he had tidied up and passed on his existing files, which were in perfect order, he would be ready to leave, in say two days. Blake nodded, remembering how soldiers were accustomed to being posted at a minute's notice and realising that if he had approached any other staff member, they would have wanted a couple of weeks to consider the proposal and at least three months' preparation to move to the other side of the world.

"If only I had a dozen men like this on my staff, life would be a breeze," he reflected, thinking of the Pareto Principle of 80/20%, meaning 80% of your business problems normally came from only 20% of your staff and conversely, 80% of your profits may also come from a chosen 20% of the staff.

Chapter 14

The following morning, Titus was in his own office by 7:00 am putting in some serious work on existing files and dictating reports, plus instructions for other adjusters to continue activities for him, allowing him to concentrate on the Ecothan case. This took him through until about 9 o'clock and the whole time he was waiting on a phone call from Moles telling him that Nicholson was in the office, but it never came.

By 9:15 am, he could not wait any longer and put a call through to Moles to see what was happening. Peter told him that there was no sign of Nicholson, nor any message from him. Consequently, he had personally just placed a call to his home. His wife Anne had answered and said that he left for work at 7:30 am, as usual, yesterday, but she thought that he was probably travelling today, but she didn't know where, as he didn't disclose details of his trips to her.

So, what had happened?

He obviously did not go home last night, after seeing me. Had he too encountered violence, or had he simply skipped town?

Titus said, "With your permission, Peter, I will come to the office immediately and providing there is no legal privacy difficulty, we should make a thorough search of Nicholson's office to see what trails can be found on any of his activities in the Middle East."

Again he warned Peter as to the need for complete security but suggested, "I think it would be wise to have your in-house counsel, Pat Curtis, present during the search to independently record what we may find."

Feeling there was now some urgency, he hailed a black cab and arrived in no time.

On arrival, Titus was again met in the foyer by Peter who took him directly to his office where Pat Curtis was waiting.

They walked from Moles' office to the opposite end of that floor, with no one in the corridor and so they entered the office unnoticed.

The office was very untidy but no one seemed to know whether that was the usual state of affairs or whether something unusual had happened recently.

Curtis had her large yellow legal notepad with her and simply stood in the middle of the room watching proceedings. She asked them how they intended to go about the search and the reason; obviously to cover everyone's backside, in case anything went wrong, but it was all duly noted.

Titus liked her thoroughness.

What a mess. Where to start?

There were papers scattered over the desk, on top of a modern white-painted credenza, and in the two-drawer filing cabinet, which fortunately was unlocked. Moles took the lead and suggested that they start on the papers on the desk, as perhaps the most recently worked on files. They started carefully examining each page, many of which were of no interest, nevertheless all were judiciously listed by Curtis.

Next, they examined his diary, which likewise had very few appointments or notes in it. Again the thought occurred, "What does this man do?"

They noted a diary entry for 4 pm, two days ago, which simply read 'EK'. Neither Curtis nor Moles knew whether that was a company or person's initials or a place and so they were no more enlightened.

Together they looked back over the 12 months and the same letters appeared several times and so the dates of those entries were meticulously noted. There did however appear to be one breakthrough with the word 'Khoury' clearly written about four months ago. This was very significant to Titus, but not necessarily the others, because he had seen the list of shareholders in New Giffin-Sen and one of them was none other than Efraim Khoury.

The final task was to check all the documents in the filing cabinet but after two more hours, there was absolutely nothing about Lebanon and certainly nothing about Jordan, or New Giffin-Sen.

When the search was completed, they vacated the office, leaving it in exactly the same condition as before, locking the door and returning to Mole's office for a final discussion. On the way, they passed a large photocopying machine, at which Curtis stopped and made two copies of the five pages of listings of Nicholson's documents. They were neatly prepared, plus she had already signed and dated them.

In the confidence of Moles' office, Curtis was the first to speak, saying that it was prudent for each of them to have a copy of her notes and then commenting that it was very strange that nothing had been found in the office relating to Lebanon and yet Nicholson had made several trips there. They all agreed saying that the absence of documents was almost as damning as finding them.

To deflect any questions, before they were asked, Titus indicated that he would now return to his own office, with the list and carefully trawl through it to see whether he could find anything worthwhile. They all seemed to understand something seriously illegal was afoot and the three of them should be the only ones privy to this latest episode's details.

Curtis nodded to them, acknowledging that her work was complete, excused herself and left the office; all very business-like.

Nicholson did not have a personal secretary assigned to him and a quick enquiry around the office failed to uncover anyone who had any knowledge of his workload or appointments, not only today but at any time.

He was indeed proving to be enigmatic.

How had he managed to get away with apparently achieving nothing for nearly two years, but at the same time taking regular long-distance overseas trips?

Chapter 15

He had been invited to Bob's London flat when details on the in-depth report on the company itself came back but it was much as expected. It confirmed the two shareholders and no adverse reports. It was very scant on financial information, which didn't assist him to advance any further.

However, the report on Efraim Khoury personally, was quite different. Bob told him that some of the report had been redacted, blacked out for security, but the remainder was no less damning.

Firstly, there was a new major security warning on him, issued by the CIA, over 12 months ago, for strongly suspected connections with a North Yemeni terrorist group based in Sana'a. However, more strangely he had connections and business around the port area of Aden, which was in the neighbouring South Yemen, at a time when there was no love lost between the two countries, after the big split-up.

So there's Sana'a again, thought Titus; definitely the town in North Yemen.

Secondly, there appeared to be a huge question mark hanging over Khoury's wealth in the UK, based on a magnificent multi-million-pound house on the River Thames, and the extensive movement of monies through bank accounts in the UK, Europe, Cayman Island and then several poorer African countries. The authorities were suspicious of it involving either money laundering and/or at worst, funding of terrorist groups' activities.

Bob was told that if he had any information on Khoury to be extremely careful, for he was a very dangerous man and to report it immediately back to SIS, better known as MI6 (Military Intelligence-Section 6).

Titus was very well aware of the operations of MI6 because he had been extensively debriefed by them upon his return from his Indo-Pakistani campaign and he trusted their judgement implicitly.

It had been arranged for Bob to accompany Titus to Century House, 100 Westminster Bridge Road, Lambeth, the headquarters of SIS or MI6, not that far from Ecothan's offices, also just off the south bank of the River Thames but at the adjoining suburb of Southwark.

It was clear that on his arrival at MI6, Bob was quite at home there and that the two operatives who greeted them knew all about Titus' military career too. In fact, there was a file on the table which clearly had his name on it!

They invited Titus to speak.

Titus told them, "Whilst investigating a writ issued on behalf of New Giffin-Sen and Mr Abdal-Monem Twal, I became suspicious of a man named Khoury and his possible connection to a massive fraud, involving millions of pounds sterling. Furthermore, because I had never met the man and legally was not permitted to contact him, I made it my business to suss him out. I knew a direct approach was out of the question so I decided on a more oblique attack."

He continued, "For complete anonymity, I organised a couple of drive-byes of his home in a taxi cab, to get some idea of the property, possibly the man himself and his lifestyle. I pretended to be doing some sort of survey of the rich and famous and so the cabbie was unconcerned at passing through the same street three times, slowly."

Titus noticed subtle eye contact between the two agents, hopefully of approval.

"I also viewed the property from the river, as part of a large unrelated group of tourists on a regular commercial tourist charter boat. I took the typical boat trip along the Thames, where they pointed out landmarks, buildings of historical interest and the homes of the rich and famous. I noted that unlike most of the homes on the river, which had lawns running down to the water, to make the most of their views and amenities, this place had fortress-like fences around it, complete with a lock-up boat shed of considerable size. My impression was of not only extreme wealth but also secrecy and possibly nefarious activities. Whereas I do not know the financial turnover of New Giffin-Sen PLC, I know that Khoury is only a 5% shareholder and otherwise a simple employee of the company in London. That fails to explain this wealthy lifestyle."

He confirmed the murder of Mr James Kingwell. Referring them to newspaper reports suggesting that a man of Arabic appearance was seen in the area at the time, and also reminded them of the attack at his home. He detailed to the agents that his preliminary enquiries suggested that Kingwell had started his own investigation into New Giffin-Sen and may have made the mistake of contacting Khoury directly.

He also pointed out that an employee by the name of Ralph Nicholson had gone missing but he wasn't sure whether this was due to foul play, or if he was in hiding to avoid scrutiny from this insurance enquiry.

The agents listened intently, without interrupting or taking notes and so he assumed the discussion was being tape-recorded, by concealed microphones.

Pretty standard he guessed.

They then indicated that they held previous knowledge of Khoury, but after contact from Truscott-Browne, they had made some further enquiries and believed that Titus had stumbled onto a major national security issue, quite aside from what could be a massive international industrial fraud.

Titus was then reminded that he was still subject to the terms of the Official Secrets Act, sworn by him during his military service and that its terms still held good.

Bloody hell, he thought, things are looking serious and these guys mean business.

It was his turn to sit back and let someone else speak and he wondered what if anything they were prepared to tell him; but these guys were good, they said nothing. He knew this technique, waiting to see if he blabbed on!

After several minutes of silence, he spoke and suggested, "Gentlemen, if there is nothing more I can assist you with, how should I continue with this investigation, into the suspected insurance fraud, without upsetting MI6's activities," thereby pushing a decision back to them.

The older of the two agents smirked very slightly, seeming to confirm that Titus had not been overwhelmed and had called their bluff, so it was indeed over to them.

Bob remained silent throughout but it was clear that he had vouched for Titus for there was no real pressure put on him, nor did they make him feel too uncomfortable.

Another silence fell over the room.

He recalled from his last visits here, after India, for his debriefing that there were no introductions and no names given by the agents and today was no different. This was their Standard Operating Procedure, tried and trusted, so he had no difficulty with it.

Still, the silence persisted, but he had nothing to defend!

Bob broke the silence by directing his question jointly at the two agents, enquiring whether they wanted to involve Lovell or to let him continue with his insurance fraud enquiry independently, but report back regularly to them, or if they preferred through him. He assured them of Lovell's discretion and reliability, indicating that he had made several attempts to coax him into a position in his own quasi-governmental security organisation, without success.

"Thank you very much, Warrant Officer, we know your military record and believe you will be useful to us now. Please give us 24 hours to consider the situation and we will let you have your orders, via Colonel Truscott-Browne. Furthermore, consider that this meeting never took place and your future dealings will only ever be with the colonel, unless we say otherwise. Is that clear?"

"Crystal clear, gentleman, thank you," Titus replied and with that; the senior agent left, giving the task of showing them out of the building to the younger agent.

They were escorted in silence across to the lifts, down to the ground floor and then signed out at the Security Desk, where their visitor's identity tags were taken from them.

Once out in the open, they walked briskly away towards Westminster Bridge, before ultimately stopping to lean on the railings to discuss what had just happened.

Titus enquired, "What was all that about orders?"

"Spooks. You must remember what they are like; from the last time you saw them."

"Don't worry about it. The department is very concerned about Khoury and I agree that for the moment you should just suspend everything for the weekend, but you should be aware that MI6 can reactivate a soldier, any time they see fit!"

"Reactivate a soldier! What the fuck is that all about, Bob?"

"Not now, Warrant Officer!" admonished Bob, automatically resuming his position as a colonel.

"Why don't you arrange to enjoy dinner again with that lovely Miss Lang over the weekend?" He said with a smile and more as a friend.

"How the hell did you know about her, Bob? This is getting weird."

"All I can say is that the spooks have been busy already, for longer than you think!" as he marched smartly away.

Well, I'll be stuffed, thought Titus, *this must be far more serious and run a lot deeper than I thought.*

Chapter 16

By now, it was about 4 pm and after the inquisition at MI6, strangely the only thought on his mind was Bob's suggestion!

He had Rose's business card in his pocket and on the spur of the moment took the brick-sized cell phone out of his brief case and found a sheltered spot, out of the wind, to make a call. He started to punch in her direct office number, hesitated, feeling unsure of himself, then continued. She answered the phone instantly, which hadn't given him time to think what he was going to say. In a very quiet but quite captivating voice, she said, "Is that you, Titus?"

He paused for a moment and awkwardly almost grunted, "Yes."

He could hear a little sparkle in her voice when she said, "I am so so glad to hear from you, Titus, especially since it has been such a horrid week here at work."

"How did you know it was me?" He queried.

"Oh, that was easy, only you and Mr Kingwell have the number!"

He asked if she was okay and she replied happily, "I feel very happy right now, thank you!"

Perhaps he hadn't misread her suggestion that they ought to get together again and so this remark gave him some courage. After some pleasantries, he took the bull by the horns and enquired, "I'd like to see you again, Rose. Would you like to meet me for a drink after work today, if you aren't busy?"

Without any hesitation, she replied, "Oh, I thought you'd never ask! Wonderful. Whereabouts?"

He laughed with her and said that they should meet somewhere and just wander around to find somewhere that suited their tastes.

Rose said, "I intend to finish work at five o'clock, on the dot today, but would like to take some shopping home first; change to be more presentable and then we can meet up at say 6:30 pm. Would that be okay for you?"

This arrangement was fine with Titus and all that was left was to nominate somewhere to meet so he suggested the Statue of Eros in Piccadilly Circus, simply as a landmark, if that would suit her too. She agreed that this was an easy spot for her to reach on the tube, so 6:30 pm it was!

Now he was really nervous! He thought he would rather go into battle than try to work out what to wear this evening.

She was going home to change her clothes: into what? She couldn't look any better than she did at work!

He thought that he would head home straight away and consider his options.

He hadn't had to do this for over a year, in fact, since he was working in Melbourne and had a casual girlfriend.

Titus reasoned that Rose dressed impeccably at work and that she might choose something more casual for the evening. With this in mind, he changed into some smart camel-coloured chinos, coupled with a light blue coloured subtly striped shirt, plus a lightweight jacket. Hell, it was a lot easier being in the army when the dress of the day was specified at all times!

He set off from home on the Circle Line to Embankment, where he changed to the Northern Line and two stations later, he was at Piccadilly Circus Station, emerging from underground into the evening darkness.

Rose would be coming from the opposite direction to him, so he presumed she would start on the Central Line and then change at Oxford Circus onto the Bakerloo Line, which was then only one stop to Piccadilly Circus.

He liked to work out these things.

He walked towards the mass of people around the steps at the base of Eros and suddenly wondered whether this had been a good choice, because he may not be able to find her in this milling, noisy, happy Friday night throng.

However, it was a beautiful clear night and he felt over the moon about this little rendezvous.

After a short time, there was a gentle tap on his arm and he turned to see Rose, right beside him, smiling beautifully. She looked fantastic and immediately reached up and forward to give him a now customary kiss on the cheek but this time with an associated hug.

"You look even better out of your work clothes," was all he could say, realising too late the double entendre and squirmed like a teenager with embarrassment but she raised her eyebrows and laughed, telling him, "Oh really! You wish! You brushed up pretty well too."

There was no awkwardness or overt 'girliness' to put him on edge and he was able to relax immediately in her company. She was wearing tight red jeans, a beautiful soft cream jumper and with a light linen jacket over her shoulders, she looked as though she had emerged straight off a modelling catwalk.

He wasn't the only one staring but she seemed quite oblivious.

Without any show of embarrassment, she linked arms with him and confessed that she had no suggestions of where they could go, so perhaps they could stroll around for the moment. He was more than happy with this and as they ambled along she chatted in a very natural fashion, with him happy to listen.

It was not very long before they turned into Great Windmill Street, the beginning of the Soho district and they both spotted the Duke of Argyll Hotel at the same time, just ahead. A quick glance of agreement passed between them and he steered her through the door and up to a small gap at the bar, which area they claimed as their own.

"Name your poison," he said smiling at her and she replied, "I'd love a nice cold glass of Riesling, please."

Strangely enough, Riesling was the only white wine that he had taken a liking to, whilst living in Australia. "I wonder if they have any Clare Valley Riesling?" He mused aloud to her and then turned to the barman making such an enquiry.

A broad, nasal Australian voice replied, "Yeah, mate, we've got a bottle of 1978 Skillogalee Riesling uncorked in the fridge, open and ready to go! It's a beaut drop for a two-year-old wine too. Okay?"

Titus ordered a glass each for them and as the barman worked his way up and down the bar they spoke to him several times learning that he was from Cooktown in Far North Queensland, hence the drawl. He was a great young bloke and kept the bar enthralled with his outlandish stories that the pub patrons were lapping up. Rose and Titus exchanged knowing looks as the tales became more exciting, if not more outrageous, involving giant crocodiles, poisonous snakes and huge killer spiders, plus fighting off boxing kangaroos in the streets.

The guy was a born raconteur and entertainer.

Soon he'd be wrestling sharks!

Occasionally, he'd glance at them and raise an eyebrow, acknowledging that they weren't swallowing any of it!

After a very comfortable hour, Titus suggested that they move on and see what else was happening. They signalled their thanks to the barman, indicating they were leaving and he shouted after them, "Watch out for those drop bears!" to the astonishment of the drinkers.

Rose was happy to follow, clinging tightly to his arm and he had to admit to feeling somewhat euphoric, like a school boy. She was warm against his arm and he could feel her body contours moulding into his side, adding to his bliss. It had been a long time!

He asked whether she would like another drink or perhaps something to eat, but she unusually became a little coy, saying she did not expect him to take her to dinner again.

Titus replied, "I'm definitely feeling hungry and the way you helped to demolish the pizza at Cardone's, I bet you are too."

Smiling at being caught out, she laughed, "I've always had a healthy appetite and I am hungry but don't want you to think that you have to feed me all the time."

She steered this time, along busy Shaftesbury Avenue, towards Chinatown, telling him that one of her favourite meals was 'Chinese' because her parents used to take the kids to The Red Dragon Chinese restaurant in the nearby town of Clare, occasionally, as a family treat, usually for birthdays.

She chatted away happily about what was happening around them, about her youth and generally, the conversation was light, with no reference to work; all very refreshing for Titus.

They smiled at the very different produce in the windows of the Chinatown shops and both pointed at the glossy brown roasted ducks, hanging by their necks on hooks in the windows, complete with their somewhat scorched heads! Yes, the Chinese certainly loved ducks!

There were spruikers outside just about every restaurant, enjoining them to enter their 'superior' establishment; most were very polite but some were unpleasantly assertive. A group of young people poured out of a brightly lit restaurant across the road from them, exuding joy and happiness and were being farewelled by the staff as they moved off down the street.

It was typically Chinese named 'The Pearl Palace' and this scene seemed to be the best advertisement of goodwill and good food. They crossed the narrow street and were welcomed in like long-lost friends, by no less than five staff members, probably covering three generations of the same family.

The atmosphere inside was just as they expected and they were ushered to a small booth for two, which was situated in a quiet corner of the brightly decorated restaurant; all red and gold, with its fair share of lanterns and dragon motifs.

He felt slightly awkward as they were put in a comfy little lovers' booth, but Rose seemed unfazed, saying, "Titus, this is an adorable spot and I really love being in here with you."

A tiny waitress, with a pretty face, was hovering just behind him and speedily took his order, returning within a minute with a bottle of white wine and glasses. She struggled awkwardly to extract the cork and then poured the bottom of the glass for him to sample. It was very palatable and beautifully chilled so he nodded his assent to her, she leaned towards Rose, poured her glass, and then filled his, before withdrawing slightly.

They quickly agreed to order the smaller of the banquets for two meals on offer and were happy to share the many small dishes, in the traditional Chinese way of eating.

Rose insisted that it would be fun if they both used chopsticks, as this was her family's tradition, even though her dad thought it was stupid when proper cutlery was laid out to use. They both initially struggled to manipulate their sticks but it wasn't long before they improved, eating and laughing their way through the seven-course mini banquet.

She said that she had talked far too much about herself and now she wanted to know something about him. Titus replied that there was not much to tell, saying that at one stage he had been a soldier and the last few years an independent loss adjuster, investigating and settling insurance claims.

Rose wanted him to talk about his life as a soldier but he told her that most of the work of an army engineer was boring and there was not much to tell. She was not easily put off and kept 'drilling' into him for details and so he told her briefly of various postings around Europe. She wanted to know what rank he reached and he found that he did not have to explain what WO1 meant, as her uncle had been a Warrant Officer Class 1 in the Korean War and she was very proud of her Uncle Jack.

Then she asked him what medals he had received but could see that he was embarrassed and apologised for being too nosey and tactless. This was the first real awkwardness between them and so he decided to be honest with her saying that it was not her fault as it was something that he hadn't spoken about for many years. She placed her hand over his, on the table, and gently stroking it, said,

"Titus, I'm really sorry that I'm so nosey and embarrassed you, but I just want to know every little thing about you."

He mentioned his return to the UK from India/Pakistan/Kashmir after eight months, wearing two Indian army campaign medals and their Vishist Sena Medal (AVSM) for Valour. Additionally, a Distinguished Service Medal (DSM) for gallantry in the face of the enemy, awarded by the British army. He had received permission to wear all of them on his British Army uniform, as they were gained on an active duty posting, for an ally.

He said that it started off with the usual difficulties but soon deteriorated into a brutal bloody conflict which he had tried to push from his mind. He squeezed her hand and said he did not need to keep any secrets between them, so all he wanted to say was that during some heavy fighting, centred on one side of a bridge, over a fast-flowing river, many men were in danger of dying. To save the situation he had managed to detonate explosives, which brought down the bridge, preventing a squadron of fast-moving Pakistani tanks from crossing over and thereby saving the loss of the lives of his unit.

She listened quietly and intently, gripping his hand and feeling his pain with him.

She waited and then asked him, "Is that what they gave you the medals, for doing all that?"

She smiled her approval at him, but as was her manner, she did not dwell but moved on straight away, surprising him by asking, "Do you have a nickname, Titus?"

He thought about several he'd scored over the years, mostly in the army but also a couple from Aussies when he was out there. Not all of them 'stuck' and so he decided to disclose only three.

"Nitro, or TG, in the army and 'Captain' from the Aussies."

"How come?" She asked.

"Nitro from my days in the Royal Engineers and short for nitro-glycerine, as I was pretty good at blowing up things!" he grinned, "and Captain as an oblique reference to my military career, from my Aussie workmates, mainly in Melbourne."

"What about TG? Oh, I know, I suppose that's your initials? What's your middle name then, George, Graham, Garry, Guy, Gerald…?" She reeled off.

Again a little embarrassed, he replied that it was the Indian Special Forces troops that he served with who had given him the nickname, 'TeeGee', straight after the bridge battle, short for 'Tough Guy' and easier for them to pronounce than Warrant Officer Lovell.

"Well, since I'm Rose, I'm going to call you TG from now on. Oh, I love it! No arguments! My brothers were tough guys, but just as gentle as you."

What could he say? An old name had come back to haunt him, but he loved the way she said it and her sentiments about it. Anyway, it was done, so it seemed!

"Please don't tell anyone what TG stands for. Okay?" He pleaded.

"Of course not, it will be our special secret," she said, still holding his hand and feeling glad he'd let her in so quickly and openly.

The meal, the service and the wine were all first class but he thought that her company was fabulous. He was absolutely revelling in her company.

Right then Rose asked him, "What are you thinking at the moment, TG?"

He felt caught out but thought he might as well tell her what had just passed through his mind and how he felt.

She was not embarrassed and said, "I'm having a wonderful time too, with the same sort of warm fuzzy feelings running through me as well."

He was thinking that as gorgeous as she was, she must be the most unpretentious and natural girl he had ever met.

Quite naturally changing the subject again, she asked him whether he thought they may serve deep-fried ice-cream because as a kid it was her unqualified favourite in the Red Dragon. He looked on the dessert page of the menu and there it was; so the waitress was summonsed and efficiently took orders for two serves, dashing off to the kitchen to instruct the cook.

It was a first for him but he enjoyed it, although watching her relish it, giving him an even more affectionate feeling for her.

When they were finished, he paid at the desk and left a tip for the young girl who had been so attentive to their needs and then what seemed like the entire staff followed them out into the street, to wave them off, with many thanks.

It was still only 10:00 pm as they wandered along Old Compton St, enjoying the sights and sounds of the evening as it became cooler. Rose's arm was linked around his even more tightly than before, again chatting cheerfully and looking in shop windows as they walked. Her body moulded against his side felt so good he just wanted to keep walking!

They passed several large newish, brightly lit American-styled flashy coffee shops, but turned their noses up at them, seeking a more traditional and cosy place to have coffee.

Their walk long Shaftesbury Avenue brought them around to Leicester Square and they soon found a lovely little old-fashioned coffee house, complete with small Charles Dickens-type leadlight window glasses forming the frontage. It was too early to be crowded, but he knew that it would be packed as soon as the big West End Shows had finished, disgorging literally thousands of patrons into the area.

Rose told him shyly, over coffee, "TG, this has been my nicest evening by far since I came to London. It is so wonderful being with you."

Again Titus did not know what to say and so they finished their coffee in silence.

He didn't realise it but he had been staring at her, when she said, "Is everything all right? Have I said something, TG?"

"No, no, it has been a perfect evening. I'm sorry if I was staring at you like a dummy. I'm not very good in female company. I have no sisters or female cousins; I went to an all-boys school and then spent a long time in a man's army. You must think me hopeless!"

"I'm more than happy for you to look at me, but you should be aware that I have been checking you out pretty closely too, and I like what I see!" she said impishly.

He really couldn't tell whether she was teasing or not but he didn't think so and felt relieved.

This time Titus asked her what she was thinking right then to which she giggled, "I was wondering whether I should ask you to adopt me or take me to bed!"

Stunned and not knowing what to say, he just gawked at her but her most natural giggle made them both laugh and again she instantly destroyed any uncomfortable feeling.

She said that this was one of her father's most embarrassing sayings from when she was a teenager, usually said after he'd spotted an attractive young girl. However, she admitted, as time passed, she had waited secretly for years for the right time to use it herself!

"God, I am really turning into my own father!" she said in mock horror, laughing.

Chapter 17

A few days later, Titus received a call from Bob requesting that he attend at his offices as soon as he could get there, to receive his orders and that was all that was said, apart from the address.

Bob's security company's office was in a nondescript building on Hartmann Road, very close to the small, emerging and newish London City Airport in The Docklands precinct. He stood back to survey the building and its surrounds noting that there were no vehicles on the street nor any people. Although there was no street action, he could hear activity at the small airport, almost alongside this building.

Noiselessly, the door clicked open as he approached it and a voice on an unseen intercom invited him to enter and go straight up the staircase directly ahead of the door. Titus climbed the stairs to the first landing, turned and continued on up to the first floor, having no doubt that further instructions would wait for him. True enough, as he topped the landing, Bob was standing at the far end of a long passageway, away to his right, beckoning him to follow.

Truly, the passageway was just plain dingy, poorly lit and very down at heel, obviously in hindsight an impression they were trying to portray, somewhat successfully he thought. A slight change of floor levels and the heavy steel fire doorway he passed through suggested to him that he'd actually entered an adjoining building. If so, it was a clever disguise of the office's actual location to the outside world.

Walking in through the dirty brown-coloured peeling door, he saw a very bare-looking reception area, with a simple steel chair and desk, both set on a faded carpet of anonymous colour. Set on the desk were an ancient Imperial brand typewriter, a couple of pencils and a similarly old black Bakelite telephone.

The sign on the wall behind the desk was dirty and faded and read, "Local and overseas transport facilitators," but with no name identified.

There were two doors leading out of this area, one left partly open, deliberately he felt, just for effect, and displaying a rather shabby office kitchenette but the other door was firmly shut.

The impression was certainly one of a third-rate business in a cheap building but once Bob magically opened the other door it was like stepping into a James Bond spy world.

They walked the length of the large room, unacknowledged by any of the staff members, something like he imagined the War Office to be. On reflection, maybe that's what it was!

At the far end of the main room was a glass-clad office and once they stepped into it, shutting the door, silence reigned, so obviously the 19 mm thick glass he'd noted as he entered was completely soundproof and if he knew anything, probably bulletproof too!

Wow, what a setup, he thought. Bob had certainly landed on his feet here; obviously, his reputation from the army and no doubt contacts from MI6 had been instrumental in the 'business'.

"Well, Sergeant Major Lovell, what do you think of my modest enterprise?"

At that point, he was still checking the view out of the window, of the old somewhat modest size building, perhaps being a temporary terminal for the new proposed London City Airport. He could see part of the runway, with a small Dash 7 propeller aircraft speeding down it, preparatory to take off. He was sure that this would be one-way glass because he knew that Bob would not be sitting there on display. Also, there was no noise at all from the airport, so it was clear that the building was soundproofed.

This must have cost a mint, thought Titus guessing there had to be plenty of financial and technical assistance from the government too. The location too would be pretty handy no doubt for covert flights when necessary, he conjectured.

"I'm very impressed, Colonel," he said with a smile.

"Okay, enough showing off, let's get down to business," said Bob, snapping instantly into full work mode and directing Titus to a comfortable chair around an expansive low-set polished timber coffee table, whilst he took the adjoining chair.

"Your investigation deals with an insurance fraud whilst my principal is interested in terrorism funded by international money laundering. My principal is in a delicate situation because the Jordanian Government is friendly and we do not think that they or anyone there is actually involved in this. However, 'our friend', Mr Khoury, is a nasty piece of work and it will probably be easier to put him away for fraud, tax evasion or money laundering than to catch him for terrorism."

"This is where you come in. We have cleared the matter at all levels, including your employer, Major Blake, who is more than willing to cooperate, by allowing you to take a trip to Jordan and obviously booked through your office, but under our eye. You will however fly on a British Airways regular flight, in your own name, from Gatwick Airport direct to Amman."

"The purpose will be for you to meet by arrangement with Abdal-monem Twal, who has agreed to cooperate on the basis that you do not try to use any information gained from him in defending the writ in the British Courts. We think that he is innocent and could be a great help."

He went on to say that they were booking Titus out of London on the 19:20 hours British Air flight that very night, from Gatwick and Mr Blake had already arranged an appointment with Twal at his Amman office at 1000 hours the next day.

"Twal is prepared to take you to the Wadi al-Abyad mine site, a little more than two hours away by car. This will give you plenty of confidential talking time in the car, as he is becoming suspicious and fearful for his own safety."

Bob followed this with a full security briefing, obviously laid out very clinically by MI6 as to what they were seeking to uncover.

To keep security tight, Titus was to leave in one of their nondescript delivery vans, as all their taxi cabs were out on jobs. He would initially travel in the cargo section but once the driver was happy, he could move through into the front passenger's seat, to be taken to St Katharine Docks, right to his apartment.

Once home, he was to pack an overnight bag and be ready to be collected by a black cab, which was also owned by 'the firm'. In turn, the cab would run him down to Gatwick Airport safely and in plenty of time for his flight to Jordan.

He wasn't quite back in the army (or was he?) but he was certainly following orders from his old OC and having everything arranged for him.

Chapter 18

On parting the previous Friday night, Rose had given him the phone number for her flat, writing it on the back of her business card which Titus was carrying. He'd walked her to a tube station telling her, "I've had an exquisite evening and am sorry it is over and I really wish it was just starting."

Spontaneously she reached up, threw her arms around his neck and hugged more tightly than he thought possible for a girl. She held onto him for ages and then he could hear her 'snuffling', perhaps as though crying.

Now he really didn't know what to do; tears, a man's biggest dread!

Eventually, she loosened herself from him and pushed back a little so that she was inches from his face. She did in fact have moist eyes and the street lights shone and glowed off them, melting his heart even more. They stood there, entwined, for a few more minutes, saying nothing, when she blurted out, "You are not too old for me, TG, if that's what you've been thinking."

He couldn't believe how perceptive and honest she was, saying exactly what was on her mind, without guile or flirtation.

For the first time in his life, he felt the unbelievable warmth of relief and love flood through his body, tingling right through to the extremities.

She saw his reaction, read it perfectly and moved closer, kissing him softly on the lips before pulling away slightly and smiling. True to form she gave a mischievous giggle and said, "There, I've done it! Cheeky girl, aren't I?"

They parted shortly after, with another kiss and an enormous hug, leaving Titus completely overwhelmed and longing for more.

Bringing himself back to the task at hand, it took him virtually no time to pack an overnight bag and then he had nearly 15 minutes to kill, awaiting the arrival of the cab. Sitting, thinking, with his mind still on Rose, he decided on the spur of the moment to give her a call.

She sounded ecstatic at receiving his call, thanking him again, "It was a lovely dinner and an evening straight out of a romance novel!"

Wow, thought Titus, *she doesn't seem to have cooled off on me.*

He did not want to go into any explanations in depth about his proposed movements and said that he had to be brief because he had been called away a moment ago on an enquiry and had to leave for a couple of days overseas. He told her that he was just packing his overnight bag and was expecting a cab to pick him up soon.

He reminded her that she should not make any further enquiries but simply do her job because the case involving Ecothan was appearing more dangerous minute by minute.

They chatted for 10 minutes, which was a marvellous distraction for him, but he had to terminate the conversation gently when the intercom buzzed from downstairs with a loud announcement, "Cab for Mr Lovell." Rose heard the announcement and said, "You had better go, but be careful and call me as soon as you get back, TG…please?" sounding more like a sweet request than a demand.

The cabbie was obviously an ex-military man and engaged him in only small-talk over the intercom, on the 28-mile journey, which in relatively benign Sunday traffic, took well less than the hour they had allowed. He could see that the driver was very alert, checking all his perimeters regularly plus changing lanes regularly and looking for any signs of being followed.

He was certainly in good hands with this guy!

To his surprise, the cabbie drove passed the British Airways end of the terminal and pulled up in front of the far end of the terminal building, reserved for mostly foreign and smaller airlines. As he stopped, the cabbie turned around, slid open his glass protection panel and said, "There has been a change of plans, details of which you can find in these orders," which he passed through to Titus. He also commented, "Your cab fare is covered," and with a wink wished him, "Good luck on your 'holiday' and say hello to the boys in Amman from Alfie."

What boys? He thought.

With his small leather overnight bag slung over a shoulder, he walked into the terminal and found a quiet corner to open today's orders. They indicated that there had been a hiccup with the British Airways flight direct to Amman and he was now on a flight 20 minutes earlier with Turkish Airlines, via Istanbul.

He worked out from the tickets that he should finally arrive at about 01:25 hours, giving him plenty of time for the 10:00 hours meeting with Twal tomorrow.

Apart from his open return ticket, the only other items in the package were the equivalent of £200 in Turkish lira and £2,000 in the Jordanian dinar. Maybe it wouldn't be too bad working for this mob, with expenses dished out like this, he thought and then set about looking for the Turkish Airline counter.

A closer look at his tickets revealed that he was flying first class so he was able to walk straight to the club counter, without joining over 100 people already lined up at the cattle class counters. With only hand luggage, his delay was minimal and he was guided through the immigration and customs counters and then invited into their first-class lounge until the flight was called.

He assumed that Bob and his team had been working behind the scenes because when he handed over his boarding pass on reaching the lounge, he was immediately reallocated from seat 7 C to 1 C.

This of course was not his customary way of travelling but something he was quite happy to enjoy. However, he wondered whether this might be the calm before the storm!

He had nearly an hour to kill but it was in a comfortable plush lounge area, with plenty on offer to read, eat and drink, so the time passed very quickly.

Too much time to think about the unknown was Titus's reaction. He'd never liked idle time when there was a job to do!

Eventually, the time came and he, plus three others, were escorted to the appropriate gate and ushered on board through a reserved air-bridge entry, into the first-class cabin. His was the front row, right side, window seat but with no one else in the whole row so he couldn't see another passenger.

Throughout the four-hour flight, the hostesses were very attentive and he was relieved when an evening meal arrived because he hadn't eaten since breakfast. It was their first class's silver service; serving up a fresh crab entrée. Then a hot dish of traditional Turkish lamb casserole, freshly baked lavas, followed by a very sweet semolina-based dessert, flavoured with pine-nuts and prunes. To finish with was an English cheese selection board with dried fruits, plus some sliced fresh pear.

Knowing what lay ahead of him, he stuck to fruit juice and tea, rather than drinking any alcohol and had time to watch a movie on the overhead screen. It was a new release film, The Blues Brothers, and was a great escape from his thoughts. He then managed a couple of hours sleep in the lay-back seats but they weren't exactly made for a hulking six-footer.

There was only a 30-minute layover in Istanbul, just enough time to change gates, fortunately without going through security again and board another jet. After the usual 'hurry up', there was the wait at the gate before the plane was cleared and raced down the wet runway, taking off steeply. It was soon airborne and heading south-east on its way for the two-and-a-half-hour flight, across Turkey, over Cyprus, cutting across Lebanon to Jordan and to the capital Amman. He was offered another meal but at nearly midnight, it was not what he needed and again maintained abstinence, sticking to water and juice to maintain good hydration.

Chapter 19

This plane was a slightly older model Boeing 737 but quite comfortable and although the seats did not lie back as much as the London flight they were more than comfortable for the shorter distance of Istanbul to Amman.

Titus dug deep into his memory reservoirs for all his knowledge of Jordan.

Jordan had been part of his study for his sergeant's exams in the subject of British military history, plus he knew some details from school days and he had also spent time recently researching the country for this particular investigation.

He recalled that the area of Jordan had been cruelly ruled for some 400 years by the Ottoman Empire from Turkey, and the local Bedouin Arab population had been totally suppressed. Nothing was about to change until World War 1 and the need for Britain to clear its enemy, Turkey, from the area.

The nigh-on impossible task was given to the now famous Lawrence of Arabia, then a lieutenant, Laurence managed to weld together a number of warring Bedouin tribes and form an army of sorts, based on the hope of creating their own nation with the riddance of the Ottomans from their lands.

The disparate groupings of tribes followed Laurence as a new hero helping them to remove 'the accursed Turks'. His next demand of them had been to ride across almost inhospitable deserts, including Wadi Rum, to approach the southern port of Aqaba.

Amazingly, they had accomplished this, taking the Ottoman fort from the lightly guarded rear, which led to the opening up of The Gulf of Aqaba, with access to the Red Sea. This secured the port of Aqaba for the British military shipping supply lines and ultimately helped to change the fate of the war in that theatre.

King Hussein, who came to the throne in 1952, on the abdication of his mentally ill father, King Talal, was still currently the leader.

King Hussein had his formal education in Britain, at the famous Harrow School and in fact, was an officer graduate of the famous Royal Military

Academy at Sandhurst, as was his father. He still received financial and military assistance from Britain and his military forces were set up along their lines.

Bob had assured him that Twal was an educated businessman who spoke English very well, having been partly educated in Britain. It appeared that the daily spoken language varied greatly but were all variants of Levantine Arabic, including a Bedouin version in the south, Levantine Bedawi Arabic, which northerners struggled a little to understand. Unfortunately, Titus knew none of the Arabic tongues at all!

His flight arrived at the international airport in Amman just before 2:15 am and to his surprise, he was whisked through customs and immigration by a British Government official of some sort, no names! *Then he was shepherded out of the terminal into the cold night air to a limousine, a huge old black Austin Princess Van Den Plas saloon, more suited for the Lord Mayor than him*, he thought. It was further explained that the driver would take him to his hotel, where, 'the account will be taken care of by your friends'!

Furthermore, another driver, who could be trusted implicitly, would pick him up at 9:30 am, to take him to his appointment with Mr Twal.

All beautifully arranged; thanks to Bob's staff and no doubt some input from MI6.

Apart from light traffic in the immediate area of the airport, the roads were otherwise quiet, as he would have expected at that time of the morning. The driver removed his chauffer's cap once in the car and Titus could see that he was most likely an ex-Gurkha soldier. Clearly from his physical size and bearing he was no simple driver and he wondered whether he may have a similar military background to his last London cabbie. Whatever his background, it was comforting to know that he was being watched over closely by his new superiors.

The short journey took him to the Zirino Hotel, just off the Seventh Circle in Amman city. The driver reminded him of his pick-up time in the morning and then, after wishing well, he saluted and quietly disappeared into the darkness.

Titus stood back, viewing the hotel noting it to be a solidly constructed four-storey building in immaculate condition and, in a flash, the concierge came running out to meet him, to guide him inside. He kept looking back down the street at the disappearing car and enquiring whether the driver had taken his bags by mistake but Titus reassured him that all was well and that he was travelling light.

He was not surprised that the desk was staffed by another ex-army man, giving credence to his thought that it was probably another 'safe' building for his new masters to use. The desk clerk welcomed him, and with a grin gave his name as 'Yo-Yo', awarded to him by his mates he said, for constantly being 'busted' in rank, for minor misdemeanours, and coming back up again to sergeant!

Yo-Yo handed him an envelope, plus a key and directed the concierge to take him to his rooms on the top floor, wishing him a happy holiday, accompanied by a broad wink.

The sinewy little concierge walked ahead of him on the balls of his feet, like a cat ready to pounce, held out his hand for the key and then opened the double doors, which were marked 'Windsor Suite'. *How bloody amazing*, thought Titus. Bob would be thoroughly amused at this opulence for his old Sgt Major; then again perhaps not, as he had arranged it.

He opened the envelope and read some further intel on Twal, which again seemed to confirm that he was not involved in this sullied situation. He absorbed the information and then tore it into small pieces and flushed it down one of the three toilets.

He explored the rooms which seemed to occupy a quarter of the top floor and found that they consisted of two reception rooms, plus two bedrooms and two full bathrooms. The decor and fittings were something he personally had never been privileged to experience before, being a strange mixture of Western and Arabic styles and showing plenty of colours everywhere.

Feeling very safe here, he didn't carry out his usual recce of the passageways and stair exits etc. as he had full confidence that no one could get past Yo-Yo, or that tough little concierge whom he guessed had been recruited from one of the British Ghurkha battalions too.

He snapped his mind back into gear and knowing that in six or seven hours' time, he would be on his way to meet Twal, he decided to kip down for the night, taking the closest of the two luxurious double bedrooms. In true form, he was able to switch off and grab five hours of sleep in a huge queen-sized bed, to be up in time to hear knocking at the door which heralded the arrival of a large tray with his breakfast.

These boys certainly think of everything, was Titus's reaction, as he tucked into the hot breakfast and a large pot of tea. An English language newspaper had been delivered at the same time and suggested that today's temperatures would be pleasant with a maximum of around 81°F (27°C) and little wind. Naturally, no rain was forecast as this was a pretty dry land.

After his obligatory exercises and ablutions, he felt ready to go but was unsure what to do with his personal belongings. He thought that all he needed with him today was his notebook, pen and his new pocket-size camera, given to him by Bob; so what to do with his bag?

He checked the phone instructions and found that by dialling 'Zero' he could reach the reception clerk and so decided to see what arrangements had been made regarding continuing accommodation for him. The Cockney who answered sounded as though he was still in the Royal Corps of Signals, complete with, 'Sir, over', at the completion of each communication.

He told Titus that the room was booked for him, "As long as you need it and your kit will be as secure as The Royal Woolwich Arsenal, sir."

"You won't do any better than trusting it to Sgt Tich Williams," he added and reminded him that his 'staff car' would be collecting him at 09:30 hours.

He was starting to wonder whether he had been reactivated into the army, without his knowledge, for clearly all those around him were military to the core and seemed to be more aware of what was going on than he was currently.

Titus was dressed in a light business suit, especially since he was seeing the head of a major firm. He was down in the lobby early, to ensure that he introduced himself to Tich, who true to his name was only 5' 4" tall but strongly built and a typical 30-year veteran soldier, lively and good-humoured. He had time to swap a few old soldiers' tales of matching postings around the world and also to make the point to Tich that he too was from the Sgt's Mess and not the Officers Mess, despite the suit he was currently wearing.

Tich grinned at him saying that Titus' reputation had preceded him and everyone at the 'Amman Station' knew of his exploits on the Indian/Pakistani border. They knew just how he had won his DSM and his Indian Army Sena Medal, both for exceptional gallantry in the face of the enemy and also why he was called 'TG' by his troops.

"It is nice to have the army's pin-up boy on board, Sahib TeeGee," Tich said with a grin, in his best pseudo-Anglo-Indian accent, accompanied by a traditional Namaste, by placing the palms of his hands together in front of his chest and bowing his head slightly; obviously enjoying the situation.

"Yeh, yeh, yeh, you clown. Just look after my toothbrush etc., if that is not too much for you, Sergeant!"

"Oh, by the way, Alfie sends his regards to everyone."

"Thanks, mate," said Yo-Yo, who had just joined them. "We haven't seen him out here for many months. He's been a great mate of Slugger for 25 years."

Who the hell is Slugger? Titus reflected but acknowledged that they all seemed to be a pretty tight group.

Dead at 9:30 am, the same larger-than-life shiny black car arrived and Tich immediately turned serious, shaking his hand, telling him to go safely but that his back was always covered. "Fear nought whilst Slugger has your back." *Again, a mention of Slugger*, he thought.

A different driver, but the same car, observed Titus.

Not meant to be inconspicuous, that's for sure, but perhaps consistent with him conducting business with one of the most respected businessmen in Amman. After all, appearances were very important, especially in the Arab world.

This time, the driver actually properly introduced himself, "Chief Petty Officer Stanley Roger 'Slugger' Jones DCM, at your service sir; ex-Royal Navy, middle weight boxing champion for seven years and now your humble driver," all said with a touch of humour and appropriate flourish.

My God thought Titus, *so this is Slugger*. He could now pass for a heavy weight boxer but still looked dangerously fit: very nice to have him around today.

Slugger looked smart in a chauffeur's suit and cap, but he knew that he would have looked magnificent in his chief petty officer's white dress uniform, no doubt with a chest full of medals.

Slugger acknowledged the greetings from those in the hotel and then opened the left rear door of the big limousine to usher Titus into the hugely spacious back seat. He wondered if Bob was having a laugh at him, first-class air travel, The Windsor Suite and then chauffeured around in a Limo.

Very bloody funny!

Chapter 20

Amman, known as the White City, was certainly true to its name.

The flat-roofed, modestly sized, two-storeyed houses, with their water tanks on the roof, were all of solid construction and painted white.

The factories and other commercial buildings likewise had whitewashed exterior walls and he imagined that on a bright sunny day, the glare would be insufferable.

Traffic was pretty disastrous for a city of about 650,000 people, because most of the roads had originated from the ancient days of donkeys being the main city transport mode and were narrow, winding, often cobbled and many quite steep.

Slugger wound the big tank of a car expertly through the edges of the city; eventually coming to what he assumed was the business area, as the white buildings were now mainly three and four stories high, with no washing extended out of the windows on sticks.

The traffic became more motorised and less animal-centric but it was no less intense.

Titus was glad he was not driving as there wasn't a straight road in sight and seemingly to him, no pattern of roads to follow. However, the sights were amazing, ranging from a Rolls Royce to a feeble overladen donkey, almost side by side.

It took about 25 minutes to travel a relatively short distance and reach the office of New Giffin-Sen, near the intersection of Khaled Bin Al Waleed Street and Jamal Al Deen Afghani Street on the eastern side of Amman. The structure was modern and quite impressive. It was constructed of stone and faced with white marble, clearly exhibiting it as a superior building to those around it.

They had arrived with five minutes to spare and Slugger took the opportunity of indicating that although Twal could be trusted, it did not mean that everyone working for him or around him was as trustworthy. Slugger knew that Titus intended to drive out to the mine site at Wadi al-Abyad and suggested that he try to persuade Twal to travel in the Austin, which had a few 'extras', such as being bulletproof, amongst other things!

Slugger positioned the big saloon car near the gateway of the car park, facing outwards and indicated that he would await Titus' advice, leaving him to enter the building alone for his meeting.

The morning air was still cool and surprisingly, relatively unpolluted he noted as he walked the 20 or so paces to the impressive marble steps leading to the entrance foyer, where an armed, but less than tidy guard, stood on duty.

Within the large foyer was a central desk, seated at which a young woman was wearing a hijab, or head scarf, but otherwise wearing modern western dress, plus a liberal application of make-up. She stood to greet him, and enquired, "Mr Lovell?"

Titus nodded and she immediately turned slightly drawing him towards the bank of three lifts, where she pressed a button and a lift door popped open immediately. She leaned inside the lift, pressed the number four button, which he noted was for the top floor, stood back and allowed him to be taken up by the elevator. The ride was smooth and swift, stopping moments later with the doors sliding silently open, leading straight into a reception area, rather than into a passageway, suggesting that they occupied the whole floor.

Waiting for him, dressed in a very fashionable European lightweight suit and looking every bit a businessman was none other than Twal. He was a lightly built man, around 5' 9" in height, well-groomed and with an open clean-shaven face, all of which appealed to Titus immediately.

He greeted Titus with a hand shake and a slight bow of his head, in the traditional way and led him to a spacious and well-appointed Western-style office, befitting a managing director.

Ice-cold grape juice was immediately poured and drunk almost ritually, presumably as a sign of hospitality and welcome.

Titus liked what he saw and was beginning to look forward to spending the day with Mr Twal.

"Because of my education in Britain and my worldwide business dealings you may find me more relaxed and less formal than you may have expected," he said with a small smile. "Despite this being a very difficult situation, I believe that you are neutral and as a matter of national security for both our countries, I am happy to work together with you."

"To start, may I say that I know you Brits have difficulty with my given name and so for the sake of working together I invite you to address me by my more familiar name of 'Abi'?"

Titus was delighted and showed it with a broad smile and, again shaking the man's hand and returning the compliment saying, "Thank you, sir, Titus for me, please," as he exchanged business cards with him.

Abi told him that he had heard the dreadful news of the savage death of Ecothan's managing director, whom he had never met, nor had any contact with. He assured him that it had absolutely nothing to do with him or to his knowledge anyone associated with his company, but qualified that by saying he had heard some nasty rumours about Khoury's recent activities. The information had come to him from Jordanian State Security, quite recently, but he was not at liberty to go into details, although Titus had no doubt that it had originated from MI6.

As instructed, Titus confirmed that he too had been directed by UK Security, without mentioning any department names, saying that he believed that New Giffin-Sen was being used for illicit purposes and together he hoped they could get to the bottom of it before any more damage was done to them.

Abi indicated that he would prefer not to speak for too long in the office as he was, perhaps somewhat unfairly, starting to feel that he was being spied upon.

Titus indicated that he had been afforded the full use of a rather 'special' car and that the driver could double as a most effective bodyguard, so it may be wise to travel together with him today.

The man was delighted saying that he was no longer comfortable driving the long distance between Amman and the mine alone and so when Titus added that the driver sat in a discreet chauffeur's cabin, he was sold on the idea, and in fact, it was a great relief to Titus.

Abi had a small portfolio of manila files plus a leather briefcase, which he said would be useful for today's discussion and intended to bring both of them with him. He said that since issuing the writ against Ecothan many things had happened and he was starting to believe the fault was as much at his end as at their end.

Chapter 21

As Twal was leaving his own office he spoke briefly to his receptionist, introducing Lovell and telling her that he would be out for the rest of the day with Mr Lovell, to the mine site.

As they entered the lift, Titus heard the phone being lifted and it appeared she was calling someone already.

Who, and was it significant?

On exiting the building, they walked across the dusty car park, towards the Austin where Slugger was already standing with the left rear door wide open, in a typical chauffeur pose. He bowed his head slightly to Twal and Titus introduced him as Slugger Jones.

Twal smiled and nodded, saying, "You British and your nicknames!" accepting the situation as quite normal and feeling very assured by the size of the man.

Twal, of smaller stature, was able to walk into the back of the car, only having to duck his head slightly.

Slugger watched as he manoeuvred into the back seat and got comfortable, giving Titus a smirk as he assisted him in as well. As Titus turned back into the car, he looked upwards and could see the receptionist looking down on them from a small balcony, but she immediately ducked out of sight. *Strange* he thought, or maybe he too was getting paranoid.

Slugger had just enough time to whisper to Titus, "We were being watched by someone on a balcony on the top floor, and I thought I saw the glint of sun on a weapon, from that building, pointing across the road."

To which Titus replied, "Let's all be careful!"

He was glad to see Slugger was on the ball and had noted the scrutiny from above too.

From the driver's seat, Slugger turned to his passengers, slid open the heavy security glass between them and asked them for instructions, despite knowing full well of their destination. He really is playing his part well thought Titus, who in turn looked towards Twal, asking if he would care to give directions.

Twal asked him if he knew how to get onto the main road south and then directed him to head south on it for about 100 km towards al-Jiza. At that point, he would give him further directions for the turn-off towards their mine at Wadi al-Abyad, but Titus was as sure as he could be that he already knew.

Slugger touched his forehead in acknowledgement, like a half-hearted salute, slid the panel shut and turned to his front. He checked his rear vision mirrors and once satisfied started the vehicle's engine and then steered it out into the traffic, turning right and then right again to head in roughly a southerly direction.

It was such a fascinating change from the main streets of London or Paris but by the same token not that different from his days in India, Pakistan and Kashmir some years ago.

He looked at the cart drivers and the men walking with loaded donkeys, giving the impression that they were all aged in their 60s or more, whereas in fact, he knew that the average age of survival in most Arabic countries was around 55 years of age and that these men would probably be in their 40s to low 50s at the most. *It was a bloody hard life*, he thought.

As they left the edges of the city, the housing thinned out and very quickly they were in sandy, stony desert country on a thin black ribbon of tarmac, heading almost due south, through glary nothingness.

Titus could see through the glass security partition, behind Slugger's head and noted a compass mounted on the dash panel, together with a couple of other items with which he was unfamiliar.

The speed limit was posted at 50 mph or 80km/h, a speed at which the big Austin purred along at minimal revs, with the engine just barely ticking over. He knew that these Austin cars were traditionally underpowered and had expressed this to Slugger earlier in the day. He was assured that although it was a big-bodied old 1958 model, the original engine had been replaced with a 1978 Rolls Royce straight six, four-litre, aluminium cylinder head engine, with a new fuel injection system and for extra 'fire' a supercharger. He said that if he asked, "The old girl would fly for me!" adding that it was also fitted with a limited-slip differential, which could be handy in muddy/wet or sandy conditions.

In the back, Abi and Titus were speaking freely, but with one of the 'extras' fitted to the car, the conversation was heard clearly by Slugger and recorded onto a small cassette recorder as well.

Abi told him of the history of phosphate rock mining in the east of Jordan and said that it was one of the saviours of their country, which apart from the productive Jordan Valley, running down the western side, was mostly desert. His company had discovered phosphorite-bearing rocks nearly 20 years ago and production had gradually increased as his profits allowed him to buy better equipment.

He said, "Almost two years ago, I was introduced by Efraim Khoury to Mr Ralph Nicholson, of the well-known and well-respected UK company, Ecothan. He explained a proposition to assist me with re-financing to allow for growth and also to take over the administrative burden, so as to increase my overseas export targets. Ecothan were to take a 7.5% commission on the value of all goods that passed through their hands but this would eliminate all the need for admin staff from this end. This would leave me free to look after the mine itself and increase production, rather than worry about marketing, permits, contracts and shipping et cetera."

"Nicholson told me that he had that authority to handle the deal alone, as he was the overseas director and so negotiations continued with some seven visits to Amman to see me."

He observed, "I found Nicholson to be a very plain, uninspiring man but without being rude have dealt with many such dreary men in London and thought no more about it because he seemed to be quite professional at his job."

"I therefore authorised Nicholson to handle some contractual matters directly with Khoury in my London office, as my UK manager."

He also mentioned that Khoury was a minor 5% shareholder, having been invited in to keep him enmeshed in the company and therefore secure his loyalty.

The contract had been in place for just over 20 months and although he was happy being allowed to concentrate on the technical side, he had become increasingly worried about the strange bookkeeping and turnover figures. He had spoken to Khoury about it but had been assured that it was all in order and profitability was up:

"It is just a delay in bookkeeping. A timing issue," he'd been told.

Similarly, his contact with Nicholson had not been very satisfactory of late, as visits had stopped and phone calls seemed to be brief and inadequate.

Accordingly, he had then spent some considerable time and money involving an independent firm of international accountants, to look through both the contracts and the books, revealing somewhat terrifying deficiencies. He had kept these confidential from Nicholson and Khoury and likewise had made no verbal approach to the Ecothan's office in London because he assumed that would have only led him back to Nicholson, as a director.

As a result of the accountant's preliminary report, he had engaged a leading firm of London Attorneys and Barristers to prepare proceedings and have a writ served on Ecothan, only because he could not bring himself to believe that Khoury could be involved; perhaps, he now thought, that decision may have been his mistake. He admitted that he really didn't understand what they had done, or how much was involved, but felt it could be a massive embezzlement or fraud of some sort.

He said that Jordanian State Security had told him of Mr James Kingwell's death, and the manner of it, saying that he was ashamed to say that it sounded very much like an old-fashioned Arabic way of dealing with a problem.

The accountants were still undertaking a forensic examination of all the available books and their next port of call was for the remaining paperwork in New Giffin-Sen's Richmond office near London. "I have been advised by UK Security that no less than three people should attend, one of whom would be from British Security, in the guise of an auditor, and so there is obviously some great concern about Khoury being dangerous."

Titus had himself become quite an expert in deciphering contracts, as they were often at the core of many legal liability arguments that he became involved in during investigations. He was pleased therefore when Abi passed him the pertinent contract between his company and Ecothan, as no copy of this contract existed at Ecothan that anyone could find. His immediate reaction was that Nicholson had gone completely rogue and was somehow organising this by himself but just using Ecothan's name.

He felt that this situation was completely extraordinary and admitted to himself that he had never seen a fraud as bold as this in is life, if in fact, that was what it was.

What surprised him next was that it was a simple three-page contract and yet it concerned a complex set of relationships, involving production, maintenance, storage, inland road and rail transport, marine insurance, customs, handling and overseas shipping, all worth many millions pounds sterling.

The contract was a sham; rubbish really, and one that spelt out very little of the respective parties' responsibilities.

He decided to take the bull by the horns saying to Twal, "This is the first time anyone has seen this contract, because no copy of it existed at Ecothan, nor had Ecothan's legal counsel ever seen it, let alone prepared it or sanctioned it to be issued."

Now it was time for Twal to show his dismay, asking Titus what he thought was going on.

Titus said, "This is completely fresh news to me and I would like to continue to examine documents, before attempting to come to any sort of conclusion."

They were both completely silent for a moment, realising the complexity of what appeared to be this massive fraud.

Suddenly, the car swung violently to the left causing the body to heave over drastically and the papers that they were working on to be spilt onto the floor. Twal was thrown against the left door and Titus slid across on top of him and onto the floor in a pile of papers.

The Austin careered off into the desert as Slugger struggled to regain control and prevent it from overturning, for the body was rolling heavily to each side. In the back, they were thrown around on the floor, with Twal upside down and Titus unceremoniously dumped on top of him. Slugger wrestled strongly with the steering wheel, also trying to prevent it from becoming bogged in sand which could leave them in a most vulnerable position.

The heavy car slew wildly from side to side as Slugger fought for wheel traction as the tyres bit deeply into the sand and small stones, shooting them up noisily onto the undercarriage. By this time, they were some 25 yards off the road but now running parallel to it rather than diagonally away from the road, which would have taken them deeper into the soft desert sand. Eventually, the car gradually steadied in Slugger's expert hands, and with both the course and speed stabilised, it allowed Titus to clamber back onto the rear seat, dragging Abi up after him.

He was on instant alert, looking through the right side and rear windows to see whether there was anyone in the immediate vicinity, for he suspected the worst.

Eventually, back on the road and moving fast, Slugger reached over his shoulder, opening the slide and apologising but telling them, "An oncoming quarry truck suddenly swung into my path, forcing me to drive off the road. I'm sure that it was not an accident but a deliberate act of trying to collide with us, or at the least to force the Princess off road, as the driver was steering straight at me!"

He said that afterwards the truck had slowed momentarily, but when the Austin hadn't rolled over, the truck driver had continued on his way and was now out of sight.

He had therefore elected to keep travelling fast rather than stop to check their car, which he felt was driving fine, commenting he didn't want them to become a stationary target!

Twal was shocked and he too turned to see if he recognised the truck but it was already a distant object, speeding on its way.

"Was it painted white, with a blue stripe across the door, by chance?" He said, but almost as though he was thinking aloud, Slugger confirmed that it was, and said, "The driver was wearing a dirty red coloured US baseball-style cap on his head and looked different to most Jordanians I know; maybe a Syrian?"

"I cannot believe what is happening, as that seemed to be one of my fleet of trucks from my mine, but it is unusual for someone to be wearing an American-style baseball cap and that does not sound like one of my drivers. They are generally more traditional in their headwear."

"How did they know we were on this road at this time and how did they identify this car?" Twal asked.

Slugger and Titus both thought of the secretary looking down on them as they prepared to depart and the glint of sun on the gun.

Abi went on to say, "This confirms my thoughts that someone from within my organisation is spying on me and I now suspect that it was either my secretary/receptionist or someone close to her. On reflection, my previous secretary of many years left suddenly about a year ago without explanation and Khoury introduced this girl to me as someone who was well known to his family, so she was automatically engaged."

"Family is most important in Jordanian culture and this wounds me greatly. How dreadful," he continued, adding, "it looks as though someone has systematically removed all my trusted contacts, contractors and even some of my personal staff, so that these evil deeds could be made to transpire."

Titus thanked Slugger for his quick reactions but he was already concentrating on the road and quietly tapping into the little black box on the dash panel. He felt that they were in the best hands possible for this journey and was happy not only with Slugger but also with the organisation behind him!

He then slid the glass shut and continued on his way, obviously by now hyper-vigilant.

This incident had happened well out of Amman and there was still more than an hour's driving to the mine, so they would certainly have to be on their guard.

Titus then opened the drinks cabinet mounted on the back of the seat in front of them and poured two glasses of water, to steady Twal before resuming their discussions, although Titus noted that he still looked pretty unnerved.

As they continued to travel south, they were able to recover the papers from the floor and put them back into some sort of order before resuming their review of what they knew.

Part of the investigation had revealed to Twal that every single one of his long-standing existing contracts had been cancelled and there was a completely new suite of carriers, shipping agents, customs agents and so forth, which caused him much angst because he had personally sourced his workforce for reliability and price. This was one of his early warning signs of a major problem and an explanation as to why now some local businessmen/friends had started to ostracise him in the city.

Another gross irregularity he had only just discovered was payments of substantial sums to Zamir Mines Coy, whom he had never heard of and did not seem to exist in Jordan and then strangely monies were coming back from them.

Whilst Twal was looking through some paperwork, Titus noticed out of the corner of his eye that Slugger was tapping on the small 'gismo' on the dash panel again and wondered what that was all about. However, the name Zamir Mines Company was not new to Titus, but he again chose not to disclose that for the moment.

Abi had a sheaf of papers relating to payments made over the months through their London office, but as all the contractors had been changed he was unsure what they all meant or whether they were value for money, although the outgoing figures seemed very high to him. Unfortunately, he did not have any invoices supporting the payments, but that was what the accountants, amongst other things, were intending to look for at his Richmond office.

He commented, "In hindsight, the Ecothan offer was too good to be true, but since it seemed to relieve me of all administrative and sales tasks, I was too easily seduced by it, only recently realising my mistake."

"I have become increasingly disenchanted with Khoury, who like Nicholson has become vague and evasive to me regarding direct questions relating to company finances."

Suddenly Twal looked at him saying, "If Ecothan did not finance this contract and in fact knew nothing about it, then where did the money and admin staff come from?"

It was like a bolt out of the blue, meaning that someone, somewhere had stumped up the initial half a million pounds or so to get this contract up and going, thought Titus. Perhaps this was the lead that MI6 was looking for, relating to money laundering and eventually leading to the terrorist cells in Yemen.

Again he noted Slugger tapping something on the same small black box on his dash panel. Titus wondered whether it was some kind of new communication device that had recently come into use, for it was a long time since he had been in the army and communications were fairly basic then, especially when compared to even the new mobile phone 'brick' on issue to him in London.

Several large oncoming trucks could be seen and they were on edge each time, but Twal recognised the drivers, so it went well.

There were no more incidents on the main road and just after the 100 km mark Twal asked Titus, "Please tap on the glass so that I can give further instructions to Mr Slugger."

Slugger slid open the glass and cocked his head to one side as if waiting for someone to speak, but of course, he had heard everything already.

Twal indicated, "In 3 or 4 km, there will be a large white sign with a blue stripe across it and my company's logo 'NGS' painted inside a circle and at this point please turn left and travel for another 20 or so kilometres, on a white-topped gravel road."

Slugger acknowledged, with a nod of his head, and waited a moment in case there were any further instructions, and in the absence of those, he slid the panel shut, resuming his driving duties.

Twal produced more documents which they pored over and discussed but many of Titus's conclusions were kept to himself. He was a careful man and would prefer to analyse a situation in depth privately, rather than randomly blabbing out his thoughts. However, a picture was building up in his mind, but the finer points of how they were pulling off the fraud were still eluding him.

The car suddenly screeched to a halt, again throwing them off their seats.

This time they feared the worst. On looking up, Titus could see no other vehicle but by now he trusted Slugger's judgement, so waited. He could see Slugger peering ahead and to his left. He followed his gaze and saw a flash of light, reflected in the sand, about two paces off the left edge of the hard-baked road surface.

What was it?

Slugger left the engine running but applied the hand-brake before putting his left hand up, signalling them to be cautious. He alighted from the car and moved to the edge of the road where he stood staring intently at the area where the flash had come from.

Titus became concerned saying, "Abi, please stay here whilst I assist Slugger, who seems to have found something suspicious over there," pointing to the roadside.

He stood with Slugger. "What do you think it is?" He enquired.

"I don't know, mate, but after the bloody truck episode, I'm not taking any chances. I think I should take a closer shufti at it."

Titus replied, "I've trained in bomb and mine disposal, so I'd better do it. Back the car up 30 yards and I'll investigate."

Checking carefully for wires running from the object to the road he saw nothing. Next, he studied for disruption to the road surface, or loose dirt, looking for a possible buried pressure plate.

Nothing so far.

No trip-wire type mechanism across the road either. He cautiously crept towards it, having removed his suit jacket and placed it on the road. On reaching it, he examined what little he could see and then started brushing away sand from around it.

What a relief!

He reached into the small depression and pulled out an empty *drink* bottle, which had obviously been thrown from a passing vehicle. He held it up and waved it to the others with a big grin, signalling them to drive forward to join him.

This time, both Slugger and Abi climbed out of the big saloon to see what he had discovered. They all laughed nervously but knew it could have been something much more deadly.

Abi explained that it was a Zam Cola bottle, which was not generally popular in Jordan but was popular in many of the more radical Islamic States. It had originally been 'Pepsi Iran' but after the 1979 Revolution, it was renamed. It had become a symbol of anti-western sentiment to drink Zam Zam, rather than Pepsi.

Chapter 22

After the search of Nicholson's office, Titus had returned to his own office where he had the facility to request 'Credit Reports' on individuals or companies in which they had a direct interest relating to an insurance claim.

He put a call through to Dun and Bradstreet's credit agency, the one he normally dealt with, requesting an urgent 'work up' on Nicholson, to be delivered to him, by bicycle courier, within four hours.

He also took the opportunity of speaking to Mr Blake, advising him that this may be one of the largest frauds ever handled and that there was some dirty work afoot, with the managing director murdered and another senior employee either involved and/or potentially murdered.

Blake listened with interest, cautioning him not to become involved in police business but to stick to the main investigation into the fraud aspect alone. He made careful notes in his diary and asked to be kept up-to-date on a regular basis, as developments occurred.

On the way to his own office, he passed the time of day with various members of staff, fielding their questions about procedures/claims and such, confirming just how far he had come and how he was respected in this profession after only 10 years. There were of course adjusters in the office who had practised for periods in excess of 30 years, but it was Titus who was the main 'magnet' for people seeking advice, strangely enough from all age groups.

The four hours passed quickly when Jenny, one of the office girls, announced that he had a courier delivery and handed him a large strong yellow envelope, confirming that she had signed the delivery docket on his behalf.

Returning to his desk, he cut open the envelope to view two quarto-sized sheets of paper, with typing on one side only of each sheet.

The report confirmed Nicholson's identity as correct and his address being the same as on his employment and banking records.

There did not seem to be any adverse credit ratings, such as late payments of accounts or mortgage defaults and the leasing payments on his Mini were also up-to-date.

There was however a record of a very large insurance claim on his Household Policy, where a succinct notation had been made, which only someone in the know could decipher. It suggested that the claim was possibly fraudulent but that point could not be proved, with the result that the underwriters paid out £98,885 cash for allegedly stolen jewellery, but in his name alone, not including his wife.

Strange he thought *that the wife was never mentioned or included.*

Very interesting, thought Titus, and immediately made a call to the Star & Eastern Insurance Co., which he knew well and often acted for them. The claims manager, Ron Gusscott, was happy to talk to him and explained that their own in-house investigator and the police had made extensive enquiries, such that they were 90% sure that the jewellery never existed. However, their legal advisors indicated that they would not succeed in proving fraud in a civil court. Nicholson had indicated that the jewellery had been passed on to him alone, not his wife, from his mother, various elderly aunts and great aunts, over many years and accordingly he had no purchase documents or valuations as proof of ownership or even photos of their very existence.

Ron asked that if anything turned up to confirm fraud he would be very happy to hear and Titus agreed to pass on anything of use, should he uncover new evidence.

Returning to the report, he turned the page to the heading 'Business Activities' and found that a payment of £100,000 had been made by Nicholson for a 50% shareholding in what was described as a holding company, named, 'K N Developments'.

This company was only registered six weeks before Nicholson had received the £98,885 insurance settlement and so Titus reasoned that it was more than just a coincidence.

Could 'KN' be the initials of Khoury and Nicholson?

Likewise, there was no trace of the money being paid into any UK bank account, and so it must have been through an offshore bank. *Why*, he thought, *did Nicholson need such an account, if that was indeed the case?*

Was the £98,885 the seed money for their illicit scheme?

The final piece of information, which he thought may fit in, was the transfer of monies to a bank on Costa del Sol in Spain, by Nicholson, about six months after the KN Developments business had commenced.

Strangely, it too was not listed in joint names with his wife. Was this also significant, he wondered?

It certainly appeared that Nicholson had made some major changes in his financial life style and they had more than coincidently overlapped with the dates involved in the Ecothan/ New Giffin-Sen fraud case. Perhaps he was not the dull grey man that everyone considered him to be.

Chapter 23

The colonel was deeply involved in a conversation at Century House with two Middle Eastern terrorist security specialist agents, reviewing what they knew about Khoury and his suspected network.

Intelligence now at hand suggested that he was very much involved in Sunni Muslim-inspired groups, who were being assembled and trained in North Yemen. Their activities initially had been in a number of Central African countries, apparently trying to join up with the North African Countries Islamic fundamentalists in an effort to swamp the African continent and either kill or convert people.

However, they were now spreading their wings introducing their brand of fundamentalism into the UK, United States, Canada and even China, in the form of training cells for the future. They were of course already very active throughout most of the Arabian Peninsula, North Africa and Indonesia, and they would need to be dealt with, especially by stopping their ongoing funding.

One of the reasons they had so much cooperation from the Jordanian Intelligence community related to the fact that Jordan had a peaceful Sunni Muslim population living with the Shia Muslim minority, and they wanted to maintain the status quo.

The agent shook his head in disbelief, saying that the ongoing 'wars' between Sunnis and Shias were very similar in many ways to the historical wars between Catholics and Protestants. In each case, they were both from the same basic religion but had taken a different path, which led to bigotry, partition, revenge, hatred and outright hostility.

It was the old story again, where, if they had Christians or Jews to fight, they would fight side by side, but in the absence of that, they would fight amongst themselves for supremacy of their branch of Islam.

SIS had been busy checking bank accounts that could in any way be connected with any combination of New Giffin-Sen, Ecothan, Khoury, Nicholson and KN Developments plus known money laundering accounts.

The results had been startling.

Literally, millions of pounds had been transferred from the New Giffin-Sen's account to a name new to the SIS, that of Zamir Mines Coy in Sana'a. Situated in the north-west of the country, the area was heavily suspected of training, harbouring and exporting the worst kind of terrorists to create hot spots all over the world.

A good slab of the money was then transferred from Zamir Mines to KN Developments, and about half that amount was retained by KN whilst the remainder was returned to the account of New Giffin-Sen, with up to a million pounds missing out of one single transaction. It seemed to be a sophisticated skimming or fraud, but without forensically examining New Giffin-Sen's books, it would be impossible to discover how they were doing it undetected for so long.

So far, the agents had been very open with Bob but said it would be better for him if he were not involved in considering or examining what Zamir did with their money. Bob knew where his security clearance ended and was quite happy to leave that part of the exercise to the spooks at MI6.

The agents indicated that it was absolutely clear to them that Kingwell's murder was directly associated with Khoury's intrusion into contracts supposedly with Ecothan but without their knowledge. Their agents had discovered Kingwell's early attempted investigation had probably been reasonably successful and their own enquiries, mimicking his, had also led him to Khoury.

They thought that a direct approach by Kingwell to Khoury had most probably resulted in his death at the hands of one of their terrorists in London. The police's main suspect was a man possibly by the name of Maloof, or Malouf, or similar, known to be visiting the London area, but he had since gone into hiding. A large task force of police was working on it currently and because they did not think they had actually managed to leave the country, they felt confident of early detention.

All in all, MI6 was certain that the whole UK exercise was being orchestrated by Khoury, not only financially but also actually directing local activities himself. However, they also considered that someone may be above Khoury in the command, but had no leads at this moment.

MI6 did not have an open slather to 'bug' phones in the UK, but were currently seeking a Judicial Order to tap the phones of Khoury and his London office and this may lead to further useful intel.

It was then resolved to get Lovell into Jordan to continue an on-the-ground investigation, quite openly, as an insurance investigation, where the evidence gained would stand up to international legal examination if necessary.

Truscott-Browne was advised to commence arrangements for Lovell's trip, in confidence, until they had spoken to Jordanian State Security and they would also put their 'Amman Station' on alert.

Titus was to be drawn into something where he was unlikely to be told all the facts but would have a large support base in the background, both in the UK and Jordan.

The question of the need to 'arm' Lovell was discussed and although it was agreed to be rational, the SIS men said it could cause too many problems if something went wrong. Accordingly, they informed Truscott-Browne that no side-arms were to be supplied, but their own men in Amman, with diplomatic immunity, would be suitably armed, as always!

He was instructed to call in Lovell in the morning, unless he heard to the contrary and then give him the MI6 formulated instructions to pass on to him for his trip.

Bob returned to his offices in one of his own cabs and engaged his staff in preparing for the task ahead and bookings for Lovell.

He would ensure every possible precaution was in place before Lovell embarked on this venture.

Chapter 24

Saleh Ahmadi was trying to work out the finer points of operating his newly and illegally acquired Immarsat satellite telephone handset, which was still secret. It had just been developed, covertly, for the most sophisticated Western Military Forces and was unknown to the world at large.

Telephone lines in Sana'a were mainly used for local calls and also through to the city of Aden some 550km south, on the coast, in the Peoples' Republic of Yemen (South Yemen). They were subject to regular disruptions, with the service and worse still, operators had to connect long-distance trunk calls, so security could not be guaranteed. He was therefore buoyant that this new phone literally promised to deliver the world to him in Sana'a, to carry on his nefarious dealings unmonitored, or so he thought!

Ahmadi was safely holed up in his home, which was more like a mini fortress, surrounded by extremely thick, high, yellowish mud walls all around, and with heavy wooden double gates being the only entry/exit to the compound. Also HQ for Zamir Mines Coy.

It was a hot, bleak and inhospitable place, more correctly belonging to hell.

The hilltop house stood towards the rear of the huge compound and, along the inside of the outer walls, built a myriad of buildings which served a number of purposes ranging from barracks for men in training or simply in hiding, to storage areas for weaponry and fuel, plus garaging for vehicles.

The cunning part of the whole exercise was that whereas the house would have been clearly visible to any aerial observations, the remaining buildings and yard were discretely covered by two layers of camouflage nets and would have given the impression that it was a simple family home with gardens, but with no unusual activities or outbuildings.

The complex was situated well away from the town centre, high on a hill, in a typical location one would expect to find such a fortified position. That is to say, a 360° view, built on high ground, and with only one dusty approach road that could be observed clearly for over two miles from the tops of the walls.

Ahmadi had chosen well and ran his little empire ruthlessly from there.

The spoils of his dealings had enabled him to buy, steal or otherwise acquire most of the latest equipment and nothing seemed to be out of his reach. He didn't realise that he'd put Western Intelligence Forces right inside his camp because Britain actually owned and controlled the satellites through which all his new communications were routed. Therefore, from that day, MI6 would be monitoring all his calls and finally, they may be able to get to the root of his brand of fundamentalist terrorism.

His very first call was proudly to one of his business partners, Khoury, in London, to report on shipping changes he recently made.

He told Khoury, "We have rerouted the Jordanian phosphates shipments, originally meant to be despatched from Aqaba to the port of Aden. They will still sail from Aqaba but now go to the smaller Yemeni port of Al Mukalla. It is proceeding better than I expected because it is cheaper and we make more! There is so much official scrutiny in the port of Aden, with too many authorities to pay off and far less here."

Ahmadi had also found a new shipping agent who was more amenable to his style of business and he was able to squeeze another 1.2% off marine transport charges, but this would be into his pocket and Khoury would not be informed. No honour among thieves!

Khoury verified, "The insurance fraud investigation continues by Lovell but he seems to have no real idea of the details of our scheme or how it works. So I feel that it is quite secure for us to continue on, at least for another few months."

Ahmadi then enquired, "Has my man, Ustaaz (Mr) Waled Malouf, managed to evade the police after dealing with Kingwell? Tell me if they are getting close and I will arrange for him to meet with an accident before arrest and prison. I do not want him talking, such that it may lead the authorities back to either of us, as there is too much at stake. Anyway, he bungled dealing with Lovell!"

Khoury told him, "Malouf is safely housed in a warehouse located just behind a historic mosque in Cardiff, Wales. Police activities, from the intelligence I have, seem to be directed around the South London area and towards the south coast, where they suspect Malouf of fleeing by a small private boat. If there is any danger of Malouf being captured, I am happy for you to take care of him in the usual way!"

At that very moment, Ahmadi was already signing the death warrant for Waled Malouf, "Why wait for the inevitable capture, because he also bungled the attempt on Lovell," he reasoned.

Their business was not based on sentimentality or the value of life!

Ahmadi indicated, "The next £400,000 will be directed to the World Overseas Trust Bank in George Town, Cayman Islands into the account of KN Developments."

Knowing that the Caymans had special banking laws, they would use them to advantage in hiding and distributing their respective shares.

Greedily, Khoury was quick to enquire about the date of the expected transfer of funds, little knowing that the conversation was playing right into the hands of MI6, who would have a full transcript of it on their desk within hours.

As a British Overseas Territory, the Cayman Islands were especially accessible to MI6 and this information would prove to be very valuable in their hands. It would also be a strong bargaining chip to use with the CIA, which was also vitally interested in terrorism.

Khoury had no illusions as to the nature of his relationship with Ahmadi, and so it was with some trepidation that he raised the next subject.

Trying to sound as matter-of-fact and calm as possible, he mentioned, "I have temporarily lost contact with Nicholson and am a little concerned with his state of mind. Nicholson is a weak unbeliever, who now seems to be much too nervous about the ongoing investigation, such that we may have to deal with him," then adding that he had probably outlived his usefulness anyway.

Ahmadi reacted quickly and violently, screaming at Khoury, "You had better make every effort to find him and test whether there is a danger so that I can decide whether it is safe to leave him alive or not. Do you understand, 'majdoube'?"

The outburst unsettled Khoury, especially calling him an idiot, for he was much more a terrorist organiser, rather than Ahmadi's style of extreme, direct and brutal action. He tried to assure Ahmadi that he was in control but in his heart, he knew that the situation seemed to be slipping through his fingers and the danger to him was also becoming quite real and imminent.

As a man of instant decision, Ahmadi directed, "Once Nicholson has been located then you will advise me immediately and I will despatch someone to get rid of him."

There were none of the usual pleasantries at the completion of the telephone call but just the veil of the anger and threat expressed by Ahmadi, leaving Khoury feeling cold and depressed.

Work was well underway through the Cayman's Courts to secure orders to place freezes on any and all accounts traceable to KN Developments, Khoury, Nicholson, Ahmadi, Zamir Mining Coy and even the three 'innocent' parties of Ecothan, Twal and New Giffin-Sen, if in fact, they had accounts.

The net was closing, but more information was essential from Lovell and an SAS patrol in Yemen, to reveal and demonstrate just how the fraudulent conversion and distribution of millions was taking place.

Chapter 25

Rose started work early Monday morning, worried about what may be ahead of her but was pleasantly surprised when she was called in by Peter Moles to act as his assistant, to clear up Mr Kingwell's desk. She had a great deal of respect for Moles who was a gentle soul, not unlike her late boss and she felt quite happy to work with him.

She felt a little uneasy when directed to go through all the papers on the desk and in the drawers, and then bring them to him, catalogued, because in fact, she had already done this for Titus. Nevertheless, she proceeded, unlocked the office and then set about the task, quite naturally finding nothing new.

She organised everything into groups and prepared them neatly into named manila folders.

The papers were duly presented to Moles and he asked her to explain them to him, which was done efficiently and simply by her.

When Moles was satisfied with all the papers displayed to him, he asked her to ring Anne Nicholson to see whether there was any sign of Ralph who had not arrived at his customary time.

It was not a task she looked forward to!

"Mrs Nicholson it is Rhoda Lang here, PA to the late Mr Kingwell and I too am enquiring after Mr Nicholson."

Through her sniffles and weeping Mrs Nicholson explained, "I have not seen my husband for three days. Initially, I thought that he was on an overseas business trip because a suitcase and his typical travelling clothes were all missing, but I later found that his passport was still in the bureau. I also noticed that his business suits are still hanging in the wardrobe, so he didn't go to work— So where is he? He left no note and I have not heard from him by telephone either."

Rose did her best to console Mrs Nicholson, saying, "When I hear from him I will make contact immediately and ask that you do the same, please."

This was duly reported back to Moles who wondered aloud whether there was something more sinister at work perhaps, thinking of Jimmy Kingwell's murder.

Both of them were missing the support of Titus Lovell's steadying presence and his sense of direction in this whole matter.

After carrying out some further, but minor tasks for Mr Moles, he thanked her and indicated he had a couple of confidential calls to make.

By then it was lunch time and Rose decided to take a walk to clear her head from the intrigue, uncertainty and dread that there was more nastiness to follow.

She bought herself a sandwich from a nearby cafe and headed towards the Thames. She knew she would be able to find a bench somewhere and sit quietly for half an hour or so to gather her thoughts, particularly about TG.

It was whilst she was doing this that she saw the temporary office girl Kim leaning against a tree, not 30 yards to the right of her position, seeming to Rose to be looking rather furtively around her, as though waiting for someone, and not wanting to be seen. She had clearly not seen Rose, who was at an angle to her, with a scarf pulled well up around her lower face because of the wind making it seem colder than it really was. Rose had been about to commence eating her roast beef and mustard sandwich but felt uneasy at what she was observing.

Titus had suggested that she not try and act the part of a detective but she couldn't help it.

Rose wasn't sure what she was seeing but kept her face down and her eyes up, angled towards Kim, to see what may happen.

Time passed slowly and the wind started to bite into her through her lightweight three-quarter coat, causing her to shiver slightly. She pretended to nibble at her sandwich as she thought this would cover her face even more but there was no sign of Kim either looking her way or recognising her.

Was she being paranoid and imagining some sort of intrigue she wondered. Yet here she was, freezing cold and thinking about spying on an 18-year-old fellow office worker!

She decided that she was being plain silly and actually started on her lunch, allowing her mind to drift back pleasantly to the evening in Chinatown with TG. She felt a surge of warmth flow through her and her cheeks felt pleasurably hot.

What did this mean? She'd never been in love before to allow her to compare her feelings to anything previously but was starting to convince herself that 'it' had happened. She couldn't bear the thought that he didn't feel the same about her, but he'd never actually said anything, although she admitted that she had only known him for a few days.

Was she racing way ahead of herself like a love-sick teenager, she questioned, although she felt that he was keen too, but how keen, she wondered, in the agony of doubt.

The sandwich was stuck in her mouth like a piece of dried-out cardboard that she couldn't swallow. Oh dear, it must be love, as she had never had trouble enjoying her food before this, she reflected.

She supposed that about 10 minutes passed when a swarthy, heavy-set woman passed in front of her, lightly brushing against her knees, seemingly in a great hurry. She automatically looked up as she strode passed but slowed her pace a short distance later and sidled up alongside Kim.

Maybe she didn't have an overactive imagination after all.

Kim appeared very nervous, looking both ways, as though something terrible was about to occur. The woman spoke for a moment but was too far away for Rose to even hear her voice, let alone the actual words uttered.

Kim hardly opened her mouth and then after exchanging business-size envelopes they both turned away and walked in opposite directions.

Rose kept her head down but her eyes angled up, observing their movements.

It had all happened so quickly thought Rose and so seemed very clandestine. She didn't like it at all; something was very wrong.

As much of the current intrigue that TG was investigating appeared to be settled around Arabian countries, Rose concluded, rightly or wrongly, that this woman was involved because she clearly seemed to be of Middle Eastern origin.

Rose thought the obvious course to take would be to follow the woman, but she could not simply absent herself from work and she was still mindful of Titus' warning not to play at being a detective; especially after Mr Kingwell's demise!

Consequently, she decided to return to work but didn't want Kim to see her or in fact, walk back to the office together. Thinking that it was getting rather awkward and difficult to try to work out, she was pleased when Kim continued to walk in the opposite direction, heading away from the office, towards a lunch stand.

She quickly dumped the remainder of her now tasteless sandwich into a nearby park bin and turned to head off towards the office, which allowed her to move, unnoticed by Kim, who was disappearing the other way.

Within five or so minutes, Rose was ascending in the office building's lift up to the safety of Ecothan's offices.

Rose went straight to her own office to contemplate the scene which she had just witnessed and convinced herself that the meeting could not have been above board.

She took a deep breath and headed into Mr Moles' office, excusing herself, saying that she needed to tell him something very important. Rose immediately reported her observations to Peter Moles, who was indeed very interested and made copious notes before thanking her and requesting that she keep the information confidential to him alone.

After she had left his office, Moles considered what Miss Lang had observed and realising that she was a very level-headed senior employee, who wasn't given to flights of fancy, he decided to act.

His decision was to pass on these facts to Mr Blake, who was Titus' employer and who had rung him a short time ago requesting that any developments should be reported only to him personally, in Titus' absence on another matter overseas.

Titus had previously told Rose about his respect for Mr Blake and she confided this to Moles who had no doubt therefore that he would take care of this new information. He called Blake and after summarising the facts to him, he mentioned that he had made his own handwritten notes whilst speaking with Miss Lang. Blake asked whether it would be possible for him to sign, date and time stamp his notes as they may prove invaluable at a later date.

"If you have a private fax machine, perhaps I could transmit a copy to you?" Moles suggested.

"Most certainly, thank you, Mr Moles, that would be most useful and very much appreciated. Please keep in contact," and gave him his dedicated fax number.

Blake of course had recently been briefed by Truscott-Browne relating to the Jordan trip and was more than au fait with the intricacies of Lovell's dangerous investigations in this matter.

He immediately called Bob to pass this fresh information on to him, whilst making the appropriate notes on Lovell's case file and adding a copy of Moles' faxed note too.

Needless to say, the information was in the hands of MI6 operatives within moments, and they no doubt would be checking CCTV cameras in the area and then set about tracking down both women to consider their involvement in terrorism.

Rose, back in her office, was wishing her TG was somewhere closer and hoping he would not only be back soon but wouldn't forget her once the Ecothan case had been wrapped up.

Perhaps she was just a useful contact and simply a part of the case to him? How could she tell him of her feelings if he didn't feel the same? She couldn't.

Chapter 26

Nicholson was a nervous man by disposition, never imbued with any great personality or physical strength, or for that matter any attraction to the opposite sex. He was dull and he knew it, but he coveted some of that James Bond playboy, rich and famous lifestyle.

After 25 years of married life, he had no children and with a greedy wife, he could not see any future or change to his insipid life. He understood that he was consigned to a loveless, boring life with no respite. That was untill Khoury had approached him with this scheme, sometime after casually meeting him at a professional function at a city hotel.

The first meeting seemed innocent enough and Nicholson was flattered by this man. He appeared to be rich and from a somewhat exotic background and yet showed interest in him, where the 100 or so other guests found him invisible, as usual.

He was now starting to wonder how accidental the meeting was, or whether it had been planned by Khoury from the start to drag him down to allow him to gratify his own greedy needs, which he spoke of, only after too much to drink.

He had enjoyed many free drinks and meals at expensive five-star hotels with his new 'friend', who had made him re-appraise his current life, whilst playing to his very dreams and discontented feelings. Over several months, Khoury had afforded him the experience of a champagne lifestyle but one which he knew needed bags of money to enjoy and so was well beyond his dreams. Why? Because his wife took all his money for her hopeless family, stupid church clubs and charities, it could never be within his reach.

Even if the Ecothan's fraud situation was completely uncovered and the authorities actually traced him to Spain, there was nothing they could do to extradite him back to Britain.

However, he was not sure what Khoury would make of him disappearing and neither was he sure just where his tentacles may reach. He knew Khoury would not be troubled by extradition treaties, as he and his cronies had a much more immediate way of solving problems! He was certain that Khoury knew nothing of his aspirations to relocate to Spain, nor of his previous trips here, because he had not travelled on his own passport; so there should be no trace of him ever having left the UK, apart from the Lebanon trips for the company.

Once all this was in the open, Khoury had sympathised with how hard his employer made him work for so little return and suggested a one-off scheme could perhaps be cooked up to make him the money he needed; then he could get what he wanted and live his own lifestyle, maybe without his wife?

Nicholson was an easy target!

He was discontent with his life, wife, income and lifestyle. Something that Khoury's promise of wealth could fix, but look where it had all led!

Khoury had said it was a victimless crime where no one would be hurt; yet more lies, in this tragedy.

Nicholson thought back to the frightful interview with Lovell at the Ecothan office and knew in his heart that he was trapped. The whole ball of string was unravelling very quickly and certainly most unpleasantly.

The death of Jimmy Kingwell had been the first real moment of truth and although Khoury had not acknowledged his involvement, he was absolutely certain that it was his doing. He was terrified of Khoury, not because of any direct threat but perhaps more because of the overall menacing nature of the man. He just thought that Khoury had now settled at what he thought to be his true level, as a ruthless completely amoral psychopath, compared to the solicitous 'friend' of earlier days.

He knew that he was totally out of his depth and dealing with the type of people who would have normally given him nightmares. Yet he had been so charming when they first met.

Completely sucked in by him? Yes.

Would he go back to his wife? No!

Would he go back to Ecothan and face the music? No!

Would he return to England? No!

Would he attempt to reimburse any of the stolen money? No!

Was he safe here in Spain? Yes, he was pretty sure.

At least he thought so, because there was no extradition treaty between the UK and Spain. Also, he had never mentioned the villa he had acquired there to anyone, especially his wife, Khoury and of course no one at Ecothan.

He had no friends! He was a loner and not by choice either.

He thought that he had planned his getaway extremely well and was therefore feeling almost smug about his current situation. He had picked up many of his ideas for his escape from fictional adventure and spy novels and they had served him well.

He travelled using his useless brother-in-law's passport, knowing that he was currently confined to a wheelchair, after a serious illness and would not be going anywhere overseas for at least six months, if ever. He figured that with the name Dennis Brown on the passport and a reasonable likeness on the photo, no one would be the wiser.

He had dumped the car at Oxford, to put them off and trained it down to the south coast. He took the evening ferry journey from Plymouth to Roscoff, in northern France, with hundreds of other people, lost in the mass. He thought the trip would never be noted and to support this, only the most cursory glance was given to the passport on leaving the UK.

He knew that he was not a person that anyone noticed anyway and so he kept very much to himself in the corner of the vessel's lounge area, sipping tea for the five-hour ferry trip. There was minimal interest by the authorities in France, where his passport wasn't even opened.

After landing, he had travelled by a combination of bus and train making his way across France to Madrid in Spain, again with no interest as he passed over the border on the train.

He overnighted in a small non-descript suburban Madrid hotel, paying cash. They asked him for his papers, but he deliberately fumbled so much, that they waved him away to his room. *Good*, he thought, *no trace of me here either.*

After a strange Spanish breakfast, of ham, tomatoes and cake-like bread, he collected his bag and walked out into the street.

He was feeling almost light-headed with joy at his success, but terror struck him as he exited the hotel to see a police car right outside.

Two uniformed officers sternly beckoned him over and he went white with fright, shaking all over. He couldn't read these foreign faces and they looked very serious. They addressed him in Spanish, but he couldn't understand a word, further adding to his terror. They'd got him already. How the hell could that be?

It was at a stalemate, as he just stared at them, trembling, as they waved their arms around, pointing.

Luckily, the hotel manager came out, spoke to the police and said they were enquiring if he had seen an African man running by. He had not, so they dismissed him and everyone dispersed, leaving him to recover.

It seemed like a close call, and he didn't need any more, for he was still shaking.

Later, he travelled by train to the city of Malaga and was disturbed to see several Middle Eastern men in his carriage. He was seeing danger everywhere, and he wondered how much more he could take.

Eventually, he arrived absolutely anonymously, and safely in Malaga.

He stayed away from the tourist haunts and the bus station, where he could have easily caught transport to his hideaway. However, now deeply into the subterfuge of his secret getaway, he mooched around the back streets of Malaga looking for an alternative to legit travel arrangements. He needed a private car for transport, not a taxi or bus.

The youth he met in a café spoke passable English and had set a price, which he knew was outrageous for a 60 km trip, but he didn't care. This kid wouldn't be talking to the authorities and would soon be back in Malaga.

The lad drove well and pointed out many tourist features along the way, so it was a mostly pleasant journey and a great start to his new life. He asked to be dropped off at a small bar, telling his driver he would be meeting a friend, who would take him inland to the bigger town of Jaen. He watched the youth turn and disappear down the hill towards the main road, happy with his fistful of money. Once satisfied, he too turned but in the opposite direction and walked a couple of hundred yards uphill to his villa, and so, even if by chance, the authorities found the youth, he would inadvertently mislead them.

Yes, he had planned well and was looking forward to the future.

Frigiliana was a small, historic village built at the top of a very steep hill, overlooked by an old Moorish castle, built well over 500 years before. The streets were narrow, cobbled and steep with the town clinging to the sides of the hill. Most of the houses were hundreds of years old, in the traditional style, all cleanly whitewashed and with contrasting black painted wrought iron balconies plus many with window bars.

Down on the narrow coastal plain, about four miles away stood the growingly popular tourist town of Nerja, which held all the facilities that he would need, but he did not intend to visit there himself, at least not for the next few months anyway. He considered that he should lie low and would arrange for his local contact to make his purchases and bring them up to him, as needed.

From his readings, he knew that many, UK criminals had fled with their ill-gotten gains and were living very well here in Spain, where the cost of living was so much cheaper than in England.

Yes, he thought to himself, *this will do me very nicely and with the money he had already purloined, he could see a good 20 to 30 years ahead of him, plus whatever he could make out of his investments in the ensuing years.* Anyway, he thought there was another payment imminent and as soon as it hit his bank in the Cayman Islands, he would withdraw it and the rest of his money from there. Then he'd move it around a few times and eventually transfer it to a new account in Spain where no proof of identity was required, unlike the UK. He could then 'play' the stock market and increase his fortune further.

The name he intended to use was simple and easy for Spaniards too and he said it aloud, "Matt Bond, yes they can all call me Mr Bond!"

He estimated that his share of the next tranche could be as high as £200,000 and that would set him up forever, especially without Anne and her dead-loss family to drag him down, with her constant demands for more and more money.

The villa he had purchased was not ostentatious from the outside and fitted into the general presentation of the village. However, it had been completely rebuilt inside to immaculate standards and was the height of luxury. The kitchen spilt out into a dining area, which in turn ran into a large casual lounge area, opening to the back of the house.

Looking out of the rear sliding doors of the lounge area was a magnificent outdoor entertaining area, with a built-in barbeque and clay pizza oven. Nicholson had never cooked anything in his life and so these items were unlikely to be used, at least in the near future.

To top it all off, an in-ground fully tiled swimming pool had been added at the rear.

Pity, he couldn't swim!

There were no immediate neighbours nor was the property overlooked, giving him a feeling of safety brought about by semi-isolation. There was an olive tree orchard of sorts, surrounding the property on two sides, but set well back from his fence line, giving clear views all around.

He felt secure in a typical local-looking village home.

On his way through, he had stopped briefly at a small village, the name of which he could not remember; something like Torrox or Torres. He had stocked up with a couple of bags of supplies which should keep him out of sight for at least two weeks.

He had purchased the villa privately from the vendor, who had previously been renting it out to another Brit.

The rather slick Spaniard told him that he could arrange anything Nicholson wanted, to be brought up from Nerja, subject to an hour or two's notice. Nicholson felt that this arrangement would suit him perfectly as he could enjoy himself, lay low and yet not be starved of the new luxuries he deserved.

Arturo said that he could find him a car to use if he needed it, either to buy or rent casually.

More interestingly, he also offered to find him a beautiful girl or boy, from time to time, if he would just let him know his preference!

This offer was somewhat staggering to Nicholson and initially offensive but the more he thought about it, the more he was tempted, as sex had eluded him for many years. Yes, this was something that he would definitely act on at a later stage, a young, well-built beautiful Spanish girl; and with big tits, oh yes!

What Nicholson did not know was that MI6 already had this address, after following the money trail and knew exactly where he was at this very moment! The only thing they did not know was the name on the false passport that he was using.

Nicholson's number was up, or should they say, Mr Bond!

Chapter 27

Truscott-Browne had passed on the information received from Blake, but initially coming from Moles at Ecothan, to MI6, who moved in several directions at once.

Indeed, police viewed council, railways and street closed-circuit TV videotapes of the area where Kim was seen by Rose to meet the unknown woman. Because of it, they had an exact time and place. The incident was found quickly and still photographs were isolated and printed.

The swarthy dark-haired woman was unknown to MI6 but on checking immigration entry records she was found to be Shada Al Shammari, a distant cousin of Khoury, arriving from Saudi Arabia some two years previous. Her address was shown as being the same as Khoury and likewise, she was traced as working for New Giffin-Sen PLC at their Richmond-upon-Thames office, as Khoury's only employee.

A watch was immediately placed on her, but no direct approach was made to her or her employer, for the moment.

Kimberley Potts's background was thoroughly checked and she seemed to be exactly as she presented, that is an 18-year-old semi-skilled office worker, living with her parents in Kennington, South London in very average conditions. None of her family had any known criminal or suspected behaviour histories; nevertheless, she had been seen with Al Shammari, exchanging envelopes in a park.

Agents requested that Moles invite Kim to his office at 3:00 pm, whereupon they would ask him to leave and they would interview her before she could leave the premises.

At 3:00 pm, Kim knocked nervously at Mr Moles' door and was invited to enter, not having any idea why she was there, nevertheless somehow feeling a little trapped. Ahead of her, she could see Moles standing behind his desk, not looking at all threatening or angry and so she started to relax.

"Thank you, Mr Moles, we will take it from here," a deep booming voice came from behind her, causing her to spin around in shock and observe two tall, official-looking men in dark suits staring at her. She turned back towards Moles to see that he had walked around the desk and was heading for the door, leaving her alone with the two men.

Oh God, I've been caught spying in here and taking a bribe, she thought with shame.

The agents saw the sheer terror on her face and softened their approach, suggesting that she take a chair so they could speak to her about a couple of matters causing them concern.

She burst into tears and it took a good couple of minutes before she composed herself enough to blurt out, "She told me that if I did not do what she wanted, she would inform the police that my brother had been buying dope, and was in debt to a dealer." She again burst into tears, but for a shorter period, and then said that she did not steal anything from Ecothan or do anything bad.

As yet the agents had not asked her any questions but already they had most of the answers!

"What exactly were you asked to do and how did you do it?"

"She wanted me to give her a list of all visitors to the office, a list of all the staff travelling overseas and their destination, and anything else that seemed to be different around the office each day. I don't know who she was, or how she found out that my brother had been smoking weed or that he was in debt. She was very menacing and frightened me into doing as she demanded. She told me where to meet her every second lunchtime and to hand over a note with the information on it. I was surprised when she gave me £50 each time to pay off my brother's drug debt. That's all I know!" and burst into tears again.

"Will I go to gaol?" She asked through her tears.

The agents indicated that they would speak to Mr Moles and tell him that she had been threatened and had done nothing to damage the business but they warned her not to speak to anyone, including her family, of what happened as they may need her as a witness later.

"Do you understand this young lady?" The older of the two men said sternly.

"Yes, yes. I won't say a word to anyone, **ever**!" she bleated in a tiny frightened voice.

"Kimberly, would you please use the intercom and call Mr Moles back into the office, after which you will leave us quietly, without mentioning this to anyone and you should just go about your normal duties here."

Meanwhile, at MI6, all stops had been pulled out regarding Al Shammari and they found that the Saudi Arabian Security authorities had indicated that she was a known disruptive due to her anti-government activities. They suspected her previous seditious actions could be taken as bordering on terrorism but she had left the country before they were able to take proceedings. However, she remained a person of interest to them and they would be grateful to see her returned to them to deal with.

This information was of great interest because it could be used as a lever when interviewing her, as they felt sure that she certainly would not want to be returned to her native country, knowing what could be in store for her.

Chapter 28

Slugger had been correct in assuming that the old Austin was not damaged for it continued smoothly along the tarmac highway and then after turning onto the white-topped gravel road it continued to travel without any problems at all.

She really was a Princess!

He knew that his well-trained hearing would pick up any strange warning sounds from her but all was well.

Talking in the back of the car had wound down because they were more interested in what was happening by way of traffic and knew that they could examine the documents later.

Twal had regained his composure but was looking visibly anxious as they drew closer to approaching his mine site.

After about an hour of very tense driving, they approached the security gate where they were directed to stop but on seeing Twal the traditionally dressed gate-man was clearly pleased, giving him a smart salaam and raising the bar to allow the car to pass through.

The security guard must have signalled ahead, because as the car moved along, the workforce appeared on the roadside and waved to them, indicating that even though Twal was the boss, it was clear that he was a very popular man, which was somewhat unusual in Arab countries.

The main administration block had been built of local white stone and was a single-storey building with a flat roof but as a concession to the desert heat, there were canvas window awnings and a large evaporative air-conditioning unit set on the roof and blowing loudly.

After the air-conditioned comfort of two-plus hours in the car, they stepped into the glaring sunlight and the desert heat struck them like a hammer.

Numerous men approached Twal obviously excited to see him when suddenly there was a somewhat familiar roar from the administration block and the men dissipated, apparently back to their jobs, without getting any closer.

Titus was relieved because in view of recent happenings, he was not looking forward to an unknown group crowding around him and Twal, as that had obvious security implications.

They were only a few feet from the building when he was dumbstruck to see his old foe Pieter Coetzee, whose voice he thought he recognised in warding off that crowd from approaching Twal.

Now that Twal was on familiar ground, quite clearly surrounded by friends he turned to Titus drawing him towards Coetzee saying, "You know, Mr Coetzee, who came ahead of you, and has been invaluable in sorting out all these changes."

Titus stepped forward to shake Coetzee's hand, and as he pulled him in, Pieter whispered, "I told you that I would do it my way—we can talk later."

Twal invited them all into the office block but Slugger declined, asking, "Sir, could I run the Princess into one of your workshops and check her out mechanically, because the old girl has had a rough ride today."

Twal called over one of his men, saying, "Give this gentleman the full run of the mechanical workshop and any help that he needs to affect repairs. I will be returning in this vehicle, later and I want it to be completely safe. Make sure he has fuel and everything that he needs and refreshments too."

The workshop was not air-conditioned but Slugger had worked in the bowels of ships through the tropics and so heat was of no consequence. He stripped off his chauffeur's jacket and shirt and worked bare-chested to the amazement of locals, whom he did not think had seen anyone stripped down to work. He was probably twice the size of anyone there, and with his barrel chest and meaty arms must have looked like a giant.

A huge pot of mint-flavoured black tea was slowly brewing over a methylated spirit burner in the workshop and it was just what Slugger required to re-hydrate. He needed to get the sweat pouring from him, to enable him to cool down naturally. He knew that very cold drinks were the worst thing to have in extreme heat because they made the body work even harder to warm them to body temperature and eventually added even more internal body heat.

In his long service with the Royal Navy, he had spent time in Egypt and Palestine and was aware of some of the Arabic customs. He remembered that when not under pressure or under radical religious direction, most Arabs were generally respectful, polite and helpful people and the older men in the crew seemed to be very cooperative and obliging to him.

One of the bays of the workshop had a two-post hydraulic lifting hoist, capable of lifting a small truck and this was just what he needed to elevate the Princess to head height, so that he could make an inspection of the undercarriage, without having to crawl under it.

Once elevated, he was able to see minor scratches on the engine sump pan, and also on the exhaust system but nothing had been deranged or broken.

A thorough check of the suspension and steering rods again showed no damage and likewise, there were no leaks from any of the hydraulic braking system's pipework.

He used the compressed airline to blow away all the rubbish from the undercarriage and felt satisfied that nothing was amiss.

He brought the Princess down and whilst sipping a mug of tea, he listened to the engine, looking for any inconsistencies but the old girl was running perfectly. The compressed air hose was used again, this time to blow all the bugs and vegetation out of the radiator, air conditioner's coils, and air filters, to help prevent possible overheating on the return journey.

By now, the locals' fascination for him had worn off and he was left alone in the workshop, to the huge, almost industrial-sized pot of tea.

There was a second group milling around, and they appeared to him as less than friendly.

He watched the five men wander off in their long flowing garments which he knew were called thawbs, made of cotton and being ankle length, with long sleeves. During the summer, they were worn with or sometimes without 'izaars' underneath, as a lower garment. They always looked so hot to him but their traditional dress seemed to suit them, only changing into darker colours and sometimes a woollen thawb in the winter months. He supposed that they didn't overheat because they wandered around in slow motion most of the time and in the hour that he'd been here he had not seen one of them do a scrap of work.

This was the opportunity he needed to get into the cabin of the vehicle and operate some of the equipment which Titus had noticed him using during the trip here.

He dictated a few more notes onto the recorder and then transmitted the whole day's recordings back to the 'station' in Amman, in a coded form, knowing that in a short time, it would be repeated through to London for action.

The tiny printer under the dashboard, which was connected to the little black box, produced a printed slip, similar to the Telex print-out, which he knew was for Titus and so he had to pass the message to him quickly.

Slugger was able to wash himself under a running tap where the water was hot from the sun beating on the steel pipes. Out of the corner of his eye, he could see a couple of the workmen looking at him in puzzlement, for it was their tradition to bathe infrequently and this crazy Englishman was washing in the middle of the day, in public!

Once he was dressed again, complete with chauffeur's cap, he drove the car back to the administration block and parked it in the shade, facing outwards, as always, and ready for a swift getaway, if necessary.

Inside the building, he came face to face with a rather ugly gent, wearing the traditional Palestinian red and white headgear and asked him, "Could you find Mr Lovell for me, please?"

It was met with a puzzled look and the reply of, "No Eeenglish!" with his hands thrown up, indicating that he did not understand.

"Boss-man!" said Slugger in a commanding voice pointing towards the office area, to which the man nodded and wandered off in that direction.

Within a moment, Twal returned asking, "Is everything all right with your car, Mr Slugger; I'm sorry if there is a problem."

"No, thank you, sir, the Princess is ship-shape and ready to sail again. I need to report the status to Mr Lovell, to assure him of the situation, if you'd be so kind as to fetch him for me."

"Certainly, I will send him out straight away, but then I need him back to continue on with what we are doing. Have you been offered a drink?"

Slugger acknowledged Twal's words saying, "Thank you, your mechanics have been very kind and allowed me to fill the tank with petrol too."

"Good, good, please simply ask if you need anything else."

Titus appeared shortly afterwards looking worried but Slugger assured him that the Princess was, in tip-top nick and ready for the trip home at a moment's notice, if he required.

There was no one in the reception office at that time and after a quick look around Slugger indicated, "This message has just come in from HQ so I will leave you to deal with it."

At the same time, Titus was able to whisper to Slugger, "Tell them that Pieter Coetzee is here, of his own initiative, certainly not authorised that I know. He is working with Twal's approval, doing his own enquiry."

"Okay, TG, I'll get onto it straight away and see what they can find out for you. Watch your back! Whilst you're in there, I'll have a poke around the yards and make sure there are no weapons or other nasties out there."

Just then one of the workmen entered the office and so they parted without any further words, with Slugger returning to the car to transmit a message regarding Coetzee and Titus walking back into Twal's office.

Titus confronted Coetzee in his office, asking, "What the hell are you doing here? You idiot."

"I'm no fool," and then in a whisper, he confided, "I have had my eye on Ralph Nicholson for the past six months and as the head of security I took the opportunity to come here and see what I could learn. In fact, it has been very interesting with Twal's original staff feeling very side-tracked by a new group of Syrian and Yemeni staff brought in to take many positions. What surprised me was that all of the changes have been made in the name of Ecothan, under directions from London, so who is responsible?"

"I made myself known as a security specialist and told Twal of my suspicions. I have noted that the newcomers are steering well clear of me, probably for very good reasons. Not a lot of English is spoken by the foreign workers, but some of the qualified mechanics and technicians do, as they are ex-military. They have been here for years, saying that the working atmosphere has become very unpleasant, and they feel something is very wrong but just don't know what it is."

"With what you have found out since you have been here, I can tell you that you are probably in danger as I have had an attempt on my life. I could have ended up the same as Mr Kingwell."

Coetzee looked a little chastened, saying that he had not connected Kingwell's demise with this issue, and would now be far more mindful of his own personal safety.

A gut feeling told Titus that he was looking more like a friend than a foe; nevertheless, he decided to take information from him but not impart any back to him. Hopefully, in the next few hours, Slugger may be able to give him some more background on Coetzee to put his mind at rest, or otherwise.

"It is not only the change of staff/management that is the cause of concern but also the fact that the old reliable cartage contractors for example have been replaced with a pretty rough, slippery lot of characters who do not mix with any of the staff except their new supervisor."

"The trucks come and go at all hours of the day and night and the old staff can't keep track of all the tonnages leaving the mine but they are told to mind their own businesses or they will be sacked. They suspect that somehow the stock is being stolen and Mr Twal is being cheated."

All this seemed to tie in with the basic premise of Titus' investigation but a lot more information would be required by way of documentation of shipping volumes et cetera.

"What documentation have you come across to support the staff's suspicions?"

"I have bundles of shipping documents which appear to be originals and I am trying to match them up against what actually leaves the mine site here and later arrives at its delivery point at Port Aqaba, down south. There also seems to be some discrepancy relating to the next port destiny after Aqaba, which should be Aden but may have been changed to the smaller port of Al Mukalla, also in Yemen. However, I do not know whether that is significant or alternatively if it is possibly the very heart of this fraud."

He has been doing his homework, thought Titus and most of this matches up with what I suspected and will need to be passed back to London smartly if they are going to intercept shipments and check tonnages against mine records.

"I am going to give you the benefit of the doubt; keep your enquiries going and don't let me down!" said Titus as he turned on his heel and headed back to Twal's office.

Ducking his head into Twal's office, he called out, "I'm going to step outside for a moment to clear my head and then we can resume our investigations."

Twal nodded, still engrossed in the bookwork.

Outside, he found Slugger behind the steering wheel, with the engine running and the air conditioner keeping the car cool. Slugger was actually working on some of the gadgets that he'd seen before and now knew them to be some sort of modern sophisticated radio communication system. He quickly communicated to him the information which he'd gleaned from Coetzee and asked him to pass that back to his masters.

Only then did he find time to read his Telex message.

Chapter 29

The confirmation from different sources that Khoury was directly linked to Saleh Ahmadi at Zamir Mines Coy in Yemen was enough for both British and American Security Agencies to conclude that it was more than just a possible terrorist threat but that this was in fact part of a wide and dangerous terrorist organisation.

Truscott-Browne had reported the findings coming back from Jordan, via Slugger's radio system and although surprised about Coetzee's involvement at the mine, full security checks in the UK, United States and South Africa found nothing untoward in his background. To the contrary, he had an exemplary record in both the civil and military police in South Africa but he still felt that some caution was required in allowing Titus to take him into his confidence.

This was duly transmitted to Titus.

Messages were flowing freely between London, Amman and the mine and the real-time delay was minimal, allowing matters to move forward very quickly.

The next message received by Slugger, for Titus, read, "Action imminent against EK and SA. Instruct A-M T to sack all staff not engaged by him personally and have them escorted off-site. Jordanian military will arrive shortly to assist. Situation still dangerous. Remain vigilant."

Titus read the message carefully and then shutting the door he approached Twal, saying, "I have just received a message from joint security forces and it seems that we are surrounded by danger and so I would like you to read this message before we move forward."

Twal read the message slowly, looking puzzled and said, "I recognise EK as Khoury but who is SA?"

"I was puzzled by that too and was wondering whether he was one of your staff here at the mine."

"I don't recognise the initials but I had been thinking about the manager who was supposedly engaged by Ecothan, Abbas Refai, a Syrian national who works in the next building. He is certainly not one of my men, but obviously, he is not SA."

Titus thought for a moment and suggested that he send someone over to bring Refai back to the admin block and then they could review the list of all new staff members to make sure they picked up everyone in one sweep.

"I will request Pieter to find Refai and bring him back and in the meantime, we can check the staff list and their locations around the site and plan this exercise."

Twal buzzed Coetzee on the intercom, asking him to come immediately for an important and confidential task.

Coetzee appeared in the doorway instantly and no doubt because of the word 'confidential', he closed the office door behind him.

Titus had already received information via Slugger that Coetzee was a man to be trusted and so Titus elected to take him into their confidence.

"We have a major security issue on site here and in a short time, a unit from the Jordanian military will be arriving to detain and remove all staff recently employed by Ecothan."

"Your task now is to track down Abbas Refai, and to bring him here, preferably of his own free will, but if persuasion is necessary, so be it."

Coetzee's head swung around to Twal, looking quizzically at him saying, "What is going on? What do you want me to do?"

"Please follow Mr Lovell's instructions immediately, and as indicated, explanations can follow later."

"Mr Coetzee, this is more important than you can know and your help will be of great assistance, especially if there is no fuss seen on bringing Refai here."

He acknowledged Titus' last instructions with a nod and set off like a man on a mission, closing the door as he left.

After a moment's pause, Twal indicated that the timing was ideal because it was approaching the mid-day meal break and virtually every staff member should be in the close vicinity of the main buildings where they lunched.

"Just how do we go about this?" Twal asked, "As I abhor violence of any kind?"

Titus considered the matter, realising that if it got out at hand it may be beyond them to regain control of so many men, who may even be armed. "Do you have a large lunchroom or shed where perhaps the men could be asked to assemble for a management announcement, without causing them any undue concern?"

"Apart from Refai, this list shows that there are 18 other new men on site so they could easily be assembled in the lunch area, which has breeze-block type construction on three sides but the front is completely open."

"That should be adequate in the short term, whilst you address these men, explaining that your contract with Ecothan has expired and that their services are no longer required. Hopefully, your country's military troops will be here shortly to ensure that they behave, before they are removed from the site and out of your life!" said Titus.

There was a heavy knocking at the office door, following which Coetzee let himself in, escorting a seemingly relaxed Refai ahead of him. *Good work*, thought Titus, who half expected him to arrive with the man in a headlock; perhaps he does have some diplomatic skills.

Twal, ever a businessman stepped forward to greet Refai, saying that he had a major announcement to make to the new workforce and he intended to call them together for a meeting at the mid-day meal break.

Refai nodded, giving no indications of being suspicious.

Titus noted Coetzee about a pace behind Refai, looking like a tiger and obviously ready to pounce if necessary. He was now starting to think that Coetzee could indeed be a useful man to have around at a time like this.

"Mr Refai, would you please sound the meal siren early? Then use the public address speaker system to tell your men to gather immediately in the meals area. Thank you."

Coetzee stepped out with Refai into the adjoining area where he sounded the meal siren, giving two long blasts and then after a short pause, made an announcement in Arabic, which caught both Titus and Coetzee by surprise, not knowing what had been said.

Twal caught Titus' expression and realising that he had not understood the announcement, reassured him saying, "Mr Refai said nothing untoward and followed my instructions exactly."

As they watched through Twal's large office window, Titus could see men drifting towards an open-fronted shed, positioned alongside the workshop where Slugger had worked on his beloved car, a couple of hours ago.

Refai was standing at the door watching the men assemble and so Titus beckoned Coetzee towards him, whispering, "Keep a very close eye on him as he is the leader of this bunch of foreigners, who we have to contain until the Jordanian Army arrives, to remove them."

Coetzee nodded, with a new respect in his eyes for Titus, slipping back into military mode himself and replying, "You can rely on me, sir."

Titus just hoped that Refai would behave, as the results could be very nasty if Coetzee had to deliver on his skills as a military policeman, who by nature was not known to be gentle!

Twal was looking anxious but Titus suggested that they not rush the exercise. "Let's give them time to settle down with their food and drink and feel comfortable before you arrive to make the announcement. It may allay any suspicions building up in their mind."

"You seem to be very calm and organised at this, for an insurance man. Have you done anything like this before today?" Twal asked.

"In my past life, I had a career in the British military, which took me around the world and so I am accustomed to awkward situations which need to be calmed, rather than inflamed."

"I will be glad when this is over but I must say that having you, Mr Slugger and Mr Coetzee here are giving me great confidence for a peaceful outcome."

"I'll just slip outside and put Slugger in the picture, as he too has hidden skills."

"I have no doubt that he would make up for ten men," said Twal, with admiration for his new team of bodyguards.

Titus had to brush past Refai as he exited the door and on excusing himself, he turned towards the man and thought that he was looking anything but calm now. In fact, he was looking quite agitated but Coetzee was sticking to him like glue and seemed to have that situation under control, for the moment at least.

So as not to alarm Refai any further, he stretched as he went out, looked around the yard generally and then sauntered over to Slugger who was standing beside his Princess with his arms folded and across his barrel-like chest.

"Things are starting to look a bit edgy, TG, what's happening now?"

"Coetzee is on our side so I've got him keeping an eye on the renegade manager, Refai. That announcement was to get all his new men to gather, in the meal area, for an announcement by Mr Twal. However, that may be the easy part because we have to keep all 18 men contained in there until the arrival of the Jordanian Military, who I believe are going to cart them off as illegal foreign workers."

"Okay, I can help here. I will move the Princess into that shade, opposite the lunch building," pointing to an area about 20 or 30 yards forward from where the men were starting to assemble.

Titus could see that as a good strategic defence position and nodded as he turned to re-enter the administration block.

Chapter 30

The North Yemeni patrol watched from the top of a dry, dusty, stony hill as two figures approached from the north-west. The patrol commander was using his Chinese-made binoculars whilst sitting in his BTR-40, a Russian-made light armoured car. Prominently mounted at the front was a USA-made 7.62mm general purpose machine gun, manned by a toothless youth, dressed partly in a uniform of sorts and partly in traditional dress and looking very trigger-happy. The vehicle was about 20 years old and had been captured from a South Yemeni patrol which had strayed over their border, the year before.

It had seen better days!

They were a ragged lot of would-be soldiers, kitted out with gear acquired from anywhere and everywhere; and certainly not worn with pride.

The leader observed two men and a laden donkey making their way slowly across the barren landscape under the blazing sun. Knowing that he could catch them in minutes, in his vehicle, he elected to watch and wait. They travelled painfully slowly without deviating as he watched them closely.

But then he became bored as they continued plodding unhurriedly and decided to investigate.

He signalled the third man, who was the driver, to head diagonally across the plain and cut them off before they reached a small dry wadi crossing point, which he pointed to.

This old tub suffered from every conceivable problem except rust and that was only because the area was so dry. The vehicle shook and rattled its way down the rocky slope, heavily blowing smoke from its exhaust pipe giving every indication that it was in imminent danger of disintegrating. Nevertheless, the driver steered it downhill effectively and across the plain, stopping at the edge of the wadi. He manoeuvred the heavy vehicle and turned it to face the approaching men, blocking their path.

The patrol leader watched as the two men continued towards him, without deviating or changing their laboriously slow pace and took a full 20 minutes to arrive at the wadi crossing.

The men were wearing the traditional headdress for the eastern Yemeni areas, clothed in filthy thawbs and wearing open sandals. As they drew closer, he saw nothing amiss, as both were dark-skinned with dirty black beards and downcast eyes. "Filthy peasant traders," he spat.

The corporal stood arrogantly beside his vehicle which was positioned across the wadi crossing path and stared nastily at the approaching group. He was sizing them up and felt no fear as they not only looked harmless but he was well covered by his half-witted nephew manning the machine gun right above him. Allah forbid that he had to be stuck with this worthless son of his sister, day in, day out!

The two men stopped about 10 paces from the armoured car and gave a traditional respectful Arabic salaam to the soldiers, bowing deeply.

The patrol leader signalled them to come forward, so they crossed the short distance pulling their worn-out, unwilling donkey behind them and then stopping as directed, only a few yards from the vehicle.

"Where have you come from and what is your business?" The soldier demanded.

The reply came, but not in the familiar Yemeni Arabic of the area, but in a Gulf Arabic dialect, which the corporal found a little difficult to fully understand, especially since the men mumbled and kept their heads down.

"We have come from the coast with our load of salt and camped last night out of Amran," pointing to hills in the distance behind them.

They waited.

"What is the salt for and where are you taking it?"

"Good master, we are taking it to Sana'a to trade for onyx, which our Egyptian brothers covet above all else." Again bowing deeply in a great show of deference to the high-ranking corporal.

The mounted machine gun was pointed down directly at the two men from a few feet away but they kept their eyes down and waited.

"Come here you," instructed the corporal, pointing at the smaller of the two men and so he stepped up to the side of the vehicle as commanded, maintaining his downward glance.

The man stunk of burnt animal dung and urine, as he would expect from a nomadic peasant, so he kicked him away, out of the range of his nose and beckoned the other to come forward. The smelly individual backed away to restrain the donkey allowing the other to come forward to be inspected by the corporal. He told the peasant to lift his head so that he could check his face but all he detected was a hollow-faced, dark-eyed, sad, bearded peasant, whose odour was just as bad.

He put a foot in the man's chest and kicked him backwards causing him to fall into the sand, flat on his back, where he turned and lay cringing.

"Bring the donkey here now, you filthy dogs!"

He doubted whether these miserable creatures could possibly have anything of value but as it was his 'right' to take a share, he intended to do so.

If the men were smelly, the donkey was far worse and after a quick prod and feeling the granular salt in the sadly worn sacks he gave the donkey a nasty swipe with his cane, causing it to run off into the wadi. The two men ran off in a panic trying to catch the donkey causing the youth on the machine gun to swing it around following the men into the Wadi, his finger already on the trigger. The men knew they were taking a risk but to a peasant, the loss of a donkey meant a loss of income and possible starvation. The corporal saw their fear of losing the donkey and signalled to the gunner to let them go, watching them run down the wadi and laughing at their distress.

Amused momentarily, they soon got tired of the sport and the signal was given and they drove off, back to find another hilltop vantage point. The corporal guessed that this was likely to be the most exciting episode of the day, and so felt that they were to be faced with another very boring afternoon.

The armoured car was out of sight in a few minutes, leaving a cloud of choking dust for the two men to cope with and catch their breath after corralling the donkey.

"I didn't like that toothless bastard on machine gun, Dodger," said the hollow-faced man, whilst taking a measured drink from his goat skin water container.

"Fortunately, that corporal was as dumb as dog shit, as are all the so-called military around here," replied his mate.

"Intelligence suggests that there is only one patrol vehicle active in this area, so we should be able to move much more freely now as I don't think they will come near us again. Christ, you stink!" he laughed at his mate.

"Bloody good idea to roll in the dung fire ashes and splash donkey piss all over us though. I nearly pissed myself when he called me over and the stench hit him. Fuck! You should have seen his face," laughing loudly.

Dodger and his sergeant had been dropped in the desert by an unmarked light plane, in the dead of night and met by a 'friendly' who had supplied them with the donkey, complete with its load and their already dirty second-hand clothing.

The pair had worked together many times, covertly, through Egypt, the Gulf States, Kuwait, Saudi Arabia, Syria, Iraq, Iran and South Yemen, all hot spots of discontent in some way or another.

They spoke several Arabic dialects but had chosen a peasant Gulf dialect from the Oman area as their cover. The dirtier, more ignorant and poorer they appeared, the less they attracted any serious attention from the authorities.

Another 30 km to Sana'a and then they would pinpoint a suitable OP on the edge of the target and use it as an LUP (Lying-up-point), until sometime in the early hours.

The Yemeni patrol had in fact been a blessing in disguise for now they could let the donkey loose and travel quickly and freely. If stopped again, they could say that the patrol had frightened off their donkey and they hadn't been able to catch it.

They felt a little guilty about leaving the donkey heavily loaded so Jonno took a rough piece of stone, which was naturally sharp and dragged it across the two packs allowing the salt to escape but giving the impression that the donkey had rubbed the side walls of the wadi. They knew that someone would grab the donkey within a few hours because they were still highly-valued work animals throughout the Arab world.

It was in the full heat of the mid-afternoon and so they elected to kip in the shade of the Wadi's walls, for a couple of hours' rest, knowing they could easily cover the last 30 km by midnight and then the fun would start in earnest.

Jonno stood watch for the first hour and Dodger the second, allowing them both to refresh for the trek ahead, which in fact was nowhere near as daunting as it sounded, as their training would allow them to cover well over 50 km in a night.

Unencumbered by the donkey, any backpacks or indeed heavy weapons, they set off at a low trot in the early evening, eating up the distance quickly and efficiently. They were well hydrated and had just consumed some dried beef jerky and prunes and felt 'pumped', looking forward to the task ahead.

Dodger was a small wiry man who spent his early years growing up in British Army bases all over the world, especially in Africa, Aden (Yemen), Oman, and Egypt, so his understanding of the culture and language was sublime. He was 32 years old and had been a soldier himself for 15 years, the last five years in 22 SAS Regiment based in Hereford.

Jonno had grown up in London as the son of a bank clerk and rather than follow his old man he too joined up at 17, just to get away from what he saw was his father's dreary life.

As a fitness fanatic, he sought more and more physical challenges but even as a PI (Physical Training Instructor) he felt there must be more. He had three years with 2 Para, The Parachute Regiment, with active service in Borneo, Malaya and 'The Troubles' in Northern Ireland, before winning a place in the SAS, where he had to surrender his previous rank of sergeant to become a Trooper (Private). This was his calling! He excelled at every facet of his training and was even better in the field. He took Arabic culture and language courses and could pass almost anywhere as an Arab peasant or even a middle-class worker.

He'd regained his sergeant's stripes within four years and was now one of the wise old men of 22 SAS Regiment at 39, and had hopes of serving another five-year stretch at least, before being put out to pasture!

They knew their target in Sana'a, although neither had been into the North Yemeni highlands city before but had closely examined satellite photos of Ahmadi's compound and surrounds. Some local intel had been made available but was not always accurate or even trustworthy from such a remote place and so was treated cautiously.

They had rescued their scant possessions from the salt sacks, which included a satellite phone, before letting the donkey go free. Other items retrieved were their modest food and water supplies, plus their personal and very prized Applegate-Fairbairn combat knives.

Further weapons, if needed, could be 'liberated' at Ahmadi's fortified compound, as it was suspected to be a weapons store and training area.

Moving quickly and quietly was second nature to them and the going was easy on lightly rising ground, but there were steeper slopes to come, as they'd have to climb another 2,000 feet from the plateau they were crossing to the 7,400 feet elevation where Sana'a was situated.

Nothing moved nor was there a sound, as this was a poor country and almost every bird or mammal, right down to rats had been caught and eaten many years ago. Accordingly, every sound would be magnified and was probably man-made, so they had to be doubly careful.

The moon was waning in its third quarter, and so the light was about 50% of a full moonlight and ideal here, out in the desert, but not quite so good for their entry to the compound.

Jonno felt things were going a little too smoothly, so moved closer and whispered, "It's a bit too bloody comfortable for my liking. Let's keep our eyes wide and ears alert because we're only about 5 km from the target."

Dodger gave a thumbs-up and they continued, spreading back out to 20 yards apart, extra alert to their surroundings.

They yomped on for another two kilometres as it became darker because of passing cloud cover, making them feel more invisible and safer.

Suddenly they heard a single shot fired, probably no more than 100 yards from them and at 2 o'clock ahead. Jonno didn't have to look around to know Dodger would be plastered to the deck, dead flat, silent and part of the landscape Not a military weapon?

Too light.

A .22 rifle?

They waited!

Voices.

Two men?

Getting closer and coming straight at them, trampling carelessly over the sparse growth and stones.

Too noisy to be an army patrol? But who knows out here, they're all bloody cowboys!

Closer and closer and straight at them.

Shit, shit, shit, they're going to go right over us, he thought.

Jonno rolled to his right and knew that Dodger was rolling the other way, widening the gap. They were so close now that he could see the forms of two adults and a kid, with one of them holding a rifle of some sort across his chest. The kid was carrying something but he couldn't see properly.

Knife gripped in his right hand and a rock in his left fist he waited. His blood pressure hadn't altered and was steady and low. No sweat here, just a job; everything in his favour.

The kid passed within five yards of his position but fortunately was not looking his way, as he was trying to keep up with the adults and puffing heavily.

Jonno could see what he now recognised as a small desert sand cat in the kid's hand, with half its head missing. *Shit, these bastards will eat anything,* he thought, realising that it was nothing more than a family hunting party, out to get their dinner.

Lying perfectly still he watched the group saunter passed him completely unaware of him or Dodger, fortunately for them, otherwise the family's fate may've been similar to the poor bloody sand cat.

As the sounds moved away and soon disappeared he lifted himself into a crouch and moved left, seeing Dodger's shape appearing in the half-dark.

They squatted and listened to ensure the group were gone and once satisfied Dodger said, "Another day at the office, Sarge! What did you make of them? I could see one had a small rifle, probably a .22, but what did the kid have?"

"A mangy little sand cat. It looked like it weighed no more than a couple of pounds or so. Not much of a meal for a family!"

"Yemeni version of takeaway food, eh?"

"Ok, let's concentrate. That would have been a bit too close if it'd been a patrol. We don't need to be eliminating a patrol and causing a diplomatic incident—again!"

They laughed nervously, thinking of a recent rescue assignment in Iran and knew they didn't need any more of that sort of grief.

They set off again at a steady pace, knowing that barring any difficulties they would be within striking distance of the compound well before midnight. In fact, they didn't want to go in till around 03:00 hours when even the diehards had finished their gambling. Unfortunately, as radical Muslims, it was unlikely they'd be drinking, which was a bummer, as drunks sleep heavily!

By 02:46 hours, they had been observing the northern or rear wall for nearly two hours. The place was as quiet as a graveyard and as dark too. There was no watch tower at the rear but there was a small tower above the front and only gate, but it didn't seem to be manned, although the guard may have been asleep up there. "Take nothing for granted," said Jonno.

The rear mud brick wall rose out of the hillside to a height of 10 feet, so it didn't present a problem, as Jonno could easily give Dodger a spring lift up to grab the top and then haul himself up after.

Time for a final check that nothing on them was loose, or was likely to make any noise.

This entry would be silent, using their knives only if absolutely necessary.

Their exit however could be very different.

Chapter 31

Bob had passed the instruction to the Amman office. He requested that Jordanian authorities despatch a platoon of armed Special Forces troops to speed forthwith to New Giffin-Sen's mine to assist in the arrest of their foreign staff, all of whom had suspected terrorist backgrounds in their home countries. He knew Titus wasn't armed but had confidence in him to manage the situation until reinforcements arrived.

He also knew Slugger's background and how very useful he would be if the situation became dangerous. He had proved himself more than once, both in the Navy and in his current vocation.

The next situation to deal with was far less dangerous but very intricate and needed full government sanction. Well, not exactly the government but the combined intelligence branches acting in their place!

The World Overseas Trust Bank in George Town, Cayman Islands, was actually a direct subsidiary of a major well-known UK national bank, although that was not published publicly. Under terrorism laws, the banking records for all suspected companies and individuals had been accessed and noted by MI6, with a staggering £9.2 million located in various nominated relevant bank accounts, although not all from Twal's business.

The next delicate phase was two-pronged, involving infinitely tracing the accounts and tracking the locations where any monies were being transferred, followed by freezing and seizing all the assets in the Cayman accounts.

It was far too delicate to involve the government itself because it was known that a number of British MPs and trade unionists had salted away their ill-begotten gains in this very same bank and so they would not be likely to sanction any raids, for fear of their own records being checked.

Truscott-Browne had despatched two of his men together with an MI6 agent and between them, they had degrees in law (specialising in the international area), accounting, international banking, forensic accounting and criminology, plus they were all big scary characters!

What a team to frighten the crap out of anyone, let alone a colourless bank Johnny, he thought.

These men were all professionals and would be arriving in George Town within the hour, via Miami, as direct flights from London were booked out and even he couldn't swing three direct flights.

On arrival, they were picked up by the police commissioner's driver in a Rover 2000 which fortunately was fitted with air-conditioning because it was putridly humid and hot at this time of the year. They only carried an overnight bag each as they did not expect to be there more than 24 hours: they were not there for a holiday!

The bags were duly tossed into the Rover's boot for the short journey to the island's intelligence headquarters for any updates and further orders that may be available to them from London.

The journey was short with the three gazing at palm trees, lush gardens and sandy beaches and thinking what a great posting this would be.

The office itself was housed in a bungalow on a small estate, with only overhead fans for cooling, although the expats in question looked very much at ease in their shorts, short sleeve shirts and sandals, considerably more comfortable than the visitors' suits.

In fact, there were no further orders or fresh intelligence for them and since their local contact had booked an appointment for 10:00 hours at the bank, for the manager to see a new corporate customer they set off in a taxi to arrive anonymously, rather than arriving in a government plated car.

They arrived five minutes early but obviously, their visit was anticipated and the staff members were all on stand-by, as they didn't often actually see their clients, for most business was conducted by letter or through professional intermediaries.

A well-presented young lady greeted them, enquiring, "Mr Samuels?" and on his nodding, they were immediately ushered up a carpeted staircase and into the manager's office on the mezzanine floor.

To say that it was plush would be one of the world's biggest understatements! It was magnificently opulent and completely over the top.

So this is where the crooked money ends up? Samuels thought, the leader of the team and the legal expert, as his eyes took in the 24' × 20' office, complete with a full wet bar, lounge area and washroom. This, he noted, was properly air-conditioned and very comfortable cool at about 71° F, compared to the main banking chamber downstairs with only overhead fans.

"Welcome to the World Overseas Trust Bank, George Town. My name is Mr Albert Thompkins and I am the general manager, at your service, gentleman," he said with a flourish, obviously pretty happy with himself and his position.

My God, that smugness is about to change very dramatically and very soon! thought Smithers, the accountant and banking expert; and one who detested anyone introducing themselves as 'Mr'. How bloody insecure and pompous!

Deere, the largest of the three men, had his eyes firmly on the GM, who without a word being said, sensed something was terribly wrong.

In a not-so-confident tone, he enquired whether his guests required refreshments and in receipt of a negative reply said, "Gentlemen, how can I assist you today and into the future?"

Samuels had his tactics planned and launched immediately saying, "Do you know Sir George Rolfe, as I have a personal letter from him to deliver to you."

Thompkins looked bewildered stuttering, "Yes, of course, he is the chairman of the board of my parent company, in London."

"Correct, read this carefully and understand fully the instruction you are under!"

Thompkins read the letter which was short and succinct and in part was as follows.

Consider your position at The World Overseas Trust Bank in considerable jeopardy, as may be your very freedom.

It has come to our notice that money laundering from fraudulent activities and theft has been passing through the bank and forwarded on to terrorist organisations.

The people who hand you this letter have the authority of not only this Banking Group but also of the British Government's Intelligence Agencies.

You will extend every possible assistance to them including allowing full reviews of all the accounts and particularly the names listed at the foot of this letter.

Furthermore, the entire amount of £9.2 million is to be withdrawn and paid into the British Treasury Account, also listed at the foot of this letter…

"This is highly irregular. I will have to verify this, before taking any action."

"Your orders are clear and before any of the money disappears from the accounts, you will embargo the funds immediately," said Deere, towering over Thompkins' desk.

"These are the account numbers, as listed by your chairman, so stand back and allow me access to your computer, right now."

"I must check with my head office," said Thompkins in a frightened voice.

"You can check using that phone but in the meantime, I need to use your computer now."

With that statement, Deere crossed behind the desk and signalled Thompkins to move away, to the phone on the far corner of the desk.

"I can't allow you to do that without first checking with Sir George."

"You make your call as it is 16:00 hours in London and you may just catch Sir George but in the meantime, stand back from that computer, now!"

"I don't need your assistance, as Sir George has supplied me with the necessary passcodes and procedures to operate this banking system and if you attempt to foil us any further, you will be placed under arrest as a terrorist suspect, which you may well be."

Things were going from bad to worse as far as Thompkins was concerned and so he stood back and buzzed through to his assistant, requesting that she place a call to London, to Sir George personally, and immediately.

Deere took Thompkins' position behind the desk and within moments was accessing the list of clients' accounts known to them. His extensive background in forensic accounting and banking, together with full disclosure of passcodes from Sir George allowed him to rapidly restrict all funds in the accounts, none of which had been operated in the last 24 hours, so they were in good time.

The old-fashioned bell rang on Thompkins' phone on his desk and he grabbed it quickly, listened to his assistant, paused and then said, "Good afternoon, Sir George, I have with me three gentlemen who have handed me a letter purportedly sent under your hand."

Sir George was obviously not happy with being doubted and his booming voice could be heard throughout the office, as he berated Thompkins, telling him to follow his instructions exactly and reminding him what a precarious position he had placed the bank in.

The call was short but certainly not sweet, leaving Thompkins pale and shaking.

He felt that he had to sit down because his head was spinning and for the reason being that he had fallen from the lofty heights of being the GM to a terrorist suspect in the space of five minutes.

In his trembling hand, he held the letter, looking at the list of account holders, thinking that he did not know, nor had he ever met any of them, which of course was not unusual. Many of the accounts were opened by local lawyers or accountants, on behalf of overseas clients, so he felt they were entitled to take them at face value. Surely they could not think he was involved in terrorism but he knew the penalties for laundering money and his bowels were starting to feel terribly weak.

Once he sat down, both Samuels and Smithers pulled out a notepad and started to question him in earnest, causing him to rush to his waste paper bin and vomit into it.

"Get a hold of yourself, man, and then call someone to get rid of that," said Samuels, so Thompkins used the intercom system and directed his assistant to take away the fouled bin.

She stepped into the office and looked surprised to see the large man operating Thompkins' computer, whilst he sat in a visitor's chair, looking decidedly ill and pointing at the bin to take it away.

"Thank you, Miss, please see that we are undisturbed for the rest of the day," said one of the men.

She immediately looked to Thompkins who nodded his assent to her, saying, "Everything is quite all right, Sally. These men are here on behalf of our head office in London, investigating possible international banking irregularities, so there is nothing for you to worry about. Please keep this confidential until I say otherwise. Thank you."

She nodded, looked placated and left with the offending bin, showing clearly that it was well beneath her position to act as a domestic servant.

Smithers and Deere then set about interrogating the computer data to see where it led them on the numerous accounts they were interested in. Some two hours passed before they sat back with a look of satisfaction on their faces and pages of notes, printouts and lists of figures in front of them.

In the meantime, Samuels had been grilling Thompkins, satisfying himself that he was nothing but a slack, greedy banking official who was fixated on turnover/profit, leading to his regular bonuses and therefore had not put into place the proper financial risk management procedures. However, he did not enlighten him on that conclusion, leaving him sweating, as he may prove to be useful on a later occasion, perhaps in another case.

"We need to speak confidentially and I need you to step into your washroom whilst we do so," said Samuels, pointing to the manager's en-suite facilities.

Thompkins disappeared quickly closing the door behind him and they heard water running as he attempted to clean himself up.

Nevertheless, they spoke quietly and succinctly.

They agreed that this part of the investigation had been completely successful and now the only item remaining was to transfer all the funds to the British Treasury's account, operated by MI6.

They summoned Thompkins back into the room indicating that, subject to further investigations, they may not be charging him with funding terrorist activities. However, things may well change during the ongoing investigation and they reserved their judgement relating to the money laundering aspect.

"To conclude our involvement here for the moment, we need you to reactivate the accounts and under Mr Deere's strict supervision, you will transfer the collective £9.2 million into the British Treasury Account, which Sir George has listed for you," commanded Samuels.

"Leave only a nominal £10 in each of the accounts, to keep them active."

"But our accounts require a minimum balance of £10,000 at all times. We are not a Savings Society, you know!" submitted Thompkins.

Steely looks from all three men left him in no doubt that £10 would suffice!

Initially, Thompkins hesitated but another look from Deere caused him to take up his seat behind the computer, with Deere hovering over his shoulder, to ensure nothing untoward was about to happen, commenced the transfers.

Once completed, Thompkins was instructed to 'open' the accounts and to insert a warning on them, that any attempt to operate them was to be directed to him only, and furthermore, he was to transmit any attempted transaction immediately back to Samuels, at any time of day and night. The ledger account books were similarly adjusted to the same figures;

The three men left the office quietly after Thompkins had arranged a taxi, leaving him in a state of confusion and fear for his future!

They returned to the bungalow for a final debriefing and then were to go to the airport. Hopefully, a London flight had been sourced, as a direct flight hopefully, rather than via Miami.

"A great day's work, chaps. We don't get to recover £9.2 million and potentially starve a terrorist organisation of funds every day. Well done, everyone," complimented Samuels.

"Time for a G & T, I believe, gentlemen."

Thompkins was left to sit alone in his office, contemplating what appeared to be a rather bleak future. Nothing seemed so grand in here anymore, he thought and rushed to the bathroom, as his bowels gave way.

Sitting like a lost soul on his toilet, he wondered if he would be receiving a call from Sir George, or would they just send in one of their heavy 'arse kickers' from London to remove him.

What about the legalities of the accounts?

What if the account holders called him and demanded their money? After all, they were apparently terrorists and wouldn't take the loss lightly.

What about his bonus?

Would he go to prison?

If he did, he knew his new young trophy wife wouldn't wait! He knew she was there for the lifestyle and money, and she'd be gone before the cell door slammed shut.

Fuck! How did it come to this in less than five hours?

At least, the staff members didn't know.

Or did they?

Shit!

Chapter 32

"I think we may have been a little optimistic in expecting to confine these men without a confrontation of some sort, especially knowing their backgrounds," Titus said to Twal and Coetzee, looking towards the shed and noting that the men were milling around, looking quite unsettled.

They had finished eating their lunch of ara'yes, spiced mincemeat-filled oven-baked flatbread sandwiches and were now becoming restless, perhaps suspicious.

Twal appeared very nervous and a little twitchy but Coetzee was the epitome of calmness standing within inches of Abbas Refai, who like his men was becoming slightly disconcerted and fidgety.

Now that the foreign workers were all in the shed, Titus nodded to Twal indicating with his head that they should move out to make the announcement, which they had previously discussed. Coetzee picked up the signal allowing Twal to lead with Titus and then he followed closely with Refai.

Coetzee's problem was that he did not know whether Refai was armed with either a gun or knife, concealed under his long thawb and that was another reason he detested loose garments as potential security breaches. However, he was under instructions to keep Refai on his side for as long as he could, otherwise, he would have frisked and cuffed him a long time ago. After all, he thought he had always been a man of action and not of diplomacy!

As they advanced across the dusty car park towards the meal shed, the rumbling of voices and shuffling feet on the sand-covered concrete floor was becoming louder and louder. It quite evidently was not going to be an easy task!

Titus could see the Austin Princess parked in the shade, close to the shed, with the engine running and guessed that Slugger was most likely in the driver's seat.

I'm not sure what he has got in mind but as none of this seems new to him, I will leave it to his judgement, thought Titus.

Advancing through the dust was like a scene from the old black-and-white Western film, Gunfight at OK Corral. Nerve-wracking!

As they approached the front of the shed, he and Coetzee in unison ushered them back into it and Coetzee eased Refai in with his workers.

Twal started to speak but his voice was not strong and no one appeared to be interested in listening. It was not going well until Coetzee's voice boomed out like a cannon, shocking then into silence, because it was not the Arab way to raise voices in such a manner.

Twal started speaking again in Arabic, "Some of you men have been here for over six months and I thank you for your service. However, there has been a change of the mine management contractor and the company that you work for is no longer involved. As of 12 noon today, the contract ceased, with the result that you will accompany Mr Refai off these premises in the next 10 minutes. Your wages are due from Mr Refai's company and you can settle with him off-site."

Refai shouted something to his men, which neither Titus nor Coetzee could understand but the intention was clear as the men surged forward, en-masse, shouting and producing Janbiya curved knives from under their thawbs.

Only a short distance of 30 feet separated Twal, Coetzee and Titus from the mob and being unarmed placed them in a very vulnerable position.

Hell! thought Titus looking for a safe option, but seeing nothing.

Coetzee and I against this rabble, with their Janbiyas waving in our faces, it doesn't look good.

However, he had forgotten about Slugger, for at that very moment, the Princess came charging forward with its headlights flashing wildly and the loudest wailing siren he thought that he had ever heard was screaming towards them as the car tore up the dust and gravel.

Hell, even he got a scare!

The Princess skidded to a halt creating a huge cloud of dust which drifted into the shed, enveloping the men completely, choking and temporarily blinding them too. The shouting stopped and when the dust had cleared the men timidly started to move forward again but were met with the view of a formidable half-naked figure of a giant standing on top of the Princess. Slugger was holding an intimidatingly long-barrelled, fully automatic Remington shot gun pointed in their direction.

Before they had time to gather their thoughts or become brave, he fired two shots in quick succession at the ground only 10 feet in front of them, so they were assaulted by not only the blasts of hot grit but also kicked up sand peppering them. The effect was immediate with the men rushing to the back of the shed and their Janbiyas were suddenly out of sight.

Not at all fierce now!

By this time, the three of them were beside the Princess and Slugger indicated, "On the seat, you'll find two Heckler & Koch VP 70 semi-auto pistols; grab them quickly and cover the left front area before they get heroic again."

As they were grabbing the weapons, he shouted down, "Don't worry about them being so light, they're polymer-framed, but they have an 18-round magazine of 9mm slugs, loaded with my special 'extra kick'. They'll stop a horse! Only use them on a single shot as the weapon goes wild on automatic!"

"As soon as the authorities arrive, slide them out of sight into your pocket, because they are pretty touchy about handguns in Jordan. I'll be ok, as I train their Special Operation Forces (SOF) guys and they sort of tolerate my use on the appropriate occasions."

The Princess was angled at the shed from the right side with Slugger maintaining his impressive position, with the sun behind him.

Titus suggested that Twal stay behind the car so he and Coetzee could move to the left covering the entire frontage effectively. They took up position, with pistols at the ready but the figure of Slugger standing tall and bare-chested, on the car was so dominant that he didn't think anyone even noticed them!

The stand-off was now calm and under control and so Titus called to Twal, "Abi, could you please go back to your office and call the authorities to see how far away they are? The number is 'Amman 444', thanks."

The day was starting to really warm up but all three of them were hardened to hot weather and stood their ground stoically, surprising the workers who always thought that all British were soft and would collapse in the sun.

No one moved and there was very little dissent by voice. All the fight disappeared with Slugger's dramatic entrance. Talk about a sound and light display!

Slugger looked like a bizarre bronzed shirtless statue on a plinth, glistening with sweat but unmoving.

The shotgun, with its 30-inch, long barrel, beautifully Parkerised in a non-reflective black finish, looked particularly sinister and experience from earlier told the workers that it would be very dangerous to think it wouldn't be used against them. Some were still nursing stinging hands, plus burning eyes and faces to prove it.

Half an hour had passed and still silence reigned, although a low rumble of discontent was just starting to surface.

Titus was beginning to work on a backup plan of how and where they could lock up the workers and how to feed them, if it continued much longer when there was the roar of vehicles approaching. They were travelling fast and although they hesitated as they entered the main area, looking for the trouble spot, it was clear they identified Slugger quickly and skidded to a stop beside him.

Titus and Coetzee slid in alongside the Princess, having slipped the H & K's into their pockets leaving Slugger appearing as the only armed person.

"Hi, boys, I couldn't wait for you, as it got a bit hairy," said Slugger with a grin, "we've bagged the foreign terrorists, who seem to be frightened of 'Betsy' here," patting the shotgun.

"They're all yours now, but watch them as most of them have a Janbiya concealed in their thawbs."

The SOF showed their stuff, surrounding the open-fronted shed, weapons at the ready and shouting orders in Levantine Arabic, Jordan's national spoken language, but probably not the chosen tongue spoken by these foreigners. Nevertheless, they understood the intention of the orders barked at them and resistance was nil.

Slugger jumped down off the bonnet and ushered them to the rear of the car where he opened a sliding panel and secreted the two H & Ks, but not before wiping them down carefully. *Well-oiled and no fingerprints; he is a true professional*, thought Titus.

The SOF boys knew their stuff and went to work immediately.

One by one the workers were called out, ordered to throw down any knives and then place their hands behind their heads. This was followed by a thorough pat-down search, by one of the expert troops, who, once satisfied, used plastic handcuffs to fasten their wrists tightly behind their back following which they dropped a white cloth bag over their head. Then they were forced to their knees, in lines, to wait whilst the remainder were processed.

The commander of the unit was a Captain, well known to Slugger, who said to him with a smile, "You didn't really need us! You had it all under control."

Slugger replied, "Yes, but I want to be home for dinner tonight and besides I know the SOF always arrive late and then take all the glory!"

"You are a funny man, Chief Petty Officer Slugger, but I thank you, as I'll probably get a medal for this," laughing quietly.

"Nevertheless, I commend your bravery for taking on and capturing 18 terrorists alone and unarmed! So I suggest the shotgun disappear fast before I notice it."

Slugger grinned at the captain whilst standing at the car boot, which was already open and gave him a Navy salute. He then expertly stripped the Remington down to its basic parts and had it cleaned and oiled in seconds whilst conversing with Captain Haddad, who was gript at the man's efficiency at all things military.

The SOF unit had arrived in three Ford M-151 jeep-type vehicles and two Saracen 6×6 armoured personnel carriers, leaving no spare capacity for the prisoners' removal.

Captain Haddad was already busy on the radio, apparently reporting in on 'his' success and now checking on prisoner transport, which he was assured was very close.

Processing was almost complete and as Titus watched, he noted that Refai had been separated from the main group. He was shackled hands and feet to the anti-grenade cage affixed to the nearside of the Saracen, out of voice range of his men. He was subdued and hooded, like the rest of his now dishevelled crew and slumped down, giving every appearance of being beaten.

Titus moved away from Slugger, watching the proceedings and remembering assisting with the processing of Pakistani POWs in India some 10 years before. A lifetime ago but brought back in a flash and this time he was not really feeling too uncomfortable about it. *His demons were almost gone*, he thought.

At that moment, the second last of the yet-to-be-processed foreign workers had sidled quietly unnoticed behind an inattentive SOF soldier. He quickly shoved a handful of sand in his face before grabbing him from behind and attempting to wrestle away his USA-made M16 rifle, complete with its full 30-round magazine. He was trying to swing the weapon around, whilst still attempting to subdue the temporarily blinded soldier with his other arm. The carbine was clearly swinging towards Haddad and his men, who were dealing with the bulk of the captives, unaware of this action taking place.

Shit, they don't stand a chance, here I go again, thought Titus.

He was off to the right side of the terrorist by some three or so paces and launched himself like an enraged rugby player straight into him, hopefully before the man could work out how to control and fire the captured SOF weapon. He hit him so hard that he felt as though he'd broken every bone in his own upper body and as the three of them crashed into the dirt, a two-shot burst discharged across the yard. He hoped they were wild shots, discharging harmlessly into the air.

Titus was winded but had to carry on, as the heavily built Syrian was a younger man than him and still had his knife on him, as he hadn't been processed yet.

Titus was partially deafened by the two shots, blasting so close to the side of his head and he could still feel the heat on his temple. He was badly winded but realised it wasn't over yet. He was still in the middle of a very dangerous situation and could feel the pistol grip of the weapon digging deeply into his left side and rib cage, accentuated by a body's weight on top of him. He could hardly breathe.

In the tangle of arms and legs in the sand, he soon sorted out his foe from the young SOF soldier and concentrated on immobilising him. He placed his left hand over the trigger guard to prevent any more rounds from being discharged and smashed away the man's hand with a vicious blow.

He was then able to grab the back of the terrorist's neck with his other hand, slowly forcing his face downwards but the man was kicking wildly trying to escape. The three men were still entangled but he knew which one he was attempting to subdue. They rolled over and the pistol grip jabbed into his ribs again causing further excruciating pains in his chest. He somehow managed to continue the effort and forced his face deep into the sandy surface under them. He struggled to maintain a steady pressure as his own breathing was becoming even more laboured and he felt himself weakening from his shallow breathing.

He pressed down as hard as his painful ribs and shoulder would allow but the prisoner was still resisting, with a somewhat weaker effort, trying to squirm his way out. Not knowing if he was feigning, which he recalled was a pretty standard trick, he made a final effort to re-apply the pressure, again forcing the head down into the sand, despite potentially suffocating him.

Pain everywhere; but he didn't dare release the pressure on the captive, who by that time had ceased to move altogether.

Was he dead?

He didn't care! Titus had his own problems just breathing.

How quickly his training and instincts had come back!

Too easily perhaps?

Time stood still for Titus. "Where the fuck is everybody?"

He looked up and saw that he was finally surrounded by troops, he rolled away, pulling the M-16 carbine with him, just in case, but there was still no movement under him, except for the young SOF soldier scrambling to his feet rather sheepishly.

He pulled himself up to his knees and handed the weapon back to the soldier, after first removing the round in the breech and applying the safety catch.

Old habits die hard!

Always make the weapon safe!

The Syrian didn't move but he could see that the man had actually got his hand on to his Janbiya and so he was certainly justified in not releasing the pressure on him.

He could see a soldier bent over his adversary, checking his neck pulse and then shaking his head, looking up at the rest of his squad.

Titus felt no regret, it was him or me, he recognised.

He remained crouched over, on one knee and when he looked up he saw Slugger approaching on the double, like an angry bull.

"Shit, I'm sore! I'm getting too old for this rough stuff," Titus gasped, as Slugger rocketed up to him, looking like a half-naked man, possessed by the devil.

He dropped to one knee to support Titus saying, "That was a stupid fucking thing to do, but it probably saved a dozen lives; me included because I could see him eyeing me off and the captain too. Thanks, shipmate."

Titus was still bent over double, trying to catch his breath and ease the pain in his upper chest, caused by the impact of the tackle, plus by the two men landing on him and then the rifle's pistol grip smashing into his rib cage. He gingerly felt his left collar bone and unfortunately could detect the deformation of a fracture, added to which he couldn't effectively raise his left arm, without excruciating pain.

"It's busted," he concluded glumly, followed by a not-quite-silent expletive or two.

Slugger helped him to straighten up slowly and ran an expert hand over the clavicle, with him agreeing that he indeed had a nasty fracture. "We'd better get a sling on that until we can get you proper medical treatment, and your shoulder is bleeding too from where you hit the deck! Come across to the Princess to my first aid kit," helping him to walk, semi-upright.

Looking back, he could see that the last man had now been processed and they were removing the corpse and placing it into the shade of one of the Saracens.

Whilst Slugger was organising a sling from the Princess's medical kit, the captain had restored order and came across to Titus with his hand out, "You must be Warrant Officer Lovell. I've heard about you, TG, and it appears the legend continues! Thank you! One lax moment by a young commando and we could have had a disaster here. I can't thank you and CPO Jones enough on behalf of King Hussein and my country for ridding us of this nest of vipers."

"Now we have to keep these extremists under close restraint until transport arrives shortly, so please excuse me."

Obviously, another RMA Sandhurst graduate, thought Titus, judging by his language and bearing.

Slugger reappeared from the cavernous boot in moments with his medical kit and like so many ex-military men he was an outstanding medic. After expertly cleaning the shoulder area with medical alcohol, which stung like hell, he applied gentian violet and several sterilised pads to the deep abrasions. He then fitted and adjusted an arm sling and Titus felt much more comfortable, with the weight of his left arm supported to relieve pressure from the fractured left clavicle. The pain subsided to an almost bearable level and after satisfying him that it was fitted in its optimum position, he nodded his thanks to Slugger, who winked back at him and gave him the thumbs-up sign.

"Here, swallow these heavy-duty painkillers," but Titus declined, waving them away, as he felt that he wanted to maintain a clear head.

"Don't be an arse, man, take them and you'll feel better much more swiftly," and as he was not prepared to argue with an unyielding Slugger, who was towering over him, he swallowed them with a swig of the water which was offered with the tablets.

"Everything appears well under control here and so I intend to go back to see Twal to collect documents for my investigation," and walked off towards the admin block.

Each step jarred his shoulder causing shooting pains in his shoulder area and so he used his right hand to hold the slung left arm tightly against his chest, finding that as it prevented bouncing it was much less painful that way.

Coetzee had partly seen what had occurred and Twal had just stepped out of the main door of the admin block when the shots rent through the recently established peace in the mine yard. They both turned in the direction of the shots to see three men lying still on the ground but Titus was not in sight.

They watched the wrestling unfold in slow motion and eventually saw what appeared to be a wounded Titus rose to his knees very slowly and Slugger went to his aid.

Coetzee held Twal back, saying it still may not be safe yet and that they should stay well way from the clash.

Time seemed to be passing so slowly as they observed Slugger giving Titus medical treatment but at least he was now standing upright, unaided.

When he turned and commenced walking slowly towards them, they could see that he was trussed up like a turkey and walking very gingerly. His suit was filthy, blood-stained and torn, with the left sleeve almost ripped off.

They were both very anxious about his condition and due to the sling, they assumed that he must have been shot by the foreigner in the tussle.

Titus made his way to them, slowly but steadily and was greeted by the question from Coetzee, "Have you been shot, man?"

However, he replied, "No, no, the rifle discharged harmlessly, I think. I'm sure it is only a fractured collar bone and yes, I'm fine to carry on."

Twal was visibly shocked but Coetzee stepped forward to shake his hand, and on observing that he was rather pale, insisted he come into the cool and rest.

"Gentleman, the reason I'm here is to assist overcome the problems with this fraud, perpetrated on New Giffin-Sen, illegally in Ecothan's name, and so we need to continue to gather documents to prove what has happened. It is my duty."

"My friend, you have done enough. You have endangered your life to save others and now you are injured and I am responsible."

"Please leave it to Mr Coetzee and me to work on this together and see what that rogue Khoury has done to me. We will prepare a joint report, with nothing hidden and hand it to you as soon as it has been completed, which I think will not be far away. Now you go with Mr Slugger for medical treatment. I feel quite safe here and will stay overnight at least until all my original staff members are safe and this investigation has been completed."

Titus heard the sound of traffic and gauged that a heavy vehicle was approaching, and as he turned he identified it as an old Diamond-T truck converted into a prison cage/bus, surrounded by a motor cycle escort consisting of ten MPs.

He also saw Slugger pulling up right outside the office, in the Princess, again leaving it facing outward, and walking the few steps to the admin block. Having put his shirt back on he was now looking far less formidable than when he had been standing on the car bonnet with that huge shotgun.

"Excuse me, gentlemen. TG, it's off to our Honorary Medical Officer for you, under strict orders from above," said Slugger, with a 'take no prisoners' look and again appearing quite inflexible.

"Say your farewells, because we're off to the MO in Amman right now, before he knocks off for the day and gets stuck into the Gin & Tonic!"

"Did you tell Captain Haddad about our road incident earlier today and the red-capped truck driver?" Titus asked.

"Too slow, fella. He was arrested over two hours ago as he tried to enter the port of Aqaba's security road block, together with three other foreign drivers a little later in the day. So that's the lot of them locked up. A good day's work, I'd say."

That gizmo on the Princess's dash had done wonderful work, thought Titus.

"Mr Slugger, I must thank you for helping to save not only my business but also my life today I now feel in control of my future for the first time in over 12 months. I feel blessed. *Shukran, Shukran*, thank you, thank you."

"Please take Mr Lovell to safety and proper medical attention in Amman, as you suggested and drive carefully."

Without further ado, Slugger assisted TG into the rear of the Princess, ensured he was as comfortable as his injuries allowed and drove back to Captain Haddad to advise that he was evacuating TG to Amman to the MO.

Haddad stuck his head into the back of the car, asked after TG's well-being and wished him well, allowing Slugger to set off for the capital.

Chapter 33

Bob's team, under the direction of and with the help of several security agencies, was coordinating activities on several fronts.

One task to organise concerned Nicholson in Spain. He was aware there was no extradition treaty with Spain and even if some of the 'heavy' boys extracted him, he could not be tried in the UK, if he had been extradited illegally.

His initial plan was to fly Titus directly to Spain to see if he could talk him into returning, providing that he was willing to cough up to the whole fraud and all the finer details of financial arrangements.

Names, addresses, dates, accounts, the lot; that's what they needed to tidy up.

However, when he heard of Titus' injury and that he was receiving medical treatment in Amman, for several bone fractures, he had to resort to an alternate plan.

His team, which had been so successful in the Cayman Islands, was back in London already and he decided that their leader Samuels would fit the bill very nicely for what he had in mind.

So a phone call was made.

"Mr Samuels, I have another job for you and Mr Deere to tackle and it will involve a nice trip to sunny Spain but is connected with your last assignment. We need to confer this afternoon so if we all meet in four hours' time at my premises, I will have your orders and full travel documentation for you. Be ready for a short trip!"

Working in Spain would be somewhat different to Jordan where they had tacit government permission and similarly in the British Cayman Islands where they had full British jurisdiction.

Spain was a sovereign country, with no extradition treaty and the Spaniards rather enjoyed having retired British ex-cons living there with their stolen millions, as it was actually very beneficial for their economy.

Later that day, Samuels and Deere were given their brief and travel documents, which took them from Gatwick Airport to Malaga International Airport in under three hours flight time. They cleared customs and immigration effortlessly, with papers as salesmen on an exploratory trip to establish a market for British pleasure craft.

They found the car rental booth where a car had been organised and paid for, so collection time was swift.

He and the Deere again travelled lightly, with a small overnight bag each and without any weapons, as their instructions were to resolve the issue with diplomacy (helped along with some pretty unsubtle threats, if necessary, but no violence!)

They were supposed to collect a mid-sized car but were given a piddly, half-arsed-sized Spanish-built SEAT, being some sort of undersized Fiat look alike. They didn't care what it was, but they could barely fit into it, even with the front bucket seats sliding back to the extreme. Deere was designated to drive but his knees kept hitting the steering wheel, to the extent he couldn't steer it effectively and so Samuels who was only slightly smaller took over the driving duties.

They made their way east along the main coast road and following maps that they had memorised, they had no difficulty in finding the hillside village where Nicholson was no doubt feeling very safe and smug.

Frigiliana was indeed perched high on a hillside, as described, typical of many Spanish, Greek and Italian villages built over the centuries. All the houses were whitewashed and clean, with the red terracotta roofing and bright window sill tiles shining under the harsh sun, in contrast to the white walls.

Everywhere was as dry as a bone and the only living plant life Samuels could see was bright red geraniums in whitewashed terracotta pots on almost every dwelling. They seemed to thrive in the dry hot atmosphere of the Mediterranean climate where nothing else did, whereas they were hard to keep alive all year round in most of England.

The sparse hillside grasses were burnt yellowy-brown by the Mediterranean sun, which seemed able to tear the life from everything it touched.

A few scrawny dogs could be seen, sleeping in the shade, or plodding listlessly, but nothing else moved as it was afternoon siesta time.

"A bit like a scene from a crumby Western movie; dry lifeless and soulless," said Samuels grimly.

No one was out to see them enter the main street so they were able to drive slowly through the village, remembering given landmarks and following their instructions, all without unnecessarily drawing attention to themselves.

The plans were accurate and so quite clearly someone had scouted for them and sussed it all out. Probably a local 'agent' had made a discrete recce for them.

They followed the exquisitely detailed instructions which led them to the eastern edge of the village, to the very last house, positioned on the high side of the road, with a sign '*el sueno*' on the low gate.

"Nothing spectacular that I can see, his '*sueno*' (dream) is about to end," said Samuels, nodding to Deere indicating that this was clearly Nicholson's hideout. They could see that behind and to the right of the house was a very steep drop away towards the coast and so they had no immediate fear of Nicholson making a run for it. "Besides, he isn't the type," surmised Deere.

"Thump loudly on the door and frighten the shit out of him," instructed Samuels, "let's rattle him and keep him that way; he's no pro, but just a grubby little cheat."

Deere's huge paw pounded fiercely on the door causing it to rattle on its hinges and probably the sound clattered right around the village, in the dead silence of the siesta, but no one bothered to investigate. A dog gave a half-hearted bark somewhere in the distance and then gave up.

After a few short seconds, Deere repeated the exercise, knowing that he had not given Nicholson nearly enough time to respond.

All part of the unnerving treatment, he thought.

They could hear the scramble of feet on the tiled floor as Nicholson came running to the door, pushing it outwards to open and see who could possibly be there. The sight of two very large men, dressed in charcoal-coloured, pin striped and very English suits, made his blood run cold, for they looked like English officialdom of the very worst kind.

He opened his mouth to speak but nothing came out and fear exuded from his every pore and hung over him like a bad aura. He tried to speak again but nothing happened and shock was added to dismay when one of them said, "Mr Nicholson, we need to have a serious talk!"

He had never seen either of them before and yet they knew his name and where he lived. *Oh god, already,* he thought.

He was about to tell them his name was Bond but suddenly it sounded very foolish and he didn't feel at all like Mr Bond at the moment!

One of the men pushed straight past him into the house and the other followed behind him escorting him back into his own home. He had to follow them as they pushed deeper into the building.

Clearly, Nicholson liked his comforts, for the house was stylishly furnished but in particular a large air conditioner was blasting cool air throughout the house bringing it to a beautifully comfortable level.

Outside were a magnificent covered patio/BBQ and entertaining area, adjoining an in-ground blue-tiled swimming pool of huge dimensions. The water was crystal blue and sparkled under the hot sun as a large fountain spilt over into a waterfall at the far end of it and splashed continuously into the main pool.

"What a place," spat Deere, "you crooked little bastard!"

Part of the effect was them arriving in dark suits, in the middle of the hot Spanish summer, when everyone else was in shorts and tee-shirts, and it had certainly worked, as Nicholson was trembling with fear so badly that they made him sit down on a kitchen chair.

So far so good, they both thought and without giving him time to settle, they commenced to work on him.

"Mr Nicholson, we represent certain authorities and point out that we have no legal standing in Spain. The affairs that you are involved in interest Her Majesty's Government, who take terrorism, fraud and murder very seriously."

Nicholson's face blanched even further as he spluttered "Terrorism and murder?" and slumped further into his chair.

His eyes rolled in fear at the two men, seeming to plead, but they were not swayed even slightly, repeating, "Yes, terrorism, fraud, money laundering and multiple murders to be precise."

"You can't touch me in Spain and I will not return to England," showing a streak of forced bravado.

"Your partner, Efraim Khoury, the terrorist, already thinks that you are the weak link in the chain. If we were to let it slip that you put us on to him but are hiding safely from justice, in Spain, I'm sure he'd organise one of his little Yemeni friends to be here in a flash and slit your throat, just like he did to Mr Kingwell. Remember?"

"No, you can't do that!" shouted Nicholson having at last found his voice.

"Oh yes, we can, as we are simply here on holiday and bumped into you. I'm sure he'd be more than interested in organising a surprise for you. Nothing official, you understand."

"The British Authorities don't work like that," pleaded Nicholson, looking decidedly ill.

Sitting in dead silence, they let him sweat.

"Is there no way you can help me?"

More silence.

They've made no attempt to grab me, thought Nicholson, "so maybe it's all just a bluff?" Then he looked at their faces and decided it was no bluff!

These two men frightened him with their intensity, but on the other hand, Khoury absolutely terrified him and the thought of a visit from one of his henchmen chilled him to the bone. In fact, he now found himself shivering uncontrollably at the thought.

Samuels' booming voice broke the silence with, "The choice is yours, Nicholson; with your voluntary return to England, full cooperation, disclosure of documents etc., plus the return of all funds and properties, we may be able to persuade the prosecutors to reduce the charges to fraud alone, rather than include money laundering, funding terrorism, terrorism and several murders."

"But we were only taking money from a filthy rich Arab in Jordan. Who cares in Britain?"

"Think what you like, it won't change the facts. You got into bed with Khoury and his cronies and facilitated funds being siphoned directly to a terrorist training camp in North Yemen and those people have already committed atrocities in many countries. Who do you think chopped Kingwell to pieces and slit his throat? It was all a direct result of your actions, without any doubt!"

More stunned silence.

Samuels continued, "When you're convicted of funding terrorism and accessory to murder, as you most definitely will be, you will be placed in the same gaol as Khoury, possibly even the same cell! However, with a fraud-only conviction, full cooperation and a good word from us, you'll go to a remotely located low security prison farm for a shorter stay, held under a pseudonym and somewhere they will not find you."

"I don't have to go back with you, I know my rights," erroneously sensing the men were negotiating with him.

Both Samuels and Deere stood up. "That's it then, we're back to the UK to complete the charges against Khoury; you've had your chance. Good luck, but we don't like your risk profile!"

"Wait!" shouted Nicholson in panic, "You won't tell Khoury, will you?"

"No, much as we'd like to, we won't, but I suggest that when his barrister requests a copy of the prosecution's papers, it will be clear where you spent your money and your 'hideout' will be blown. What a pity!"

It was obvious to Nicholson that they were on their way now and he was doomed.

"Let me think about it for a few days!"

"There is nothing to think about. You know the facts. Come with us now voluntarily and do a deal, or stay here and end up painfully bleeding to death at the bottom of that crystal clear pool, when they find you!" he said pointing to the pool.

No more persuasion was required! His bladder felt as though it were about to give way to him as he nodded in concurrence.

'Mr Bond' returned with them that night, on his stolen passport, but with a ticket arranged and paid for by HM's Government.

It was an uncomfortable trip sandwiched between these two 'giants' in small airline economy class seats. He was permitted to eat, but not drink as they warned him he would not be allowed to visit the toilets. Still, even his bowels threatened to let go.

He was held overnight in a special security cell at Gatwick Airport, under what he felt were terrifying armed security conditions. The lights were left on all night and he was placed in a cage-fronted cell, in full view of two hulking monster guards. He had a blanket and a wooden bench for a bed, but he did not feel like sleeping!

What could he possibly have done to deserve this harsh, even inhumane treatment? He thought.

He actually pissed himself at one stage under their cold savage stares, despite there being a bucket in the cage, as he couldn't bring himself to urinate in front of them.

He was frogmarched out of his cell whilst it was still dark and transferred very early the following morning, in a prison van, under a heavy armed guard, all of which caused him no end of terror. There were no windows and he bounced around in the back of the van like a puppet, with each movement causing the handcuffs to bite a little deeper. His wrists were beyond chafed and when the van finally stopped, he could feel warm blood trickling down his wrists onto his hands, but he couldn't see this due to the hood over his head.

He was soft! He had never experienced pain before and almost literally shit himself. Oh god.

He was in pain, stinking of piss, mortified and feeling utterly terrified and degraded.

How could matters become any worse? But they were about to go off the scale.

Much to his ongoing and increasing distress, he was under intensive interrogation very soon that morning by counter-espionage/terrorism experts, in a secluded farmhouse, obviously having no idea that Khoury was in the same building. Hour after hour, two men teams alternated and subjected him to a constant barrage of questions, crushing the last drop of information from him, ringing him dry emotionally and leaving him empty.

By then, most of the heinous story was already known, but a thorough interrogation of Nicholson revealed a more complete and provable picture for the prosecutors to prepare their briefs. Plus, revealing valuable modus operandi data as to how these groups set themselves up financially for operations.

Chapter 34

The same day that they grabbed Nicholson, Shada Al Shammari and Efraim Khoury had arisen as usual, with her making him breakfast of lentil soup, falafel and pitta bread, plus sugary sweet coffee. She was more like a slave to him, but she knew that was the way life was meant to be for her type.

It was just after 8.10 am when they were preparing to leave for their office, not far away at Richmond. The woman carried his heavy briefcase and a bag of food that she had prepared for their lunch, whilst he stepped out and turned to lock the magnificently stained oak front door.

He had just closed the heavy door and was turning to face outwards when he heard the woman gasp. He looked towards his luxurious Jaguar V8 saloon parked on the neat gravel driveway but was confronted by a group of six men, forming a semi-circle around the two of them.

They must have been waiting for them to exit the house and he hadn't even checked. It was then he realised that he was becoming as slack and lazy as these infidels. Too late!

"Naghil," he called out—"Bastards."

They were all wearing black Special Ops gear, with balaclava-type ski masks and were heavily armed with what he knew to be silenced Heckler & Koch MP5A3 slimline style submachine guns, with 'waffle' 30-round magazines and were looking like they meant business. They all looked young and confident, poised on the balls of their feet, like panthers. Unmistakably, they were the cream of the security forces, exceptionally well trained and so no chance of even considering making a dash for it; not with this array of weaponry! Anyway, he wasn't a fighter; he had others to do that for him and a plan was already forming in his scheming brain.

From behind them appeared a slightly older man, the only one in a business suit and showing his face. He introduced himself as Chief Superintendent Scott of Special Branch, flashing his warrant card and after formally addressing them each by name, he arrested them and stipulated that they must accompany his group immediately for questioning; not that they had any choice.

Before either had time to react or comment, they were searched, hooded, cuffed and hustled into different vehicles, both being green Range Rovers fitted with blacked-out windows, then driven away from Khoury's home, with a minimum of fuss.

The neighbours probably hadn't even noticed.

Despite Khoury's protests and demands for information, the officers gave him no satisfaction and soon they were travelling in complete silence. As an extra precaution, one of the officers had applied a set of ankle manacles to Khoury, before they climbed in each side of him, settling down with the muzzle of their weapons poking painfully into his ribs on either side.

It was similarly silent in Al Shammari's vehicle with her apparently being too stunned to even open her mouth but she was aware of a massive guard on either side of her, pressing into her side and the smell of gun-oil very close to her. She was not comfortable with being so close to men who were not related to her but they were only '*babi*', filthy pigs; they did not understand.

Khoury tried to work out where they were going from ambient noise and road turns but soon all traffic sounds were gone and still they drove on. Into the country somewhere?

The two cars did not travel together for security reasons, allowing Khoury to arrive alone, or so he thought, for he could not hear a second vehicle or any other movement.

Where had they taken Shada?

Could she be trusted under pressure? He hoped so as she was cognisant of all their business dealings and almost their entire illicit network.

Would she be seduced by a deal? If she did, she'd die; cousin or not.

Although he didn't know his whereabouts he was manhandled from the car and felt gravel under his feet and he noted a fresh smell in the air; a farm?

With his legs shackled, he could only manage mini steps but nevertheless, he counted 43 before he was heaved up two steps, or was it three steps and then set back on his feet, this time onto something shiny. Concrete or tiles? He wondered.

Then he knew he was no longer in fresh air; so he was inside. Where?

A timber floor underfoot and then the smell of infidels' unclean food assaulted his nose.

As he was guided through a door way, he suddenly felt brave and shouted, "Allah yin3al abuuk. May god curse your father!"

What he didn't know was that he was being delivered to a soundproof room in a semirural property, somewhere in Surrey, south-west of the Thames, into what appeared, to all outward observation, a simple smallholding's farmhouse; but it was anything but that.

Al Shammari arrived not long after, once Khoury was safely out of earshot and she was placed into the custody of a very stern looking, lightly built, policewoman. She stood with her back to the locked door; arms folded across her chest and never moved her unblinking eyes off her, not for even a moment; despite the prisoner being cuffed to a table, although her hood had been removed once in the room.

"Where is my cousin?" She demanded, but received no reply, as her initial treatment was to be unnerving silence.

Khoury was in for sterner stuff from the beginning, being handcuffed to an upright steel chair, which in turn was securely bolted to the floor. They had both his wrists and ankles secured, whilst his head had been left fully hooded.

He couldn't hear anything and thought that he had been left alone, all trussed up to the chair, with them knowing he could not move at all.

The rooms were kept cold. Very cold!—Deliberately.

Khoury could detect a strange sweet odour, getting stronger and stronger. Were they trying some new gas product to drug him to make him talk, or was it their filthy unclean food?

Both were allowed to stew for hours in dead silence before any form of interrogation was even considered; time was a very useful tool in such investigations and they were lucky to have plenty of time in this case.

The interrogators were preparing by reviewing the evidence before them currently, but until the SAS patrol had returned, hopefully with documentation about Zamir Mines Coy and Ahmadi, they decided to let these two agonise even longer.

Al Shammari was a heavily built, sullen and unattractive woman who simply glared at the police officer who was guarding her but there was a certain cunningness and evil in her eyes. However, 37-year-old Sergeant Dee Lloyd was no stranger to these Special Ops and her personal skills in unarmed combat made it obvious that she was more than capable of dealing with any outburst from the Saudi woman, although she was well tethered.

After two hours, there was a coded knock at the door, which Lloyd recognised and without taking her eyes off her charge she made one step forward, un-snibbed the door latch behind her and allowed her relief officer to enter. Lloyd pointed to Al Shammari, instructing that she should stay where she was, and whispered briefly to Constable Shazz Bright, warning her that the prisoner was considered dangerous and to take no chances, nor engage in any conversation whatsoever.

Silence must be maintained as part of the psychological approach.

As Lloyd slipped through the door opening she reminded Bright to lock it, stand with her back against it and never take her eyes off the woman.

"Semper Paratus!" were her whispered parting words.

Be prepared!

And Bright was!

She seemed almost twice the size of Dee Lloyd at 6 feet 4 inches tall and looked extremely intimidating, especially as she towered over the seated figure.

All under control felt Lloyd.

Al Shammari was not frightened and much happier now in the female's company. She thought that she would profess to speak virtually no English when the questioning started and that would cause a delay, allowing her more time to fabricate her story. She would hope for a Saudi interpreter, who may be sympathetic to her and not translate accurately, giving her some leeway to wriggle out of the situation, where they knew very little. No, all was not lost yet.

Pity, they spoke Arabic!

Chapter 35

They had been in their LUP for over two and a half hours, lying still on the sand but amongst sharp stones, scorpions, ants and other crawling beasties, none of which distracted them. It was very dark currently as clouds had drifted across the moon only a moment ago.

They fixed their stare and tuned their ears for either movement or sound from above. Together they would stop breathing, for absolute silence and then slowly exhale when satisfied that it was silent.

The rear and western side walls of the compound could be seen darkly outlined, almost like a fortress in this light.

They had seen no movement, nor heard a sound for over an hour and were now 99%, certain that the only watch tower, standing tall at the front of the complex, was unmanned. No lights, no movements, no glow of cigarettes and so no tell-tale signs of occupation.

It was cool now at this altitude at night, even a little cold, and probably around 10 degrees Centigrade; ideal for everyone inside to be tucked up in bed, sleeping soundly. Hopefully!

They moved silently over the last 50 yards towards the 10-foot-high rear wall, with a nod of 'here it goes'.

Nerves of steel, plus of course their favoured steel blades in their belts, to be used as a last resort only, although blood would most certainly be spilt tonight, well after they were gone!

Jonno led the way as they crept forward carefully, making sure not to disturb any loose stones on the sloping ground. If a stone started to roll, it could run down several hundred feet and collect others as it travelled, starting a mini landslide, with disastrous noise effects.

They had just removed and stored away their stinking thawbs under some low scrub and were now in black cotton track suits. Faces and any exposed skin were smudged liberally with dampened sand, which became sticky and dried like reddish-brown clay.

They reached the thick high mud wall and backed up against it.

All good—so far.

There were no trip wires, anti-personnel mines or perimeter snares; probably because the rear approach backed onto a huge descent and hundreds of miles of sparse hills and desert, so was therefore a most unlikely line of attack.

The same mistake the Turks made in The First World War at Aqaba in Jordan! thought Jonno. "Let's hope this goes as well for us."

Dodger nodded to Jonno and then backed up hard against the wall, placed his hands in front of him, like a stirrup and Jonno placed his right foot into them. "One, two, three," whispered Dodger and rocketed Jonno up the side of the wall with no apparent effort at all.

The lighter man sprung up easily and grabbed the top of the wall, which fortunately had neither broken glass nor razor wire set along it. He hung silently for five seconds, listening for any response but there was none, so he pulled himself up carefully, keeping low so as not to break the skyline any more than absolutely necessary.

He lay along the top of the nearly three-foot-wide mud wall and listened further. The moon was shining now and he could see that there were no traps along the top of the wall.

Nothing!

He saw no movement or lights anywhere.

Another good sign, he thought.

He dropped his right arm down and gave a low chirping noise to alert his mate. Jonno took a run at the wall, leaping up high enough to grasp his wrist and then crawl up his arm quickly and over him to the top. "Easy peasy," he whispered.

Silently, the two of them lay there for a further two minutes observing and listening.

In the cold clear night air, they could see the compound laid out in the weak moonlight before them.

Still, nothing stirred.

"Nice and quiet, that's how we like it. Let's hope it stays that way," murmured Dodger.

"I hope there are no scabby bloody rabid mongrels down there. Dogs are a fucking menace!"

The reconnaissance satellite photos had shown a set of steps built into the inside of the rear wall and in the moonlight, they could just make them out a short distance to the left of where they lay. The top of the wall was smooth with little or no pebbles on it, so nothing to be disturbed and cause noise, plus the steps seemed clean too.

"Not often we're supplied with steps for a gentleman's entry," Jonno said softly as he led the way down, still pressed hard against the wall, so as not to create any tell-tale shadows.

His hand was on the perfectly made hand-grip of his knife but he hoped he wouldn't need it, at least not at this early point in the intrusion.

"We'll arm ourselves first, as there may not be time later if things don't go to plan," whispered Jonno as the crept forward, walking on the sandy courtyard surface.

Bloody sand everywhere, what a shit-hole of a country; but in this case, it was a blessing as it was a noiseless path for them to cross.

They headed for the ramshackle lean-to timber building on their right side, which they had been told was most likely the armoury, situated along the western outer wall.

Approaching silently, they were surprised to find no guard anywhere in sight.

"How bloody sloppy," muttered Dodger when they discovered this, "and not even a lockable door on the building! Maybe it's not the armoury."

"Too easy, I don't like it," said Dodger. "That rickety door may be booby-trapped and if so we could go up with it! Or there may be a guard inside, sitting waiting for us, nice and cosy."

Without a moment's delay, a decision was made and Jonno slipped in soundlessly, over the sill of a low unglazed window opening, to determine if a guard was waiting inside, asleep or awake.

Allowing a few moments for his eyes to acclimatise to the darker surroundings, he peered around carefully. Nothing initially but not wanting to be too hasty he scanned a little longer, taking every aspect in and analysing the information. Eventually, he thought that he saw something against the door. Sure enough, what initially appeared to be a bundle of rags against the door turned out to be a sleeping man dressed in a mixture of Russian military gear and traditional

Arabic garb. He could now hear the deep rhythmic breathing, as he stopped his own, confirming that it was a 'sentry' who was anything but on-guard!

Jonno snaked his way silently across the 20 feet which separated them and was again thankful for the sandy floor. He observed that the guard was bearded with a nasty, wide, white, irregular scar down the exposed side of his face and was clinging to an automatic weapon-easily recognisable to him as a Kalashnikov AK-74. It was an update of the original AK-47 and the choice of third-world countries, terrorists and bad guys generally; not to mention all the USSR Block controlled countries.

He knew that it would have to be dealt with swiftly before the guard could discharge it and awaken the entire barracks, bringing god knows how many extremists down on them.

Not a pleasant thought.

No delay.

His combat knife was thrust through the centre of the guard's throat, with a flat blade and was driven in swiftly, right through to the cervical spine, severing it and causing a silent, instantaneous death. Jonno's left hand was already covering and removing the weapon from the dead man's hands, lest he clasped the trigger in his death throes. As he was slumped in a sleeping position, he elected to leave him there, conveniently blocking the door, whilst they searched the armoury.

He moved back to his point of entry, mouthed "Okay," and signalled to Dodger, beckoning him in over the same window opening.

Dodger slipped in over the mud brick sill and Jonno pointed towards the door silently, giving a finger across the throat to confirm what had transpired, plus the hand sign to proceed.

Their covered mini torches soon led them through the stockpiles of both Russian and contraband USA Military hardware. "Shit, this is nearly as good as our supplies at Hereford. No wonder this mob is so fucking dangerous, armed like this, but with no proper training or discipline."

Strangely they thought the stores were remarkably well organised and so within minutes they had selected a couple of bags full of 'toys' and also stuffed their pockets with a few extra small modern powerful explosives, fitted with timers, plus a couple of fragmentation grenades and were ready to go. Adding some HE, incendiary devices and several sophisticated anti-personnel mines, plus a Beretta 93R hand gun each and a spare 20-round box magazine each, completed their requirements.

"Better than bringing our own!" whispered Jonno.

They knew the Beretta well, with its 9mm parabellum cartridge and capable of firing bursts of three rounds at a time. Yes, these would do, if they needed help, but only as a last resort, because of the noise.

A cough was heard, somewhere outside, causing them to freeze and listen, but no suggestion of movement was detected, and so Jonno signalled to Dodger to move out through the window, with him to follow 20 seconds later.

They crouched close to the wall and listened.

Nothing?

Good!

They moved off, straight across the centre courtyard area, treading very carefully. Clouds currently obscured most of the moonlight and so there were no tell-tale shadows thrown across the area.

The house itself was a quite separate building and situated at the rear of the compound, whilst the sheds and barracks were built along each side wall, leading towards the front wall.

They could detect no movement but you could never be complacent.

Underfoot it was soft and sandy; nice and quiet, thank god, as there could be dozens of half-trained fanatics sleeping in the adjoining buildings, all with itchy trigger fingers.

They reached the main house quickly, noting that no lights were shining from either windows or under doors.

Looking good, they both thought.

On the side wall of the house, they spotted a large gas bottle, probably plumbed into the kitchen and Jonno realised that it could be a readymade bomb, of devastating proportions. He earmarked it for the placement of an explosive device before they left; always use what was there!

Now the challenging part!

Assignment: Enter the house unobserved, find the office, locate certain files, grab original documents and then leave a handful of delayed ignition devices to destroy the remaining records and terminate Ahmadi. Also, they needed to deal with the vehicles and the armoury. It was required that they wipe out the entire terrorist cadre, which would also create mayhem and aid their own escape.

They avoided the front door and found that the heavy wooden side door was unlocked and they were able to swing it open with only the slightest of creaking sounds.

They waited but nothing stirred.

The house's rough layout plans had been memorised and for a pleasant change, they appeared to be reasonably accurate, which was a bonus for them. They knew what they wanted to see was most likely in the first room to their left, being nominally the office or planning room.

The floors were constructed of large flagstones, so there were no creaking floorboards to worry about like in Northern Ireland, when they regularly searched houses for weapons and explosives, often whilst the family slept upstairs.

They allowed their eyes to become accustomed to the lack of moonlight but found it wasn't too bad as all the windows were unshuttered.

They trod carefully, in their rubber-soled desert boots, down the centre of the wide passageway, keeping away from the walls, which may have shelves or even ornaments displayed along the floor. Kicking or bumping anything at this stage could end up being fatal for them and others.

The only sound made was the faint squeaking of the rubber soles on the stone floor.

Shit, could anyone else hear it?

After a long pause, they resumed movement as it appeared that they had not been heard.

They reached the office door which was partly ajar and no light was showing.

Jonno checked his watch; now 03:20 hours. Good progress so far.

Dodger knelt down and put his head around the door, only two feet above the floor level, which is not where people expect to see an intruder enter.

They listened.

The room was better lit than he had expected from the open double window and he carefully scrutinised every inch of it, in case someone was sleeping in there too.

He satisfied himself before signalling all-clear to his patrol sergeant and gently pushed the heavy wooden door wide open to check behind it.

All clear!

They stepped inside and closed the door behind them.

Suddenly a door banged somewhere outside.

The barracks?

Guards changing?

"Shit, that's all we need, with one guard dead," whispered Dodger.

They waited. No action in the house. Nothing happening in the courtyard?

Someone having a piss out in the yard, they wondered.

Perhaps just an unsecured door banging?

Then all quiet again.

Jonno nodded to Dodger and they separated to search the room. It wasn't very large, maybe 12 feet by 12 feet, with a large well-worn, painted, timber desk against one wall and shelves with manila folders on the other.

Jonno gravitated to the desk and Dodger to the shelves.

They had specific documents to look for, relating to companies named Ecothan plc, KN Developments, New Giffin-Sen, World Overseas Trust Bank and Zamir Mines Coy.

Other than that, which appeared somewhat 'commercial' to Jonno, they were to seek any possible lists of names or locations of terrorist activities or potential cells.

They had another hour to clear the place, as the call to prayer would come at dawn at around 05:20 hours when the whole area would come to life and they didn't want to be anywhere near here then!

Dodger lifted files off the desk and disappeared under it, where he could use his mini torch in his teeth and the glow of light would be unseen from outside.

Papers were checked and placed into one of two piles. The left pile consisted of discards of no use to them and the right, expertly extracted, was info as per their orders.

Similarly, Jonno was at the shelves, torch in his teeth, where after a short time he found files labelled in Arabic, 'Somalia, Chad, Niger, Ivory Coast, Ghana, Zaire, Egypt, England, USA and Canada', each containing lists of names, contact numbers and bank accounts.

"Gold! I think this is it," and signalled Dodger, with a thumbs-up.

The empty files were scattered, to ensure they burned properly and the salvaged papers were slipped into a pocket especially sewn inside their utility tops. Other useful-looking papers followed until he was satisfied that he had fulfilled his orders.

Dodger found two thick files marked 'Ecothan', written in English and two thinner files named KN and Zamir Mines Coy, with pages of bank statements too. They were similarly emptied into his own pocket.

"All done?" Jonno queried in a low hoarse whisper.

"No, still looking for anything on World Overseas Trust Bank, but I think I'm in the right area."

"Better hurry, mate, this is not the fucking regimental family picnic!"

A short time later. "I've got it. Not a bad filing system for a mob of sand jockeys!"

"Okay, I've got the commercial-type stuff. What about you?"

"I think these papers could be a list of terrorists and their contacts or cells all over the world! If it is, then its absolute gold!"

"Okay, we've got a few minutes to set charges and get out of here. You do the office with HE and place incendiaries outside each of the doors of the hall and also rig the gas bottle, then do the same outside the barracks. I'll do it inside the armoury and under the vehicles, plus the two fuel storage tanks. I'll set a charge against the front gates too, so they think that's where we came in. Set them on 35-minute delays and then we'll meet at the steps on the back wall in 15 minutes. Ok?"

"Roger. See you on the way out."

Still as quiet as death; but that was coming soon!

They moved like ghosts around the compound, placing small but powerful devices in strategic positions, especially across all doorways.

Dodger used his combat knife to slice partly through the flexible gas line, which would cause a pool of the heavier than air gas to collect around the base of the 210 kg gas bottle, containing up to 400 litres of propane. It would allow for a massively destructive explosion when their charge detonated and the entire pressurised cylindrical tank went off.

Shit, it'll go off like a fucking nuclear bomb!

Jonno set the charge at the front gate to explode three seconds before the other charges, designed to cause maximum confusion, as the terrorists would probably try to awaken and rush out to investigate.

He placed three anti-personnel mines in a line about five paces out from the front of the barracks and Dodger did the same outside the main house, just in case anyone managed to get out.

Not that it would be necessary, as he didn't expect there to be any survivors from the initial blasts, especially when the propane bottle, the fuel storage tanks and the armoury went up!

The compound was isolated, on a hilltop, well way from the town, by chosen design. Accordingly, they didn't expect a rapid response from the town but knew they'd have to make a pretty smart getaway.

They crept up the rear steps, the same way they'd come in and still moving silently, tightly pressed against the back wall.

Taking one quick look at the silent, motionless enclosed group of buildings, they slid over the ten-foot wall and down the steep hill into the sparse, stunted and scrubby growth.

"Let's make tracks out of here, like famished ferrets!" said Jonno grinning and they set off at their best cross-country fast jog, which they knew that they could keep up for several hours, especially downhill.

They were making very good time, eating up the distance between themselves and what was soon to be Armageddon.

Better a bloody big blast here, than on some innocent civilian targets later.

That was their job!

Four minutes yet until the gate blew and then a further three seconds before 19 other charges blew simultaneously, covering any tracks of them having been in the office in particular. Maybe it would be put down as an accidental electrical failure and fire in the armoury resulting in a series of explosions.

Maybe not! Ha-ha!

On their way out, they had collected their discarded thawbs, sandals and the Sat phone and had raced away into the darkness. They sprinted downhill, not now concerned with the slight noise they were making over the desert floor but putting maximum distance between them and Ahmadi's HQ. They were as sure-footed as mountain goats but knew a slip or fall could cause an injury that may slow them down so placed their feet prudently.

Suddenly they heard a dull explosion. "That'll be the gate going," panted Jonno as they kept running steadily, downhill and deeper into the desert.

"Three, two, one," they counted and turned to look up the hill.

Nothing happened?

Then the sky above the hill lit up like World War 3 but soundlessly.

All in one almighty brilliant red flash and a moment later, the sound of the exactly timed multi-explosions reached them, assaulting their ears, even at this distance.

They watched in awe and then after moments, they heard further erratic explosions as the ammunition in the armoury overheated and started going off in a staccato fashion. This was likely to go off for a fair while yet, preventing anyone from investigating the compound or getting anywhere near it.

"Holy shit, let's get out of here, Dodger!" as they raced due north, navigating by the stars.

A minute later, they turned again to see what appeared to be the whole hilltop on fire, followed by a giant explosion as the propane gas cylinder ignited sending a flame higher than they could have imagined. Shit, it would have demolished the entire compound, razing everything in it.

Then an unnatural silence hung over the scene, only occasionally broken by what seemed to be erratic gunfire in the distance; probably the contents of the armoury still detonating.

Getting out was hopefully going to be easier than their entry as peasant traders with a stinking, slow donkey, for within just under three hours, at a fast jog they had covered almost 30km and they were approaching the DZ number 1, for their pick-up. They were well on time and so they wouldn't have to run another 10km, to DZ number 2

Dodger sent a pre-arranged single transmission blip on the sat phone, which confirmed both their location and the fact they were ready to go, plus that it was safe to land at the first DZ.

Situated at the foot of the slope, under the cover of the lee of a hill and right on time, they were ready to be picked up by a Royal Navy low-flying helicopter.

It had been despatched from the aircraft carrier HMS Hermes, travelling north up the Red Sea towards the Suez Canal, after joint manoeuvres with The Royal Australian Navy, in the Indian Ocean.

Waiting was never a problem for these two troopers, just another part of any patrol; a time to rest and revive.

Set a guard, hydrate then wait and use the time to rest.

Heart rate normal!

It was standard patrol procedure. No sweat!

It was a familiar and very welcome sight as the heli dropped down noisily, almost on top of the designated yellow-coloured flare and set off at the last moment to mark their exact position. The showing of the flare was a necessary and calculated risk, as they wanted a quick extraction, without any stuff-ups or a delay looking for them, for this whole area was going to be under huge scrutiny very soon.

The dull grey-painted Wessex had hardly touched down when they were beside it, bent over double, keeping low and clear of the massive rotors. They clambered in quickly and as the leading rating pointed out their harnesses another crew member slammed shut the sliding door.

The pilot lifted off the moment that the door was secured.

"We'll drop you off in about 50 minutes for your next pick-up," was all that was said initially as the crew concentrated on flying low and ensuring they weren't detected by radar over foreign soil. The side-mounted machine guns were manned and ready, but they all hoped that they would have no cause to fire them over Yemeni territory.

They flew fast and continued at a low altitude across the desert floor, to the northwest. Their DZ was just over the North Yemeni border into Saudi Arabia and to where the patrol was told was an old British WWII airstrip, inland from Jazan on The Red Sea, set in the middle of a vast and fortunately uninhabited desert.

Another rest period but it wasn't over yet and they well knew it.

On arrival at the second DZ, the Westland Wessex helicopter dropped down quickly and a crew member signalled for them to jump when hovering six feet off the deck, obviously very nervous to be at this location too.

The boys jumped down fearlessly into a sand storm caused by the rotors. The heli then lifted immediately, further blasting them with stinging sand, all of which was nothing new to these two veterans.

Sand up every orifice they possessed, bloody lovely!

The pilot had no intention of staying any longer than he needed, uninvited, on foreign soil, or in the air!

Why hadn't they been taken directly to the aircraft carrier? Thought Jonno, and then thought that they must want complete deniability.

The Wessex was gone from both sight and sound in seconds, leaving them in total isolation.

They sat and checked their surroundings. Not much to see. No buildings, no lights, nor any sounds! Just a hard-baked level landing strip in remarkably good condition for its age, but then it never rains out here.

After 10 minutes, their ears picked up a sound in the night air and soon a dot appeared in the pre-dawn western sky of a low-flying jet aircraft, which on watching seemed to be heading straight for them.

"It might be ours, but just in case it's a Saudi F-15 Eagle fighter jet, we'd better conceal ourselves in that ditch, under a sand 'blanket', as this is no place to be caught with our pants down," indicated Jonno.

The plane drew closer and closer but they still couldn't identify it yet. A twin-engine jet for sure and still possibly a Royal Saudi Air Force smaller jet on patrol, although by the lighter sound now, not a fighter, but still someone could be checking out the recent helicopter activity!

Shit, everything had been going so well.

Closer viewing confirmed that it was not a large fighter plane but a smallish, possibly civilian passenger jet.

Eventually, they identified it as an unmarked, plain white, Lear Jet 35 as it descended steeply, landed, turned and taxied back to the two-man SAS patrol's agreed DZ position.

They quickly dismantled their two Berettas, hurling the pieces in all directions, followed by the magazines and the cartridges, tossed individually to the winds.

The door was lowered and a distinctly American voice called out into the night, "Yellow Cab for Hereford?"

The boys appeared out of their ditch, shaking the sand off them like dogs shaking off water after a swim, whilst the crew member signalled them to hurry, with a flurry of arm signals beckoning them to board without delay. They needed no second invitation, bounding up the short steps and the door/steps were pulled up briskly behind them.

"Geez, what the hell are you guys doing out here, for Christ's sake?" came the rhetorical question, which the Yanks knew would never be answered.

"Obviously the powers that be have called in a little help from our US cousins. No less than the CIA, I'd guess!" said Jonno as the slick, well-appointed business jet sped along the hard sand and took off steeply.

"No doubt they don't have air clearance in Saudi Arabia either and want to be back over the Red Sea as soon as possible," murmured Dodger.

"Ok, you guys, settle back, next stop RAF Northolt, on your own fair shores in about six hours."

"We will take on fuel over the Med, near Sicily, in flight, from one of The Marine's Boeing Stratotankers, to give us a non-stop flight right through. ETA about 17:00 hours, you'll be home for dinner boys!"

"As soon as we reach 33,000 feet, above the cloud level and the Red Sea, we'll let you guys use the facilities to shower because I don't know what you've been through but we can smell that you've had a damn hard time! We've got some spare clothes, hot grub and plenty of good coffee, of course, so just sit tight till I give you a hoy."

"Bliss. A shower, a nice ride home with no one on our tail, plus a hot feed and a kip; are these jobs getting easier, or what!" laughed Dodger, sitting in a plush leather arm chair type seat. They were quite relaxed and guessed that the Lear jet had probably been confiscated from a drug baron from Central America and pressed into service by the CIA.

No complaints!

Chapter 36

The journey in the Princess, back from Wadi Al-Abyad, was without incident although Titus was far from comfortable. It was late afternoon and starting to cool slightly but the sun made it very glary without his sun glasses which had been smashed in the affray.

Slugger's assessment of her condition was right as she performed perfectly; yes, she was a tough and reliable old bird, with plenty of secrets! He didn't understand women but loved his Princess.

They were accompanied by an MP motorcycle escort of two units up front and two trailing, just for extra safety.

The MPs had their own road rules in this very military country, which allowed them to travel fast, well over the 50mph speed limit, usually at around 75mph (120km/h). They made exceptional time and guided all the way to the door of the Honorary British Medical Officer for Amman.

The four MPs saluted Titus as he alighted from the car and he acknowledged the special compliment respectfully, as he was neither a commissioned officer nor serving with the Royal Jordanian army. They waited and only sped away once he was safely inside the large private medical centre, attached to the main public hospital.

Dr Bleechmore was larger than life and physically a very commanding man.

He had the well-earned and proud reputation of being a real ladies' man in town and was already preparing to 'party' when they arrived. Smartly dressed, in fact, immaculately turned out and cut a rather dashing figure. However, he knew his business as he'd ended up a colonel medical officer/surgeon in the British army, after serving in Korea during the early 1950s and later in many other difficult zones in Africa and the Far East.

Well after dark, Slugger drove Titus back to the Zirino Hotel, where he was welcomed by the boys as a conquering hero, much to his chagrin. Yo-Yo and Tich were both there and they already knew the bulk of the story, amazing him how communication practices had changed in the years since he had been demobbed from the army.

However, they recognised that he was in need of rest and allowed him an early exit from their celebrations, which they generously continued on his behalf. He found that his body was stiffening up and Slugger handed him his medications which included painkilling and anti-inflammatory drugs and by this time he was happy to take them.

Back in the Windsor Suite, he found his paltry belongings just as he left them and was pleased to have a long hot shower, for he was filthy from his rolling in the sand plus there were small patches of dried blood on his shoulder, arm and chest. Luckily, the MO had applied a fully waterproof dressing on his shoulder, saying to shower in it and leave it on until it literally fell off.

A large drink from the bottle of water in the fridge and he dropped into bed.

Titus couldn't really get himself into a comfortable position in bed for any length of time, so deep sleep eluded him mostly that night.

When he arose early, he found that they had attempted to repair and clean his suit but the jacket still looked rather neglected. However, beside it was a smart pair of linen trousers, a shirt and a blue blazer, all in his size and miraculously procured overnight. He didn't have the energy to shower again, but shaved and made himself presentable for the day.

A very early flight booking had caused him to be summoned at 04:30 hours for breakfast. It was a fine meal in the dining room, in the Amman crew's company and this took him back to rather comfortable days in various bases in quieter times in the past, in the sergeant's messes.

These certainly were the salt of the earth types and an excellent recruitment strategy for such work. Just what some old servicemen, who never married but needed a family and useful work for virtually the rest of their lives. Then off to the Chelsea Pensioners' Home to see out their old age together, back in uniform.

Titus said his farewells to the boys at Amman Station, better known as the Zirino Hotel, as the MO had already given him the once-over and cleared him for air travel.

The night before he had been given two injections, one of which was an anti-tetanus shot and the other an antibiotic, just in case of any infection from the dirt in the shoulder abrasions. The doctor applauded Slugger's first aid efforts and told Titus to take it easy for a minimum of two weeks but told him that no active treatment could be offered for any of his fractures. "Just time, my boy…that's all you will need and you'll have to give the wee lassies a rest for a while," he said with a grin as he set off for his night out on the town.

Slugger was there at breakfast too, looking as though nothing unusual had happened and he really did admire the man's aplomb, now taking on the role of head of the sergeants' mess, for that's what he was, in truth! A continuation of their 30-odd years' service being rewarded with an ongoing job, a home and still being able to serve their country.

Slugger insisted on driving Titus, for this one last trip in the Princess, to Amman International Airport to catch his flight. He had the tickets all organised and carried his bag to the car for him. He had been busy, as the old girl was sparklingly clean and showed no signs of her rough ride yesterday. He must have worked on her for half the night!

On arrival at the terminal, he shook Titus' hand solidly and genuinely thanked him for his input into the whole exercise but especially for saving a disastrous situation at his own peril.

"We could do with a man of your steady temperament and talents out here and I'm sure the entire Amman Station would put in a good word for you if you'd like to join us."

Titus thanked Slugger too, saying, "It has been a pleasure serving with you and all the boys here, but my soldiering days are behind me! I hope to see you around, somewhere, but not in uniform again for me! Good luck."

In a way, Titus was sad to leave, as working with these ex-military guys was a very comfortable feeling, despite the danger; but surely he was past this?

He boarded his early morning British Airway flight and was afforded a first-class seat for a direct flight, straight into the London Heathrow Airport, in a Lockheed L10–11 (Tri-Star) long-range aircraft. With his shoulder and ribs causing him quite some discomfort, he was especially glad to have the comfort of the wider seat, plus the lay-back facility for a good rest on the approximately five-and-a-half-hour flight home. Luckily there was an empty seat beside him because he didn't want to have to explain his injuries or what he'd been doing in Jordan.

An hour into the flight, he was fed again, too well, and decided to take a couple more of his painkillers to help him drift off to sleep, as sleep had eluded him for a day or so. He was able to manage almost three hours of sleep and felt much better for it.

Arrival in London at just before 11:00 hours, revealed a miserable, grey, cold and wet day. Nothing new, but at least he was home and glad of it!

Clearing customs and immigration was no more than a passing formality; more of Bob's work.

He was met, after passing through immigration, by the same cabbie, Alfie, who'd taken him to Gatwick at the beginning of this little adventure, so it was nice to see a familiar face. This time the driver shook his hand warmly, taking his kit bag and carrying it for him to the cab which was parked quite some distance away.

Once in the cab, he introduced himself properly this time as retired Petty Officer Alfie Crews a lifelong friend of Slugger. He said he'd heard a condensed story of the Jordan escapade, commenting that anyone who could impress Slugger, let alone save his life was pretty special.

"If you ever need any help, just call Colonel Truscott-Browne and Alfie will be there for you."

The drive took a little over an hour due to traffic conditions and he was driven back to Truscott-Browne's location, through a side factory gate, about 50 yards away and around a backway. How many different ways could there be of entering these premises unobserved?

Alfie escorted him through a maze of passages and up a set of concrete stairs, leading him into their rather swish canteen for lunch but he only required a sandwich, as he'd eaten on the flight as well as having a very early breakfast at the Zirino. He received many sideway glances and the occasional thumbs-up sign of approval, apparently from those in the know of the Jordan escapade. Obviously, the Jordan assignment had become relatively common knowledge in these protected rooms and after a bite and a hot drink, Titus was ready to be whisked off to Bob's office.

Bob was straight down to business, saying that they had, together, cracked a massive terrorist organisation but more details were required to nail it all down and MI6 were on his back for the complete story.

Almost immediately, Bob began a detailed half-day debriefing of his movements, discussions, actions, observations and activities in Jordan, as MI6 were impatiently waiting on him for info to complete their side of the equation.

Bob was nothing short of thorough in dragging out every minute detail of the two days, leaving both of them exhausted at the intensity of the concentration required.

Then it was Bob's turn to share what he knew and it was extraordinary.

Titus learnt that Ralph Nicholson, who had done a disappearing act, had soon been traced, through the money trail, to a property he had recently purchased in southern Spain.

"Guess what alias he chose?" Bob laughed showing levity for the first time.

Titus shrugged, having no idea and really being too tired to play Bob's game.

"Matt Bond. He wanted everyone to call him Mr Bond. What a piss-whit. Mr Bloody Bond, can you believe it," shaking his head in disbelief.

"A specialist team had been despatched, strictly unofficially, resulting in him being found and recovered from Spain. He had quickly agreed to return, despite there being no extradition treaty, because he knew the game was up and it was made clear to him that he was safer with his own people than being exposed to Khoury's gang. He is securely in custody, still being interrogated but now safely well out of sight and he was being particularly cooperative."

"Just a greedy, despicable little turd, sucked into something he had no idea about. That's my summary of him," exclaimed Bob. "He literally pissed himself and then later shat his pants, in the interrogation room."

"Likewise, Khoury had been rounded up by an anti-terrorist unit from the Special Branch, together with his female assistant Al Shammari, who is not only his accomplice but also a cousin. Both of them are in the custody of our masters at a safe house until charges are served on them," explained Bob.

"Khoury hasn't spilt much yet and probably won't, as he's an experienced and trained operative, but on the promise of full immunity by us, Al Shammari has literally spilt the lot and is still talking. She was the one who actually contacted the cells worldwide, on either Khoury or Ahmadi's instructions and put men into action, so she may be doubly useful. She is a nasty, dark piece of work, if we ever met one."

"How can you sanction letting an animal like her escape charges, as she's probably responsible for dozens of deaths?" Titus fumed at his old friend.

"Ah, if I may go on, please let me explain that she has complete immunity in the UK but she will later learn that we will be required to allow extradition to Saudi Arabia to answer long outstanding offences of sedition against their royal family. The Saudi royals treat that offence particularly seriously and so she will most likely never see freedom again. You see, there is more than one way to skin a cat, my friend."

Titus was duly chastened, realising that he'd shot from the hip, without all the information; lesson learnt.

"Sorry, Bob, I should have known better, but I guess I'm a bit tired and cranky and not thinking 100% clearly."

"Understood and apology accepted. I fully comprehend your outrage, especially after you saw them in action only yesterday. By the way, I'm sorry too, as we didn't expect anything to erupt like that. Thank god for you and CPO Jones."

Bob went on, "A North Yemeni man named Waled Malouf, a crony of Khoury, and who had been working illegally here as a courier driver in Bradford has been arrested. It now seems that he was trained at the Zamir Mines HQ in their Sana'a compound and he has been identified as the man who attacked you with the knife and had most certainly been the one who killed Kingwell."

"Malouf is now in custody, having been arrested in a terrorist hideout, in a rather rundown part of Cardiff. His arrest has also directly led to the dismantling of what could have become a major operating terrorist cell in the Cardiff area and so the hierarchy at MI6 are preening themselves, taking all the glory of course!" he laughed.

The arrest of Malouf brought some measure of relief to Titus, not only on his own behalf but for Jimmy Kingwell's family too.

"Other enquiries were carried out in various countries and have netted a huge embedded terrorist organisation covering cells in about a dozen countries including here on home soil. This of course is covered by the Official Secrets Act and not to be mentioned anywhere," explained Bob.

"Understood," replied Titus.

"Now, I have here for you a detailed commercial report, as promised by Twal and Coetzee, who by the way has turned out to be a real asset. It sets out in clear detail the nefarious financial dealings by Khoury who really conned that dead shit Nicholson into something he didn't have a clue about, except the money of course. Even there, the supposedly 50/50 deal was more like 75/25 Khoury's way, plus Khoury retained all the Marine Insurance Policy's commissions and some healthy illicit rake-offs from the shipping, freight, customs and export taxes."

"You can read the report at your leisure tonight but it notes the procedures and how Ecothan's identity was used illegally, without anyone, except of course

Nicholson, having any idea of what was going on. Furthermore, I have the piece de resistance so your instructing client will be very impressed with your work."

Titus was intrigued as the report seemed to be all he required to resolve his investigation satisfactorily.

"Again I must remind you of the Official Secrets Act when telling you that certain information was gained by Her Majesty's Government of illicit banking, on a worldwide scale and as a result of other specific enquiries, huge sums were identified as being 'skimmed' in various ways by our two friends. Due to the rather plucky and open cooperation by Mr Twal, it has enabled us to recover a truly handsome sum."

At that moment, a sturdy-looking, but not unattractive young woman knocked on the glass door to Bob's office and on his invitation entered carrying a tray supporting a pot of coffee, two mugs and a plate of hot sugary doughnuts, so they broke their concentration for the first time in over four hours. As she left, she gave Titus a knowing smile and nod apparently acknowledging his work.

Titus was surprised at how much mental energy had been drained from him in the time since his lunchtime sandwich and was thankful for the snack. It was still awkward eating/drinking one-handed but he guessed he would get used to it, knowing it was only short term anyway.

Noting his discomfort, and feeling abashed that he'd launched straight into business, Bob enquired how his collar bone was feeling, realising that this should have come first.

Titus was not one for fuss and was able to say that the collarbone would not require surgery or fixation in any way but would heal itself in time.

"What about your ribs?" He asked, surprising Titus. "Bleechmore says you've got three or four broken ribs on the left side."

Obviously, Bob had received a medical report from Jordan; can a man have no secrets! "Pretty painful to be honest, Bob, but they'll settle down too."

Back to business!

Still, under caution, Bob explained that they had recovered monies from the overseas bank accounts of Nicholson and Khoury, plus undistributed funds in both KN Developments and also in Zamir Mines Coy's accounts, to assist in building up the windfall.

"We have also seized Nicholson's luxury villa in southern Spain and believe it could be a very useful asset to retain into the future, without showing any connection to HM Government."

"Due to a most unfortunate 'accident', after a covert visit by a SAS Patrol to Sana'a, neither Zamir Mines HQ, their records nor any of their staff survived a massive explosion. So the balance of the other funds of nearly £3 million will be retained to assist Her Majesty's Government tackle terrorism, as the Zamir business simply doesn't exist anymore! Plus of course, it was a weapons store, training camp and barracks complex and they are all gone," Bob said with a wry grin.

"I have taken the liberty of setting up an appointment with Deke Collins for tomorrow at 2:00 pm at his offices for you to meet with Mr Twal, who will fly in tomorrow, late morning. We need to tidy this all up, so no more enquiries require to be followed up and MI6 can have a free run. Also attending will be Peter Moles, who has just been appointed managing director of Ecothan by his board. I will list shortly how much information can be disclosed but preliminary advice from Twal suggests that he is now disinclined to proceed with his legal case so less is better. Oh, also attending will be your boss, Major Blake, who is thrilled at the audacity and success of your assignment and I must say he has been right behind you all the way; a great guy."

"Finally, I have it on good authority that you will be awarded a Bar to your DSM and you will be granted Her Majesty's permission to accept King Hussein's honour of 'Medalat alSharif', which is Jordan's Military 'Medal of Honour' for gallantry, on the basis of you being an Army Reservist on duty. There will be a ceremony in the near future but keep this under your hat for the moment."

After concluding the debriefing and accepting further documents, Titus left in one of their in-house taxis, via a rear exit of an adjoining building. This time out into the airport car park, around the back of what appeared to be an aircraft repair facility and therefore totally anonymous.

Beautiful setup, he thought.

As he was leaving, Bob shook his hand telling him that he'd done a sterling job for his country and may even be called upon again.

What did that mean?

By now it was dark, so he requested to be dropped off at his apartment, rather than face the office and become involved in lengthy detailed explanations, especially after such a long gruelling day.

He was pleased not to be looking over his shoulder as he entered his building's foyer and glad that the Yemenis were incarcerated at last, leaving London a safer place.

His apartment never felt so good he thought as he closed the door behind him.

Chapter 37

Whilst preparing their report summarising the fraud Twal and Coetzee worked very well together, hour after hour. They were helped by some information sent in from the UK, after the MI6 raid on the Richmond office. They discovered that Khoury had illegally increased his commission from 7.5% to 15%, withheld $10 per ton, falsified tonnages to his advantage and cooked the books relating to cartage and sea freight charges, but the exact figures were unclear to them.

Coetzee politely pointed out to Twal that some serious risk management measures were needed, sooner rather than later, and he could guide him through implementing them effectively, if help was needed.

The older mine staff, who had been forced to work under the Syrian manager until yesterday and had been pushed to one side by him, were now somewhat at a loose end and production had become erratic and slow.

Coetzee had moved in on them, without invitation and re-organised then into two teams, plus a maintenance crew, appointing reliable men as foremen and within 24 hours the mine and transport were ticking over beautifully. The men respected him and were happy to be back in a safe and proper workplace again doing their old jobs.

This had not gone unnoticed by Twal, who had been suffering a personal crisis of confidence and unable to properly deal with the calamities facing him on several fronts. Titus had saved his business and probably his life and now Coetzee was resurrecting his mines to a good working model. These men deserved every accolade that could be heaped upon them and he decided to make representations to the king for official recognition.

With Captain Haddad's help, his secretary-receptionist in Amman was removed and gaoled for assisting with the attempt on his life. His original girl was located by the authorities and brought in to the office. She thought that she had simply fallen out of favour and had been sacked by him and so she was happy to be back, increasing his confidence in the future to maintain effective control of his own business.

A whirlwind of events had overtaken him and he needed a rest, or help, or both!

He was frightened that the Syrians or Yemenis may infiltrate his staff again and he wouldn't be able to face another such crisis. He was going to have to work hard to save his business but knew he had to do something and quickly and suddenly he knew what he must do.

A phone call was made to Mr Moles at Ecothan, whilst Coetzee was out in the yard organising the men and after a long discussion his mind was made up.

On Coetzee's return, he asked him to join him for sage-enhanced tea, setting the scene for a more formal discussion, as is the Arab way.

At the conclusion of tea taking, he took a deep breath and started, "Mr Coetzee, I think you and I are two very different men from quite different backgrounds but working together with you I believe we complement each other's skills as a working team. I sense that you too feel happy here and whereas I have no wish to cause you any embarrassment I have a proposition for you to consider, if you will."

Coetzee was puzzled, as no one seemed to warm to him and vice versa really. He was aware of being 'prickly' and thought that he actually enjoyed it, but sometimes he wondered if life could be more pleasant if he lightened up.

Anyway, he was happy to listen, so he nodded respectfully.

"I will come straight to the point, as I know that you like directness. I would humbly like to offer you the position of risk manager and operations manager here at my company and based in Jordan. After 12 months of satisfactory service, a 5% shareholding will be presented to you as a bonus, but it must be relinquished back to me, at fair market value, if you choose to leave. Your salary will be 50% more than Ecothan currently pays you for the first three months, and then it will be increased to double. At the end of two years of satisfactory service, I will hand you another 5% shareholding, taking you to 10%, again to be sold back to me if you leave."

He went on, "There is a very nice house on site for your use as your own because I intend to spend less time at the mine and will not need this accommodation. Also, I will make available to you a modern two-bedroom apartment in Amman, to use when you are in Amman City, either on business or for leisure if you have visitors. I think you are a very worthy man to join my firm and I enjoy working with you, as do my men who likewise respect your integrity."

"Finally, I will provide two fully paid air fares each year to either London or South Africa, as you choose. Please consider my humble offer."

How completely unexpected, was Coetzee's reaction, but he was very pleased. He sat there for a moment, taken aback and eventually said, "Mr Twal, I am overwhelmed. I will have to clear this with Ecothan in London before considering it all, as there are current legal proceedings between your company and mine. However, I must admit that I've enjoyed my life here more than in London," was all he could say.

"Of course and for my part, I would not even consider poaching Ecothan's staff without speaking to them first. In fact, I've advised them today that I intend to abandon all legal proceedings immediately against Ecothan, so there will be no conflict of interest for you either. As such I took the opportunity to ask them whether they would be offended if I offered you a very senior position, plus a share in my business within 12 months."

"I can also reveal to you that Mr Moles, who you should know is now the newly appointed MD, recommends you highly for your initiative here in this delicate matter and would support you wholly."

Coetzee's head was reeling, it was something he'd always wanted, a share of a business, rather just an employee and strangely enough he too felt very comfortable with Twal and his men.

And Moles recommended him highly! Wow.

He had no wife, nor any family in the UK and only one surviving brother in South Africa, which was easily reached by a flight direct from Amman to Johannesburg.

He liked the climate here, hot like home, rather than dreary, wet English weather, and he was in the open air more: so it was decided!

"Mr Twal, I thank you for your confidence and gratefully accept your proposal. I will not let you down."

Strangely, both men had acted out of their usual characters by making almost impulsive decisions on major matters and were both feeling very pleased with their respective choices.

Twal felt that things were returning nicely back to normal and Coetzee was elated at the proposed change of lifestyle.

Chapter 38

Bob called Titus at home the next morning, joking that as he was an invalid he would organise a cab to collect him from his apartment at 1.40 pm for his big meeting at Deke Collins' office, reminding him to carefully read the report, as he'd have to explain it at the meeting.

"And don't forget that lovely Miss Lang!" he said, with a knowing smile on his face.

His little joke thought Titus. *Ha-ha.*

Anyway, he was pleased to accept the taxi as it would not be too much fun being jostled on the crowded trains and both his collar bone and ribs were certainly painful without the need for bumping.

He was waiting outside when a London black cab pulled up and called out his name and destination. The driver negotiated the streets expertly despite the rain, heavy traffic, poor visibility and pedestrians scuttling all over the roads and arrived at the lawyers' premises with five minutes to spare.

"Good Luck, Guv," called the driver as Titus ducked through the now heavy rain being driven by a cold wind and into the building's foyer for some protection. He shook off the excess water but it didn't seem to help much.

He took the lift up to Deke's offices, where he was recognised by the receptionist Belle, who knew him well. After taking his soaked coat, she escorted him directly into the large well-appointed boardroom where he was offered refreshments. He was immediately brought a steaming cup of tea and told that Mr Collins could still be a short time yet.

Sitting alone for five minutes, he had time to collect his thoughts and again consider how this meeting may unfold with so many facts, many of which could not be disclosed.

He had his 'Report', courtesy of Twal and Coetzee.

He'd read and absorbed the guts of it and found that it exonerated Ecothan as a company, with the exception of the actions of one renegade employee,

Nicholson. It was detailed, covering nearly two years since the massive scam started and showed pretty well how Khoury had worked it from inside of New Giffin-Sen, raking off millions by fiddling both prices and tonnages of product in this favour, overcharging on shipping and associated freight charges and taking an overgenerous management fee.

He was deep in thought when the door opened and Deke ushered in Abi Twal, Peter Moles and Cyril Blake who all approached him, sympathetic to his condition and saying how pleased they were to see him safely back in the UK.

A shade embarrassed by all the fuss Titus mumbled that he was fine and they all sat down in specified seats, as directed by Deke.

Deke's resonant barrister's voice welcomed them individually, leaving Titus to the end and declaring him as the most incisive, bold and brave person he'd ever had the pleasure to work with.

It was becoming plain embarrassing, thought Titus; let's get down to business.

"Mr Twal, you have elected to attend without your legal representative and I believe that you want to open the proceedings. As you requested this conference to be kept as informal as possible, I'll hand over to you, please," announced Deke, gesturing to him.

Twal stood up, saying, "I need to be a little formal if you can bear with me, Mr Collins, as this issue is of the utmost importance to me. The last two years have, if you will excuse the expression, been an absolute hell for me personally and for my business. It was with some trepidation that I commenced legal action against Ecothan but the honest and straightforward way that they, their lawyers and in particular their investigating Chartered Loss Adjuster, Mr Lovell, dealt with this matter have literally saved my life and my company from ruin. I have lost much money but that is trivial compared to what could have been if I'd been dragged down further by these rogues, my man Khoury and your Mr Nicholson," nodding in Moles' direction.

Becoming very emotional, he stopped to compose himself and turned to Titus, saying, "Please accept my heartfelt thanks and tell your principal that, due to your outstanding investigation and bravery, I have discontinued my legal proceedings. No further action will be taken and I seek no reparations. Your actions are far beyond duty. It is ended!"

The unpretentiousness and humbleness of the man filled the room, leading to complete silence.

Before Deke could take over, Titus stood up beside Abi and thanked him saying that he'd like to fill in some blank spots.

Abi sat down and Titus continued.

"The two main perpetrators you referred to are both incarcerated awaiting trial on a string of charges and are unlikely to see the outside world for a very long time. I am told that Mr Kingwell's killer is also in custody awaiting trial and if he is ever released then the USA authorities want him for acts of gross violence on their embassies."

"Much of what occurred is a matter of state security for both our countries and will not be made public but with Mr Twal's openness and unreserved cooperation I am permitted to say that the world is generally a safer place."

Abi bowed his head in acknowledgement and he too looked embarrassed.

Titus continued, "Mr Twal, I know you are satisfied with this result and require no payment from Ecothan but I'm delighted to hand over to you as much of the defrauded monies as could be traced for your company. All only occurring after a massive effort reaching halfway across the world, in a top-secret operation, the details of which must never leave this room."

He gestured to Abi, inviting him to stand and to everyone's astonishment he shook his hand and then reached into the sling supporting his left arm, pulling out a banker's cheque which he presented it Abi.

Abi took the slip of paper and turned as white as a ghost and gasped in Arabic, "*Mis ma3'uul*. I'm sorry, in English I mean, incredible and unbelievable. It is for £5.9 million. It cannot be! How is this so?"

He was shaking so much that Titus assisted him to his seat and told him that a combined effort, including unspecified governmental assistance in several countries, had allowed this conclusion to be reached. Monies had been located, salted away in a number of bank accounts overseas and happily accessed and recovered for him.

After composing himself, Abi profusely thanked all present admitting that the fraud was so devious that it was well beyond his full comprehension, even now. Furthermore, he admitted that he thought that he may have lost considerably less than the nearly £6 million just handed to him. He just didn't know.

Cyril Blake was astounded. This had never been achieved before. The entire insurance claim being defended was one thing but recovering nearly £6 million cash for the plaintiff was just so far beyond the call of duty he couldn't believe it.

He knew that he would be able to dine out on this one for the rest of his life. Even better than one of his Loss Adjusting friends and competitors, Tony Hart, who had his 'Great Train Robbery' investigation story, which had kept him in the limelight for over 15 years!

After some further formalities, Abi suddenly remembered and handed a card to Titus saying, "My Saville Row, tailor has instructions to make you two suits to replace the clothes that you so gallantly ruined at the mine. Please use this authority with my humble thanks. It is the least I can do for you, Mr Lovell." He then excused himself and indicated that he must deposit such a large cheque, as his business was approaching the brink of failure, due to an almost crushing cash flow problem and this would absolutely resolve his firm's difficulties.

He invited all present to be his honoured guests at a dinner, when he was next in London and also if they should ever visit Jordan, they would be made welcome at his home. He then bade his rather formal farewell.

Deke arranged for one of his young, rather formidable-looking rugby-playing lawyers, to accompany Abi to Lloyds Bank in nearby Fenchurch St and then arrange a taxi cab to his hotel in Paddington. Abi was grateful for all the help he had received and being rather overwhelmed he accepted Deke's offer, with further thanks.

After Twal's departure, it was Peter Moles' chance to thank Titus, as the writ hanging over their head had begun to affect their business and a successful claim of this size would make them uninsurable, and which would also kill off Ecothan's reputation. With this result, their reputation and name would most likely suffer no damage at all.

Mr Blake then spoke saying that he'd been liaising with the Secret Service and was able to say that Titus had been in great danger but had triumphed personally and also professionally for his firm and country, disposing of a multi-million-pound matter to all parties' satisfaction.

Deke took it all in quietly.

There really wasn't much for him to say, as his secretary had just excused herself into the meeting and handed him documentation confirming the abandonment of these legal proceedings.

This was indeed a coup for both Deke's practice and Blake's adjusting firm and would rate highly on their resumes, for there was no doubt that at law

Ecothan would have been liable for the actions of their renegade, uncontrolled employee, Nicholson, and with legal costs it may've been a £10 million payout, taking years to resolve Deke indicated that to preserve 'Legal Privilege' he did not require any written report on the matter and that Titus should simply submit his bill of fees direct to the underwriter, who would be delighted to pay it.

Deke would summarise the legal side in his own way and both their files would be concluded. He also urged them to be very circumspect as to most of the background and security aspects, for he had received a briefing from Bob, only this morning.

This was an added bonus to Titus, as a big part of any job for him was laboriously preparing a multi-paged detailed report, with supporting attachments, often taking a day or two to complete, to his level of detail.

As they were leaving, after additional congratulations to Titus, he asked Blake if it would be in order if he took some annual leave, straight away.

Blake wouldn't hear of it, saying, "You were injured on duty, my boy and will be placed on fully paid sick leave for as long as you need to recover. Truscott-Browne has alerted me to the full list of your injuries so let's commence with two weeks and see how your recovery progresses!"

Titus still had a pocket full of cash, over £2,200, in the form of his 'expenses' from the Jordan trip, as supplied by Bob, but when he'd offered it back he was told, "Keep it, you've earned it and more!" so he had enough for a nice little trip if he wanted.

A short time later, a shared cab dropped him off on St Katharine's Way and he walked the short distance to his apartment whilst the cab turned and drove on to the office, taking Cyril Blake to the office. The weather was milder than earlier in the day and so he enjoyed the five-minute walk home.

He opened his apartment door, juggling his bunch of keys one-handed, with some awkwardness, but eventually managed to open the two locks.

The image and scent of Rose swept back into his mind and he thought that he might call her in the morning: but still, he might give Rose a call tonight, before she leaves the office.

Yes, he would, right now.

He rang her office direct line but the phone rang and rang, unanswered.

Disappointed, he was about to hang up when suddenly a breathless voice answered, "TG is that you?"

He couldn't speak at first, as she seemed to have that effect on him, but then managed to splutter that it was.

She gushed on, "I've really missed you and was so worried but a friend of yours, Bob, called me twice to tell me you were okay. Who is Bob? You never mentioned him. How are you?"

"Slow down, Rose, I'm all right, just back today from overseas and can now tell you I've been to Jordan on the Ecothan file, which has worked out really well. I've just had an important meeting with the parties involved and everyone is smiling."

"You sound so tired. Are you sure you're okay?"

"Well, I did have a little mishap whilst at the New Giffin-Sen's mine and my shoulder is a bit uncomfortable, but I'll live!"

"Oh, I knew something must have happened when Bob called to reassure me, I could feel it. Can we meet somewhere later today, or if you're not up to it can I come and see you at your place, please?"

"Well, I've been on the go since 4.00 am yesterday in Jordan but it'd be great to see you here. Can you get yourself to Tower Hill tube station after work and I'll meet you by the old Roman ruined city wall? Do you know it?"

"Yes, yes, right by Tower Green, I know it and I've got some news for you," she said tantalisingly. "I can be there by just after 5.30 pm. Is that all right with you, TG?" It certainly was!

Chapter 39

It had been a long couple of days but he was happy to be here waiting for Rose, with crowds thronging around him, coming and going in the evening rush hour. Yes, this was his London! Standing waiting for Rose, he didn't even notice the misty rain falling as he anxiously scanned the thousands of faces coming up the steps from the station. He realised how much he'd missed her and was pleased that she still sounded so keen to see him.

He started forward a few times as he thought he saw her long dark hair in the crowd but on properly observing the girl he stepped back, feeling a little foolish at his anxiousness, although they hadn't noticed.

Still, he was happy in anticipation of her arrival.

What a period of tumult!

Only three weeks had passed but had involved him in travelling from England to Turkey and Jordan. Insurance fraud, murder and terrorism all rolled up together in a nasty parcel; but there was now Rose, yes Rose!

Was she just being polite or was there really the flame here that he felt so strongly and he fervently hoped that it was real for her too?

He really couldn't read women.

What if she lost her job at Ecothan with all their turmoil and decided to return home to Adelaide? What would he do? Could he try to get her a suitable job, or perhaps she just wanted to go home after 10 years? Was this just a passing phase for her?

Lost in his thoughts, he felt a gentle tug at his right sleeve and looked around to see Rose, glowing, right beside him, apparently oblivious to the rain on her face. This time it was him that took the initiative and swept her to him with his good arm and hugged her tightly, but he couldn't stop himself wincing as his ribs and collarbone twisted slightly.

She tried to pull away to relieve the pressure on him but he didn't let her go. He couldn't, he wanted her right there, pain or not!

She didn't know what to do, so he indicated to her to hang on to his right arm as he supported his left arm and off they went.

"I'll take you home, Rose," was all he said as he set off.

She had no idea where he lived but was happy to go with him and simply tag along.

He led her along past Tower Green, downhill and across in front of the Tower of London; over the roadway, then under Tower Bridge Road and into the St Katharine Docks precinct. She was wondering just how far they were going to walk when he silently pointed upwards indicating the building housing his apartment.

It was a beautiful old original four-storey warehouse, constructed of classic yellow clay brick and now converted into apartments, right on the dockside.

How beautiful she thought as floodlights splashed up the walls, making it look like a palace or a mansion.

He led her along the western walkway, by the marina's water's edge, to the apartment block's entrance.

In the large foyer was a modern lift, to take them up to the third floor.

The lift arrived swiftly at '3' and when the doors slid open silently, they were able to exit into a stylish lobby area which had a long wide passageway running off it in two directions.

She immediately noted several comfortable-looking sofas set along the large windows, which no doubt would make an ideal suntrap and place to sit and enjoy the views. She managed to gain a peep of a view of the top of the masts of yachts in the main marina and thought it wonderful. She wanted to go right up to the window for a proper look, but TG was already at his door, marked 301.

He fumbled one-handed attempting to select the correct key and quite naturally, without any fuss, she gently took the bunch from his hand and he told her, "The larger of the two brass keys will open the bottom lock and the other brass key the top lock, Rose, thanks."

She unlocked the sturdy front door, with its two heavy-duty locks, thinking that this building had great security, not realising that only Titus had such locks, especially fitted courtesy of Bob's team of specialists and only recently.

He pushed open the stylish, wide, polished timber-panelled door and ushered her in ahead of him.

She loved it immediately.

It was a modern open plan style, clean and tidy, really warm and cosy, plus it appealed as being well organised. Why was she not surprised?

It was agreeably furnished, with nothing glaring at her as being out of place, and it was certainly not a spoilt bachelor pad! And not overcrowded like hers.

The view through the huge window wall, out towards the Thames, and across the marina below, with expensive yachts bobbing gently in the breeze, was exquisite. Lights twinkled everywhere in the rain, reflecting off windows and the water's surface of both the dock and the river itself.

She could watch that view forever, how magnificent.

How romantic too, especially compared to her lower ground floor flat with a view of the base of a mothy old tree and some rather half-dead looking grass around its base.

She helped him slip off his coat and for the first time saw the sling, which had been hidden under it.

"What did you do to yourself?" She softly asked, somewhat as a rhetorical question for she had some idea what had occurred.

"I fell over in Jordan, at New Giffin-Sen's mine, nothing dramatic, so let's not make a fuss, please Rose."

"I don't think so, TG! Just before I left the office, Mr Moles told me that you were nearly shot saving some soldiers from terrorists, or something like that!"

He shrugged and looked down. Nothing needed to be added, he felt.

"Does it hurt a lot? What can I do for you? Can you tell me about it?" She rattled off sympathetically.

"I'd like you to take your coat off too, relax, make yourself comfortable, stop fussing and come and sit with me. I've missed you so much…Oh, sorry, I must be getting soft in my old age to say that," he said with a grin.

Her coat was off in an instant and she was plastered against his good side in no time at all, as this was exactly what she had hoped to hear from her big tough guy.

Warmth was everywhere. *Glorious*, she thought happily.

He gave her an edited version of the case and in particular the Jordan trip, as she kept pressing him for more and more details, especially on how he was injured. He gave her the basic details, after which she said, "Mr Moles said you will most likely receive a medal for your actions and that you deserve it!"

He didn't know who knew what about any awards so he simply smiled and pushed sideways against her, raising his eyebrows.

They sat together for ages, glowing in the rays of the gas fire before he asked, "Would a small kiss be in order, for the invalid, perhaps? But you will be gentle with me?" He chuckled at her.

She punched his right arm lightly and leaned across in front of him, gazing into his eyes, stirring up all that he felt for her and then ever so tenderly kissed him.

"I think I'm feeling much better already, could we do that again, but not so gently?" He laughed at her.

She too laughed and her next kisses were not as temperate!

To hell with the pain, thought Titus!

He wanted to hold her tightly but it was so awkward, so they sat in silence, enjoying just being close.

Nothing needed to be said.

Suddenly she sprang away saying, "I've got a surprise to tell you!"

"Mr Moles has been appointed to take over Mr Kingwell's position as MD, which is great news and he has asked me to be his personal assistant, with a pay rise too, so I won't have to leave now. I admitted to him that I'd been helping you, as I thought it wise to have no secrets from the start and he respected that I told him."

"Well done, Rose, I am so relieved. I was worried about all this and was ready to see Mr Blake about a job in my firm, but this is fantastic news. I don't want you to disappear back to Oz."

"Mr Moles was very sweet and has an idea that I am rather fond of you, so he insisted that I take two weeks' special leave on full pay to look after you."

"Are you?"

"What?"

"Rather fond of me?"

"Don't go fishing for compliments, mister!" she said with a radiant smile.

Suddenly, moving on, she asked, "Are you hungry, TG, because I'm absolutely ravenous. It is after 8 o'clock and I missed out on lunch too. Do you have anything here I can cook, or are you one of those bachelors who live on fish and chips?"

"Really, Rose!" in mock horror. "In the freezer, you'll find two portions of my unbelievably first-rate homemade Madras Indian beef curry, completely prepared on the premises, if you don't mind! However, you'll have to cook some rice and then heat the curry in my microwave oven afterwards. There's a jar of mango chutney to complete the meal. Will that be okay?"

She felt a little abashed at her bachelor comment but very pleased at his response. She was off like a shot, easily finding all that she needed and commencing the preparations.

He was in heaven, with Rose pottering around in his kitchen as she belonged there and humming happily as she prepared their meal, as though it was the most natural thing for her to be doing. He watched her as her hips swayed around the kitchen, looking absolutely adorable but his thoughts by then had strayed wildly from the impending meal to something far more sensual.

In less than twenty minutes, the rice was cooked to perfection and he explained how to use the microwave, as although she'd heard of them, she didn't have one at home, because they were the latest gadget for the kitchen. The curry was heated in individual bowls, as directed and in a flash, all was ready.

The apartment smelled fantastic as she finalised her kitchen activities.

She had previously fossicked around by herself, finding Splayds, serviettes and lovely modern bright red bowls, thinking how organised and stylish he was and how complete all the items in his cupboards were. This man has everything and then she reflected that she was not necessarily thinking about his kitchen or the meal either!

Her thoughts had been straying too, to the more erotic. Steady girl, she thought.

She brought the meal to him, where he still sat and they smiled together at her accomplishment, but nothing was spoken.

They sat on his brown leather Chesterfield settee, next to each other, with Titus having a cushion on his lap to help balance the bowl, so he could manage to eat one-handed, with the Splayd. She cradled her plate high up against her chest and managed very well, looking across at him like a mother hen but her feelings were far from maternal at that moment!

Nothing was said for quite a while but the atmosphere again made them both feel conversation was superfluous.

After the meal, she said, "That was chef-quality curry, TG, I could eat here all the time," with a hint of suggestiveness in her voice and her eyes teasing him too.

But in her usual fashion, she didn't dwell on it and moved away immediately, sourcing a bottle from his not immodest supply, which she had noticed in a cupboard earlier. She was chatting to him as she did, and he was delighted that she was so much at home that she didn't feel the need to ask if it was okay to open a bottle. She removed the cork like a pro and poured two glasses of the deep red Bordeaux so they could now enjoy a glass of wine, as it had been too difficult for him to manage a glass one-handed, during the meal.

They sipped slowly, savouring each mouthful and because Titus felt a little mushy, he was content to just gaze at her. He took in every feature from her dark shining hair, her beautiful eyes, her perfect facial features, her glorious breasts and felt contentment.

It was his turn to break the trance when he suddenly remembered, "I'm on at least two weeks' leave now, as well. What shall we do?" He said with a twinkle in his eye.

"I'm sure we'll think of something," she replied with more than a little eagerness and a touch of wickedness when she arched an eyebrow, all of which quickened his blood. She remained pressed against his good side, as close as she dared, without causing him pain but there was no pain now, just joy.

For his lot, Titus was as happy as a pig in poo!

Her warm breath was on his cheek, her light scent in the air and her breast was pressed tightly against his arm. Was she aware of the effect it was having on him? All this was making him feel a bit too frisky for his present condition. *Steady boy*, he thought but these thoughts raced and could not be suppressed, even if he wanted.

After sitting for ages, she hopped up to set about tidying the kitchen and loading the dishwasher, which was a feature she had never had at home or anywhere else. She stood back and admired the sparkling area, comparing it with the pathetically small kitchenette at her tiny flat, wondering how she had managed to put up with it for so many years. Then she thought it had been only her there, with no visitors to please, so it hadn't really been an issue but now things seemed to be changing quickly too.

Yes, she loved this kitchen and the owner too she thought, with a flush, which fortunately he didn't see.

She returned to his side and they sat talking for ages. Titus continued with a further abbreviated version of the investigation, as she wanted more, but he deliberately left out the security aspects, the finer details of the terrorists and the earlier attempt on his life. No need to worry her!

She asked about Bob and he simply replied that he was an old friend who was his last OC in the REs and with whom he had maintained contact.

She talked about her home town of Laura in South Australia and how she wished she could make a visit to see her family, whom she had not seen for some five years. Titus added that he'd like to visit Australia again too, which made her glow. Could they actually go together which might allow her to show him off to her family but she didn't dare voice her dream, not yet anyway.

Quite late in the evening, she announced that she'd better go, so as to be able to catch the last train but he squeezed her hand tightly, to stop her from rising. Looking into her eyes and taking a deep breath he declared, "I have got a couch you can sleep on you know, Rose," finding himself embarrassed and also now reddening, wondering whether he'd stretched their budding relationship too quickly and too far.

She picked up on his embarrassment and looked at him with make-believe horror and suspicion at such an offer, exclaiming, "Oh, TG, I am shocked at such a suggestion but then you are so disabled that perhaps I had better stay and sleep in your bed with you, to see that you'll be all right during the night. I do hope you'll behave yourself!"

He was stunned but ecstatic at her suggestion, causing them both to burst out laughing and hold each other as best they could.

And so began a wonderful fortnight, which they both knew they wanted to continue forever.